Lights! Scalpel! Romance!

Dr Jas Kohli thinks of himself as a cosmetic surgeon gone astray. He is a writer, poet, birdwatcher, singer and amateur astronomer. He has a blog, titled 'Smile a While' (www.jaskohli.wordpress.com) and can be contacted at drjskohli@gmail.com, Facebook (@Jas Kohli) and Twitter (@authorkohli). This is his second novel. Dr Kohli will continue to tickle your funny bone in times to come.

Lights! Scalpel! Romance!

JAS KOHLI

Published by
Rupa Publications India Pvt Ltd 2019
7/16, Ansari Road, Daryaganj
New Delhi 110002

Sales centres:
Allahabad Bengaluru Chennai
Hyderabad Jaipur Kathmandu
Kolkata Mumbai

Copyright © Jas Kohli 2019

This is a work of fiction. Names, characters, places and incidents are either the product of the author's imagination or are used fictitiously and any resemblance to any actual person, living or dead, events or locales is entirely coincidental.

All rights reserved.
No part of this publication may be reproduced, transmitted, or stored in a retrieval system, in any form or by any means, electronic, mechanical, photocopying, recording or otherwise, without the prior permission of the publisher.

ISBN: 978-93-5333-490-1

First impression 2019

10 9 8 7 6 5 4 3 2 1

The moral right of the author has been asserted.

Printed at Parksons Graphics Pavt. Ltd, Mumbai

This book is sold subject to the condition that it shall not, by way of trade or otherwise, be lent, resold, hired out, or otherwise circulated, without the publisher's prior consent, in any form of binding or cover other than that in which it is published.

Contents

1. A Lousy Start — 1
2. The Colourful Boss — 15
3. Beauty with Brains and Lots of Guts — 22
4. The King of Fiascos — 29
5. Some Consolation — 38
6. The Sweetest Surgeon — 42
7. A Nation of Cricket Maniacs — 51
8. The Bitter Experiences of Candy — 60
9. The United States of Desis — 73
10. So Near, Yet So Far — 81
11. Newbies Create a Stir — 99
12. Doctors in the Wilderness — 110
13. Teething Troubles — 116
14. Unkempt Becomes Polished — 125
15. Yet Another Goof-up — 132
16. The Angry Old Man — 139
17. Coming of Age — 148
18. The Serious Comic — 163

19. A Matter of Life and Death	172
20. Experience Matters	184
21. Crowd Management is No Joke	207
22. Arranged Marriage Jumble	214
23. War with No Rules	222
24. A Close Shave	229
25. Undoing Others' Mistakes	233
26. Parties Full of Surprises	238
27. Life in a Fast-forward Mode	249

1
A Lousy Start

> *Upon joining the MS course, a doctor doesn't expect to be showered with rose petals. But he shouldn't be treated like dirt either.*

A funny-looking man entered Nirog Hospital. He was swaggering like a WWE wrestler, on the move. But his spotless white coat and the stethoscope hanging around his neck were clear pointers to his type—a subset of humans often lauded as second to God, and often berated as devils in white coats.

Dr Nipun's modesty had gone for a toss because he had vanquished many self-styled Einsteins in the entrance test to bag the Master of Surgery seat under Dr Ujjwal, a superior brand in the medical profession. A career brighter than a floodlight was almost a certainty. He also hoped to get his family out of the financial mess brought about by his dad, who could have written a self-help book titled *How to Fail at Business*.

Nipun was eagerly heading towards his revered shrine, the operation theatre (OT). The day of his joining had coincided with the operation day of Dr Ujjwal's surgical unit. As he walked, his gaze fell on his right hand. He thought, *It looks like a typical surgeon's hand. But if I get a chance to apply a few stitches today, my seniors are definitely going to feel low. They will complain to God—'Why aren't my hands as dexterous as those of Nipun?'*

Nipun imagined rotating his wrist to complete the insertion of a stitch. 'That was a perfect circular motion!' he bragged to himself.

Then, his body rotated in an elliptical fashion. He had toppled over a patient transfer trolley, which had suddenly appeared out of a side corridor. After observing fuzzy stars for a few seconds, he came to his senses. Nipun felt warm breath on his neck. He was lying upon the chest of a middle-aged male patient on the trolley. Had the patient been a lady, his position would have been embarrassing.

He realigned his limbs with his torso and got up quickly—just like Tom the cat, his favourite cartoon character. Turning to the patient, he said, 'My apologies! I hope you aren't hurt?'

To his surprise, the patient flashed a smile, although a sardonic one. 'I am okay,' he said, 'but it is quite surprising to find a doctor dead drunk early in the morning!'

'Come on! In the morning there isn't even time to drink poison even if one is in the mood!'

'You were walking like a drunkard and looking at your right hand as if it were the well-manicured hand of a pretty lady! This collision was waiting to happen.'

'Actually, the saying "Pride hath a fall" has been demonstrated—verbatim,' Nipun said with a sigh.

The patient threw his head back on the pillow. 'I got injured because of a careless driver. But an accident in a hospital corridor is unthinkable!'

When he noticed that Nipun had been cornered, Jeevak, the orderly who had been pushing the trolley, decided to come to his rescue. Right after the collision, Jeevak had almost shouted out his most potent expletive. It was so insulting that the victim could go into a prolonged period of depression and even develop suicidal tendencies. But his vicious tongue had screeched to a halt after recognizing that Nipun was a doctor, wearing a white coat.

'Actually, it's my fault too,' he said to Nipun. 'While shifting the patient to get his X-ray, I was speeding. But what do I do? The other orderly is on leave while the ward is full of patients. If I take too long to finish a job, even if it is beyond my control—Savitri, the ward-in-charge, gives me a dressing down without bothering to check if the other staff are enjoying the show! Apparently her mother-in-law had beaten her with a broom in the morning!'

'That is just an excuse. Actually the hospital management has launched a covert operation to fill beds in the emergency ward! You've been instructed to knock out pedestrians by moving the trolley at a breakneck pace!' Nipun said with a wink, making both the orderly and the patient smile.

The trolley resumed its journey, making un-harmonious sounds with its un-greased wheels and moved out of sight. Nipun felt a mild discomfort in his upper thighs, just below the groin. This was the pivot around which his body had rotated.

A shudder passed through him. *If I had been just an inch shorter in height, the edge of the trolley might have crushed my nuts. I would have ended up in the OT, amidst bloodthirsty surgeons, ready with their sharp instruments. I could have been castrated and would have been teased lifelong as 'The Man without Balls'!*

Nipun had just learnt an important life lesson—sometimes there was just a thin line between good luck and bad luck.

He noticed the huge expanse of greenery from the oversized windows of the corridor on the first floor of the hospital. His eyes sparkled with joy. It was the Delhi Ridge, a real jungle, cheek by jowl with its tormentor, the concrete jungle. Nipun was such an avid nature lover that if given a choice between watching a lingerie show on Fashion TV and an African safari on Discovery Channel, he would have preferred the latter. But he wouldn't entirely ignore the topography of the leggy models either. He'd ogle at them later on YouTube.

'Hey! Lecherous!'

He heard someone shout his old nickname. Nipun turned around to find Shishir, his batchmate from MBBS. Once seen, Shishir was unlikely to ever be forgotten. His eyebrows looked as if moustaches had come up in the wrong place.

'Hey, dude—I got to know that you are joining the MD in dermatology at this hospital,' Nipun said.

Shishir chuckled. 'I am also aware that you are going to be the latest chamcha of Dr Ujjwal! So we won't be able to meet often because the junior doctors under him are rarely seen outside the wards except when they are turned out by the chief himself!'

'True. For the next three years I'll be slogging like a worker bee. But why did you call me lecherous? Presently, I am such a decent guy that any respectable man wouldn't think twice before he married off his daughter to me!' Nipun said.

Shishir gave him a derisive smile as he walked away, 'I doubt it! Catch up with you some other time, Lecherous!'

'You will pay for this!' Nipun said, although he didn't really mean it. The word lecherous triggered memories of his college days. But in order to avoid another collision, he kept an eye on the incoming wheelchairs and trolleys, as well as the hospital employees who were rushing, either to save critically ill patients or to save their skin from tyrannical bosses. He also avoided getting distracted by women who had been lovingly handcrafted by God in his spare time.

Nipun had presumed that after he left medical college, his nickname would die a natural death. Being known as Lecherous was cool during one's college days. But now that he had become a surgeon, female patients would keep a safe distance from him if his name continued to be prefixed with 'lecherous' instead of 'doctor'.

Nipun recalled that he had been naughty right from his preschool days, when he had poured cold water over an elderly relative while he had been asleep at their home. Most naughty kids sober as they age. But for Nipun, prankishness had become second nature. His dad was often seen in the principal's office at Nipun's school, tendering apologies on behalf of his son.

After joining MBBS, Nipun gave his classmates a glimpse of his sense of humour by assigning whacky nicknames to them. But he got away with something benign, Naughty Nipun.

Conceived by him, the competition for 'Most Creative Verbal Abuse' was a huge hit. It was held on the top floor of the Boys' Hostel. The surprise winner was Sujay, a refined guy. Their local slang dictionary had been enriched by the addition of new cuss words, some of which even found usage in conversations.

Learning anatomy had become easy for his classmates because Nipun had created catchy mnemonics. The mnemonics were of two varieties, straightforward ones for girls and bawdy ones for boys. Once, the girls had overheard him while he had been narrating the saucy version to the boys. They had forced him to part with his whole collection—uncensored.

For Yukti, his girlfriend, Nipun's sense of humour was his main hook. But he was not too bad in the 'looks department' and he managed to score decent marks due to the insane toiling he indulged in during the examinations. He would glue his butt to the study chair.

Nipun had made a name for himself among the teachers too. One day, in a state of absent-mindedness, he had requested two of his friends to give his attendance by proxy. When two different voices had simultaneously uttered, 'Present Sir!' Dr Hoshiar Singh, the vigilant lecturer, had detected the con. He had been more amused than angry but took all three students involved in the conspiracy to task.

Nipun even had a namesake who was a year senior to him. But the other Nipun hadn't even teased a butterfly, let alone a human being. He was called Padakoo Nipun because the only time he didn't study was while he was asleep. Even after the other students had left the cadaver dissection hall at the end of the anatomy practical, the hardcore scholar kept company with the dead bodies, unravelling their anatomies by dissecting them again. He had even given the cadavers nicknames, imagining what they would have been like when they were alive. His competitors had given up hope of ever replacing him as the topper of the class. Padakoo Nipun often joked that while other students were plain humans, he had the genes of a pack mule to boot. His decency was also exceptional. He thought of all the women in his class as his sisters, which they did not appreciate.

Six months after Nipun had joined the MBBS programme, Sarwan, his dad, visited the Boys Hostel to meet him. At the hostel gate, he found a group of medical students indulging in frivolous chatter. This was a bit disconcerting for Sarwan. He had presumed that with the exception of his son, every other budding doctor was an embodiment of sobriety.

'I am Nipun's father,' he said, 'Please tell me the way to his room.'

'There are two boys named Nipun in this hostel. One is decent and the other one is lecherous. Which category does your son fit into?' Pranay, the naughtiest in the group said with a quizzical smile.

'Guide me to the room of the lecherous one!' Sarwan said. He had sounded as confident as a mastermind at a quiz competition. A wave of uproarious laughter had spread through the group of students.

That day, Nipun had a naming ceremony during which his classmates had performed the role of the priest. Naughty Nipun was rechristened as Lecherous Nipun.

During the practical exam in anatomy, one of the external examiners had showed him a preserved specimen of the human brain and asked him, 'What is this organ?'

'Sir, this is the one that is quite underdeveloped in me!'

The examiner had laughed with his mouth open so wide that apart from all his teeth, the uvula had also been visible. However, the way Nipun had answered the subsequent questions, he had proven that he had a normal and developed brain.

His coup de grâce, however, was his mimicking of his teachers during the annual college festival, which had everyone, including the professors, in splits.

While he was studying in his final year of MBBS, Nipun found out that his dad had filed for bankruptcy after suffering from heavy losses in his business of consumer electronics. Actually, the writing had been on the wall for quite some time. Sarwan had borrowed heavily to fund an over-the-top expansion plan, which had been driven by envy instead of judiciousness. He had been trying to catch up to his cousin, Ranjiv, who was also in a similar business. It did not help that Ranjiv's wife took every opportunity to show off her solitaires to Nipun's mother, Jagriti.

Sarwan ended up doing a clerical job under one of his former suppliers, one whom he used to taunt for stinginess during his heyday. The crisis was initially concealed from Nipun so he wouldn't be unsettled. However, later on, there was no choice left but to reveal the naked truth because his pocket money had to be curtailed to such an extent that he could only book a table for one at a good restaurant.

It was a wake-up call for Nipun. Pranks were cool until life played a prank on you. Nipun took the unexpected setback to heart since he was quite attached to his family. He changed his social media status from 'Life is wonderful' to 'Life sucks'.

Nipun had trailed after three daughters in the family. He had been brought up as a modern-day prince by his parents. They saw him as the torchbearer of the family name and their trump card for elevating the family's status from undistinguished to eminent.

When Nipun had been a kid, even a mild sneeze had warranted a visit to the paediatrician. His sisters too didn't take offence when he pulled their braids just for the heck of it. Nipun did get scolded by his mom, but only when he protested against her force-feeding him milk, and that too in a tall glass.

Later, in medical college, his high-stress situation had included deciding which movie was to be seen after bunking classes and making it to the morning class on time. So he hadn't developed the soft skills needed to deal with a full-blown crisis.

Nipun stopped shaving. After a while, he got so attached to his beard and moustache that he couldn't part with them. His edginess resulted in frequent tiffs with Yukti, who had once proclaimed in filmi style, that she would stick with him, come what may! During the commotion caused by a fight which turned ugly, Yukti escaped from his emotional captivity.

He felt like burning all love epics. Presuming that Yukti had ditched him because he had revealed his family's pauperization to her, Nipun texted her—'I wish that you find a Tata, Birla or Ambani and live happily ever after with his wealth!'

Yukti replied promptly. 'Don't imagine things. I am being forced to leave you because you are trying to use me as a punching bag. Don't dare text or call me again.'

Without wasting much time, she took sweet revenge on him by going into the arms of Shreshth. Nipun had outwitted him to win the affections of Yukti two and a half years ago. Yukti also proved that she was not a gold-digger because Shreshth's family lived in a flat and they drove around in a car with only an 800cc engine.

Nipun started losing sleep. He didn't feel like eating anything and made only special appearances in his classes. After their amateurish pep talks fell flat, two of his close friends realized that he was a 'gone case'. They took him to a psychiatrist who bugged him further by asking him innumerable questions. But the mind detective was able to hit upon a diagnosis—he had reactive depression. He was put on medication. In addition, Nipun was also referred to a clinical psychologist who hammered into his head that life was a mixed bag and most humans on earth were worse off than him.

Nipun recovered quickly. The party animal made an amazing transformation into a bookworm. He had never imagined, even in his wildest dreams, that one day his classmates would come to him to clear their academic doubts. In fact, Lecherous Nipun came quite close to Padakoo Nipun in terms of lifestyle and conduct although only for a brief period.

Nipun's recollections were interrupted as he reached the pre-operative room. The patients, attired in OT gowns were patiently waiting to surrender themselves into the hands of surgeons. Some of them were mumbling prayers to their Gods, probably with the sweetener that they would worship them even more intensely if they emerged in one piece. Nipun was reminded of his mom. While facing even a minor inconvenience, she would take a vow in front of her chosen deity to make eleven thanksgiving visits to the deity's abode if the issue was resolved. With a bossy mother-in-law, a scheming sister-in-law, a good-for-nothing husband and wayward children, there was no dearth of problems for her. So she was perpetually on the move from one religious place to the other.

Nipun swung open the door of the OT. It made a creaking sound like the doors operated by ghosts in haunted bungalows. Just a few feet ahead, the floor was marked with a broad red line. Beyond this was the sanctum sanctorum, the sterile zone of the OT. One could cross the line only if one did the cutting, had to get cut up or assisted in the cutting.

Situated at the end of the side passage was the Surgeon's Lounge. Here, the senior surgeons recuperated after finishing a surgery. Resting their weary backs on the comfy sofas, they chatted about topics ranging from 'recent advances in surgery' to 'recent scandals in Bollywood'. When the seniors were in there, there was an unwritten rule that the junior doctors could come in only if they had to receive instructions or to give explanations (which were rarely accepted anyway). They were supposed to be tireless, like the swifts and the swallows. After the senior surgeons left the OT, the juniors took the liberty to sit in the Surgeon's Lounge.

A doctor walked up to him.

'Are you Nipun?'

'Yes, Sir!' he replied loudly, much like a soldier talking to his officer.

'I am your senior, Dr Nakul. Welcome to the department.'

The seniors in Dr Ujjwal's Surgical Unit seem to be more amicable than they are supposed to be! Nipun thought. 'Should I change into OT clothes and come inside?' he asked.

'No!' Dr Nakul commanded. 'Today Dr Ujjwal is celebrating his birthday by fêting the OT staff. He wants you to fetch bread pakoras from Tara Chand's shop in Munirka as nobody else is free. Take the money and leave right now.'

What the hell! Is this how they welcome a newcomer? Nipun thought. But he masked his feelings, which were anyway not of much consequence in the department.

He replied, 'Sure, boss. I will be back as soon as possible.'

'Why didn't they order a pizza that could have been delivered?' Nipun grumbled softly as he made his way to the shop which was about five kilometres away.

He reached Munirka in a jiffy. The entry to the shop was by way of a narrow street. On the way, he encountered the street goonda, a jet-black mongrel with amber eyes and oversized ears. The dog barked menacingly at Nipun but that was all he seemed to be capable of as he made no move to have a taste of him. But, Nipun noticed with amazement that the canine goonda was letting all the ladies pass without even a growl. As he moved ahead, an uncovered manhole gave Nipun an open invitation for admission to Nirog Hospital. He was able to dodge it just in the nick of time.

'Today my balls have been so lucky!' he mumbled, aware that the groin was often injured after a fall into an open manhole.

At last he reached the shop, but that was not the end of his travails. He had to stand in a long queue. A fly started planting kisses all over him. Even at 8:30 a.m., the sun was providing more warmth than was desired by warm-blooded man.

'One day, I will achieve even more name and fame than the chief. But I will never treat my juniors like shit,' Nipun whined to himself.

Tara Chand, the owner, was dispensing the bread fritters. His son, who was frying them in a huge vat, resembled his father so much so that he seemed to have developed exclusively from his father's sperm—by asexual reproduction.

On the signboard was written, 'We have no branch'. The customers were waiting patiently, as if this was a temple where one's wish was to be granted. The duo seemed to get a kick out of the devotion.

Opening a branch near Nirog Hospital would be a good way for them to expand, Nipun thought. *That would also make life easy for those hospital employees who are addicted to their stuff.*

Standing in front of him was a guy so broad and tall that Nipun felt claustrophobic. He turned to Nipun.

'Today the queue is comparatively short. Two weeks back I had to wait for an hour. Normally, they finish their stuff by 3 p.m. and then shut shop,' the big man said.

'These guys don't need likes on Facebook because they have so many diehard fans in person,' Nipun commented.

'Santosh Kumar,' the man introduced himself and then offered a handshake, which felt more like a hand-crush.

After recovering from this playful display of aggression, Nipun replied, 'I am Nipun.' He purposely omitted the prefix, Dr.

'I live for food!' Santosh said with relish.

'That is quite evident!' Nipun quickly added.

Immediately, Nipun regretted his statement. What if his sarcasm had crossed the giant's tolerance threshold? Nipun could be trampled upon, strangled or beaten into a pulp. Santosh could also lift him up, rotate his body to build up momentum and then throw him away like a discus, straight into the vat of boiling oil.

However, to his relief, the big man smiled.

Nipun liked his bindaas attitude. The world needed joyous creatures like him, not the sadu types who had a low threshold for frowning.

'What do you do?' Santosh asked. Even though Nipun was sans the white coat, Santosh had speculated that he was in some vocation which required an extensive use of the grey matter.

'I am a doctor.'

'Arrey... Doctor Sahib. Why are you standing in the queue? Your time is very precious,' Santosh said, surprising Nipun.

Then he spoke to those who were ahead in the queue, 'Please let Doctor Sahib take away the stuff first.'

Everyone complied. Nipun's fatigue disappeared in a flash.

He was reassured about his status. *There may be a few hotheads who get the doctors admitted into the trauma wards. But the average Indian respects us*, he thought.

After getting the pakoras packed, Nipun thanked Santosh and gave him his mobile number.

'Do contact me if you ever need my help,' Nipun said.

'I hope such a situation never arises!' Santosh said with a sarcastic smile.

Nipun smiled too.

2

The Colourful Boss

Doctors aren't from another planet. Like other humans, some of them are off-centre too.

Meanwhile, inside the OT, Dr Ujjwal, the chief, was in the thick of things. He was celebrating his birthday as a true surgeon does, by conducting a difficult surgery. The patient had an abnormal swelling of the common bile duct. It was known as the choledochal cyst. 'There is a saying among surgeons that such cases should be passed on to one's enemy!' Dr Ujjwal had told his juniors before starting the surgery.

His fingers were moving with the fluidity of a master craftsman. The chief liked to show off his skills. He was enthused when there were admiring spectators around the operating table. The trainee surgeons too imbibed a lot of wisdom because he kept a running commentary about the surgical steps involved. However, if any of the assisting doctors showed signs of being 'physically present but mentally absent', they were taken to task by a liberal use of crass adjectives which pricked more than a needle.

Removal of the cyst was as tough as retrieving an object lying amidst hissing serpents. Vital structures like the portal vein and the hepatic artery clung to the cyst as if they were madly in love with it. One wrong step was enough to cause torrential bleeding. The chief had called Dr Anuroop, the assistant professor of the unit, for help.

A reenactment of the Wolf and the Lamb fable often played out in the OT. Whenever something went wrong, Dr Ujjwal found it handy to offload the blame on to the lambs, which included Dr Anuroop and the other junior surgeons. The typical accusation—they hadn't assisted him properly.

The chief had been operating for more than three hours. The joints and muscles of his body were beginning to feel uneasy. 'Some doctors have converted our surgical unit into a patient dumping ground,' Dr Ujjwal grumbled after he had gotten stuck in the dissection.

This was largely true. Many surgeons posed as if they were lion-hearted. But whenever they came face to face with a tough case, they galloped away like a horse. The referral of the patient to Dr Ujjwal was disguised as a favour. However, his was the highest court of appeal, and no one could be turned back.

Then there were his former students, who felt that it was their birthright to send complicated cases to their chief. But Dr Ujjwal later extracted his revenge by calling them ham-handed surgeons who had only exemplified his failed parenting.

Sanchi, the theatre-in-charge, also known as Lal Mirchi, had scrubbed up for the surgery. She was personally handing over the instruments to the chief. Her brashness enabled her to act as a referee between surgeons of the different surgical units. They often squabbled like street hawkers in the event of a shortage of OT time slots.

Aside from Dr Ujjwal and Dr Anuroop, she called all the doctors of the unit by their first names. Sometimes she even swore playfully at the junior doctors. The chief preferred her as the main scrub nurse. The other technicians and nurses did not complain. On the chief's operating day, they preferred to do the floor job, which entailed carrying out supportive tasks. This way, they could avoid scrubbing up and thus escape Dr Ujjwal's tongue lashing to a great extent. But Sanchi had developed immunity to the chief's diatribes and took them for background music.

The saga of Dr Ujjwal's past had been retold so often that it was known to everyone in the hospital, with only minor variations. It could have been turned into a book even more titillating than the biography of Rasputin.

While he was in primary school, the young Ujjwal had realized that his body's biochemistry was aberrant. Just by gazing at an attractive girl, he could go into a trance. When he was in class five, Ujjwal had his first girlfriend; although all the couple did was to smile at each other. At the time, most boys of his class were into superheroes. They believed the only function of the penis was peeing. They also presumed that babies were conceived by women after marriage through divine blessings, without any contribution from their husbands whatsoever.

Dr Ujjwal had completed his MS in an era when the sixth sense of the doctors was more valuable than radiological investigations and lab tests. He was fortunate enough to have received his surgical training under Dr Jagdish, a legendary surgeon with an astronomically high idealism to materialism ratio. Dr Jagdish came to work on a bicycle and invariably wore a white shirt with pleated white trousers. It was rumoured that he had only three sets of clothes.

Instead of watching Hindi movies with the ending 'and they lived happily ever after', the young Dr Ujjwal used to remain in the OT during his spare time. Dr Jagdish took note of this and gladly parted with his surgical expertise. But some of Dr Ujjwal's colleagues, who envied him for being so close to the chief, were of the opinion that his dedication to the profession was just a cover-up for his 'amorous operations' with the women who were on duty. They would often say in jest that whenever he was on the night shift, a female staff or doctor was quite likely to become heavier by five grams, overnight!

However, Dr Ujjwal applied himself with equal sincerity to both cutting and flirting. Once, a consultant complained to Dr Jagdish about Dr Ujjwal's licentious activities. Dr Jagdish retorted, 'What else do you expect from a strapping young man? Have you forgotten your own times?' Such was his endearment for his student.

A bizarre incident took place when Dr Ujjwal had been a junior consultant. On the ward rounds, Dr Jagdish had asked for a pen. In his eagerness to impress his boss, Dr Ujjwal had hurriedly put his hand into the front pocket of his trousers. In addition to the pen, he had inadvertently taken out a packet of condoms which had a picture of a busty porn star on the packet. Some of the onlookers had been titillated while most of them were embarrassed. But Dr Jagdish was unruffled as he had expected something like this to have happened sooner or later. The clinching evidence convinced even the sceptics of Dr Ujjwal's double life. However, even after the exposé, Dr Ujjwal didn't mend his ways. He reasoned—since the tag of debauchery is not going to go away anytime soon, why should he waste his talent of seduction. This incident was regarded as an important 'scene' in his unofficial biography and was religiously narrated to all those who joined his department.

Dr Ujjwal's birthday celebrations on that day were limited to the hospital. His married life was like a fractured bone which had gone into non-union. He had wooed his ex-wife Meenal in style while studying for MBBS. She had been aware that he had a roving eye but had been optimistic, expecting that he would mend his ways after their marriage. However, Dr Ujjwal kept on intoxicating ladies with a heady cocktail of good looks, charm and his celebrity status as a surgeon. What made matters worse for Meenal was her inability to hire a full-time maid. She was afraid that if the maid was left alone in the house with her hubby, he would try to seduce her. In this regard, he was a socialist, above the considerations of caste, class and creed.

Once, Apoorv, his elder son, brought Gehna, his girlfriend, to Dr Ujjwal for consultation regarding abdominal pain. After just two meetings, she found the father much more interesting than the son. From that day onwards, Apoorv vowed not to bring any of his lady companions within hundred yards of his dad's office.

'Use your tool on as many women as you want without the fear of getting caught! I free you!' Meenal had shouted during their last meeting.

'But it is the fear which provides the thrill!' He had felt like saying but had refrained. They were in the living room. The few glass vases in the vicinity would have been thrown at him. If she had attacked him with the sharp edge of a broken vase, he could have become history.

Then a few events took place in quick succession as if the reel of his life had been put on a fast-forward mode.

His parents shifted from Chandigarh with the intention of staying with him. They presumed that he would be an emotional wreck after having separated from his wife. On the contrary, Dr Ujjwal was enjoying his 'free bird' status to the hilt. One day, he invited his girlfriend over for dinner at his house, along with two of her friends. Falsely suspecting that their characterless son had gone to the extent of indulging in orgies, his parents left for their hometown. Dr Ujjwal received another jolt when his two sons too broke off all ties with him. Then, there was an attempt on his life by the brother of a disgruntled old flame. Only the poor marksmanship on the part of the shooter saved him, as the bullet which was intended for his heart grazed his left shoulder.

After this event, Dr Ujjwal realized his philandering had become an addiction even worse than that for smack. A steamy lovemaking session in the back seat of a car on a deserted road didn't excite him any more. Rather, he fancied having a cup of tea in the evening with a steady partner while admiring the orange hue of the sunset from the balcony of his home. But there were no takers for him now.

However, throughout all this, his career had only moved one way—upwards. It reached its zenith when he was appointed the official surgeon for a number of dignitaries in the central government. This also gave him access to the corridors of power. Those at the helm of affairs in the hospital management chose to close their eyes to his foibles because he was a magnet to draw the public and thus a major factor in maintaining the financial health of the hospital.

Dr Ujjwal would tell his close friends, 'Whenever my obituary is published, it will mention me as a great surgeon and nothing else! No one will write: "Ujjwal was a scum on the face of the earth. His misdeeds are unprintable. May he rot in hell!"'

In fact, Dr Ujjwal's patients held him in high esteem because he went out of the way for them, sometimes even donating his own blood. They were unaware that he had won over so many stunners that even James Bond would have felt envious if he had found out.

3
Beauty with Brains and Lots of Guts

Beautiful ladies are spoilt for choice as far as men are concerned. So, most of them aren't in a hurry to fall in love at first sight.

The other newcomer in the department was ensconced within the OT all morning. As a lady, she couldn't have been told to fetch the bread pakoras. Since it was her first day, Dr Nishtha had been instructed by the chief to observe all the action from a distance, like the twelfth man in a cricket match.

The OT was all about functionality and sterility. Interior designers were a no-no here. Plain tiles had been put on the walls for ease of cleaning. If a high-society lady would have happened to look at them, she would likely have sneered, 'Doctors have no taste. Even my maid's room has better tiles!' The windows were covered with frosted glass; as if looking at the clouds or the rising sun would have induced the surgeons to compose poems on nature, making them lose concentration on the surgery.

Although more than two-thirds of her face was concealed by the surgical mask and cap, Nishtha was still attracting furtive glances. Her striking doe eyes were enjoying all the attention. They no longer had to compete against her luscious lips and rosy cheeks. The woman appeared to be beautiful, despite the tent-like OT uniform, which succeeded in only partially concealing her curves.

Nishtha had set her sights on becoming an accomplished surgeon. Her idols weren't the bimbos who gave away their poor general knowledge by crediting Einstein with the invention of the light bulb. Rather, she idolized strong, knowledgeable women who, if the occasion demanded it, could intimidate men so much that their balls hurt.

Finally, the surgery had ended much to the relief of the weary team.

The famished surgeons made their way to the Surgeon's Lounge to relish their well-earned reward, the bread pakoras from Tara Chand's shop. Nakul had just heated them up in the microwave.

Nipun bowed his head like a seasoned sycophant, 'Sir ji, happy birthday.'

'Thanks. You too have been born today! As a surgeon! And now I have the tough job of rearing you!' the chief said.

The pecking order of the unit was followed in the serving of the pakoras. For a while, conversation halted as everyone revelled in gustatory titillation. Dr Ujjwal's face looked as if it was in the throes of an orgasm.

By the time Nipun's turn came, only a single pakora was left. He dipped the fritter in the chutney, took a bite and became Tara Chand's fan. This was unlike any bread pakora he had tasted before.

'Eating this can be listed as one of the many paths to achieve nirvana!' Nipun said.

He wanted to devour more. However, everything was not lost. Nipun greedily looked at the leftover chutney. He waited for everyone to leave the lounge, poured the chutney onto a plate, brought it near his mouth and lapped it up, like Tom, the cat.

Back in his hostel room, Nipun thought about Nishtha, whom he had seen in the OT. *She is so gorgeous that the chances of her falling in love with a chutiya like me are almost nil. At Nishtha's age, most girls look at the boy's financial status apart from his appearance and I score poorly on both counts. Plus, the seniors are sure to be biased towards her. When the heroine is shimmering on the big screen, no one looks at the chorus dancers.*

'But there is no harm in being friendly towards a colleague,' asserted the optimist in him.

The next day, he invited Nishtha to the cafeteria. She was wearing a light pink lipstick. But her eyes were boldly lined with kohl; it was as if a shair (poet) had an appointment with her to write a ghazal about them. Nipun took regular breaks from staring at her so that he was not branded a cheapster.

Nishtha too evaluated Nipun. He was basically handsome but exhibited a lot that she hated in a man. She found his hair anarchic, his beard unwarranted and his moustache funny. She judged that his clothes were environment friendly—recycled ones bought at a flea market. His only saving grace was his smile, and he smiled as much as panellists in news channels yelled at each other.

Although Nipun wasn't hungry, he ordered food along with the soft drinks, so that they could have a long chat without being given murderous looks by the cafeteria staff for blocking a table.

Treading cautiously, he asked Nishtha about her school, college and blah blah. Then, he asked what he considered a pertinent question. 'Why did you choose a male-dominated field when you had other options?'

He had no idea that any talk suggestive of male chauvinism had the effect of waving a red flag in front of Nishtha.

'Why do some men practise gynaecology?' she said, her facial muscles twitching.

Realizing that he had strayed into the den of a tigress, Nipun made a quick U-turn. 'I get your point. One's interest in the subject should be the main criterion for choosing it.'

Nishtha asked Nipun about the hits and misses of his life. She wanted to come across as a good conversationalist, not a swollen-headed beauty.

Nipun spoke about himself, but he deleted many portions of his life history. Having expected some juicy stories, Nishtha was disappointed.

'It seems as if you're narrating your biodata! If you keep on talking like this, I might fall asleep!' she said.

Nipun immediately loosened up and divulged the riches-to-rags tale of his family. Then he dwelt on how he gave away his steady girlfriend on a platter to his competitor.

Nipun continued, 'But despite all this, I smile a lot. After the big shocks, I've started valuing even the minor joys of life.'

'Even when you don't smile, you radiate happiness,' Nishtha said.

'How?'

'You are such a laughable character!' Nishtha chuckled.

'Thanks for the compliment! You can add some more adjectives if you like!'

'One is enough for today!'

Nishtha felt emboldened. 'Three months ago, Arpan, my steady boyfriend, asked for my hand in marriage. However, he was adamant that we settled in Rajpur, his village, where he proposed to set up a private hospital.'

'I don't see anything wrong in that,' Nipun opined.

'I have visited my ancestral village quite a few times and know the ground reality. For men in villages, emancipation of women ends at allowing them to move around without a ghunghat! My life would have been like a saas-bahu soap opera with unlimited episodes.'

'What happened next?' Nipun was curious.

'I could have sacrificed everything for love but for that fateful evening. Arpan and I were having a heated discussion. I asserted that it was unjustified to expect all women to leave their own place and reside in their husband's house after marriage. Arpan had been on the verge of losing the argument. Then he barked, "In our country, even if women are educated, they have as much status as a man's shoe!"'

'Then you spat on him and left in a huff!' Nipun grinned.

'I can be nasty but not to that extent! But I did walk out on him.'

'So, how did you come to terms with your break-up?'

'I focused on academics. Maximum credit for my success in the MS entrance exam goes to my failed love!'

Nishtha didn't divulge everything. For the past few months, her parents had been cajoling her to agree to an arranged marriage. But whenever they raked up the topic, she acted hysterical and subsequently became incommunicado for a few days. That worked and they left her in peace. But all the while her parents were awash with guilt. They presumed that their daughter was heedless because of some lacunae in their parenting.

Both of them had thus indirectly indicated to each other that they were unattached. Nipun was hoping against hope that Nishtha would try her luck at yet another game of love.

Ultimately, the chief popped up in the conversation.

Nishtha began, 'Yesterday, I observed Dr Ujjwal while he was operating in the OT. His hand movements are magical. And he is so handsome.'

Nipun smiled. 'You mean to say that the chief has cast a magical spell on *you*!'

'Hey! Mind your language. I didn't mean that.'

'Come on. Be a sport. A conversation without some silliness is like a dish of unseasoned, boiled vegetables.'

Suddenly, Nishtha became pensive. 'Listen, everyone has been telling me to be wary of the chief. He is supposed to be a compulsive womanizer. The worst part is that he is single. What should I do if he tries to act fresh with me?'

'That is a very tricky situation,' Nipun agreed.

Both of them racked their brains. Then Nishtha rose

from her seat. 'I have a brilliant idea! Whenever I visit his office, I can take along some chilli powder spray with me.'

Nipun shook his head. 'Proposal rejected outright! The chief is going to shape your future career. You can't be enemies with the Loch Ness Monster if you live in the Loch Ness! The best strategy would be to pre-emptively quell any possible conflict.'

'But how?'

Both of them considered the problem once again with as much concentration as world leaders attending a round table conference in Geneva, in a last-ditch effort to avert the Third World War.

Finally, Nipun came up with a strange solution. 'You should get a fake fiancé to meet the chief. That puts a label on you—"Already Fixed Up"!'

'You have strong lateral thinking.'

'In addition, it is twisted!'

Nishtha's wry smile was an indicator that she was about to come up with a zinger and she did. 'There is another label on me and this one is meant for you—"Not Available"!'

'Your Highness! Whenever you do choose to descend from your high pedestal, this commoner will be glad to hold your hand,' Nipun said, gesturing like a theatre artist.

Nishtha held up her right middle finger and followed it up with a venomous look. Then, both of them exploded into laughter.

4
The King of Fiascos

Repeated failures can make humans believe that the universe is conspiring against them.

It was a special day. Even nerds were letting their hair down. Chants of '*Holi Hai*' resonated all over the city during the madness inducing festival of colours. It was a tradition for the junior doctors to visit Dr Ujjwal's home to celebrate Holi. Taking a break from his dadagiri (bullying behaviour) at the hospital, the chief played the perfect host. Also, in keeping with the spirit of the festival, he wilfully made a spectacle of himself.

After having smeared each other with dry colours in the hostels, the gang of doctors got into an open mini-truck. Most of them were high on alcohol, and low on inhibition. A dhol player provided the beats for their raucous singing, chalu (smutty) songs being the flavour of the day. Finally, they reached the terrace of Dr Ujjwal's house. There was a constant supply of hot snacks like samosas and pakoras. Here, Holi was played with wet colours, especially black and purple. Soon, many faces began to look ghostly.

'It is rumoured that the food contains cannabis, but nobody knows for sure,' Sehaj, the senior resident, told Nipun.

Since the pakoras tasted fine, Nipun felt that they didn't have the 'stuff'. So he helped himself to quite a few pieces. Minutes later, he laughed at Nishtha's multicoloured face. Then the laughter continued, incessantly, as if he was out of control like a vehicle with failed brakes, moving downhill. He didn't remember much of what happened later except that he had to be escorted by the seniors to his room. Here, he had seen a doubled image of himself in the mirror. Then he had collapsed on the bed and had woken up only the next morning.

The next day, he confronted Sehaj. 'I'm sure you knew for certain that the pakoras were laced with cannabis!'

Sehaj was nonchalant, 'Yes, I was in on it. That is why I ate so little. But you are not alone. Every year, the juniormost doctor makes a fool of himself in the very same way. Thankfully, you only laughed. Some weep or even reveal their secrets! I made a video of your antics. But don't worry; I won't put it up on YouTube.'

'Send it to me! Let me enjoy it, and also preserve it for my kids and grandkids!'

The very next day, Nipun was on duty in the indoor ward. As a first-year resident doctor, he had been assigned mundane jobs, which made him feel like a pack mule. Ward gossip and the possibility of amorous encounters of various degrees were of some excitement. But here too, the young doctors could start developing a sixth sense by keeping the other five senses in the fully receptive mode and consider ways to keep their sanity by becoming thick-skinned.

The day passed by uneventfully. In the evening, he began his rounds in the private ward. He was supposed to take the blood-pressure reading of three patients. After doing the needful on the first two patients, he was on his way to the third room.

A staff nurse stopped him on the way. 'Doctor, beware of the patient's husband. He is a retired general but he behaves as if he is still in office. Some of the nurses have come out of this room with tears in their eyes.'

But Nipun wasn't perturbed. He didn't expect a warlike situation in the event of recording of blood pressure.

While he was about to enter the room, there was an interruption again. Nipun heard a familiar voice call, 'Hey, Nipun!'

He looked back. He was not too enthused to find Sanket, although he had been Nipun's schoolmate. Sanket was also known as RH—Royal Highness. He had been the most despised boy in his class because he had enjoyed belittling others. Whenever he had been spotted at any gathering by his former schoolmates, they had stealthily moved to a different section of the venue to avoid spoiling their day.

'Hi! What are *you* doing here?' Nipun said, 'Are you making a big donation to the hospital?'

'That's a good joke! How can a kanjoos (miser) like me donate money? Actually, I've come to visit my uncle. He has been admitted into a "super-deluxe" private room in the department of neurology,' Sanket replied, with special emphasis on the word 'super-deluxe'.

'So,' Nipun asked, 'How is your job going?'

Sanket's face lit up. He seemed to have been eagerly

waiting for this question. 'Too good! Actually, I got a pay hike of 30 per cent after switching companies. Now, my monthly take-home salary is in six figures! What about you?'

Nipun felt more uncomfortable than an ageing actress when asked about her year of birth. 'I'm getting a stipend, not a salary.'

'Come on! Tell me, even if it is not respectable! I am not going to put the figure up on social media!' Sanket said with a sarcastic smile.

'Okay, I am making 27,000 bucks per month.'

'Ha ha! Even a peon in our company makes more than that,' Sanket said while he turned up his nose and pouted with his lips to make the most contemptuous expression Nipun had seen in a long while.

Nipun felt blood rush to his head. If he had not been in the hospital, he might have given Sanket such a slap that the vibrations alone would have been recorded on the nearby seismograph as a minor earthquake. Here, his only option was to use his tongue as a weapon.

'Who cares about a salary when there are so many hot women to sleep with?' Nipun said while mimicking Sanket's swagger.

Sanket was confused by such an unexpected benchmark of comparison. He looked like someone who had been demoted from an executive to a peon.

'I have to go. There's a lot of work to be done,' Nipun moved on quickly, leaving Sanket to lick his wounds.

Nipun entered the private room. The general sitting there had an extra-large body and a gravity-defying moustache. Nipun felt like a rabbit that has come face to face with a huge, golden eagle. Even before he could speak, Nipun was subjected to a round of unprovoked fire by the general.

'Doctor, it is written on the chart that my wife's BP is to be recorded at 8 p.m.! Why are you late by fifteen minutes?' he yelled.

He clenched his jaws hard and he looked like he could have chewed a bone. His eyeballs were protruding as if they were attempting to escape from their sockets. Nipun felt the earth beneath him quake. This was an overreaction on the general's part.

But Nipun was also a Doctor Sahib. He counter-attacked with equal ferocity.

'General Sahib, for all the patients in this ward, the same time, that is 8 p.m., is listed in the BP charts. How can it be possible for me to record the BP of all the patients simultaneously? I can't grow tentacles on my body!'

'Different timings could have been put on the chart for different patients! You are a typical civilian, with no concept of punctuality,' the general retorted. His eyeballs had acquired a reddish tinge. In the past few years, before his retirement, interaction for the general had been like one-way traffic. He had always been at the telling end and others at the listening end.

'As a doctor I know the value of time better than you!' Nipun shouted. He then rushed out of the room without waiting for the general's response because it could have hit him in a non-verbal form. He quickly walked through the corridor, looking back frequently to confirm that he was not being pursued. The staff nurses who were present at the nursing station smiled wryly. Although they had not heard the conversation in the private room, they had an idea of what had transpired.

But there was more to come. General Himmat Singh happened to be a personal friend of the chief. He complained to Dr Ujjwal—Nipun had not only come late, but also tried to tinker with his self-respect. Nipun was summoned to Dr Ujjwal's office.

'What happened?' the chief calmly asked. In order to resolve conflicts, he usually listened to both the warring parties before coming to a conclusion. But if the versions were contradictory, as was often the case, he resorted to his own investigations. There was no dearth of secret agents in the department. A number of doctors and staff members were ever ready to suck up to the chief.

Nipun described the incident as it had happened.

'I agree that you are not at fault. See, my friend, Himmat Singh, is a war hero. Unfortunately, he has a fixed notion—that most of the civilians are a depraved lot. This is actually true to some extent! See, when you face a vastly superior enemy, it is better to follow guerrilla tactics. You are so skilful at making excuses! So instead of arguing, you should have pretended that you were stuck in an emergency. That would have had the effect of pouring icy water over his hot head! Be straightforward with the disease, but be tactful with the humans!' the chief said.

Nipun stuck to his guns. 'Sir, I respect the faujis a lot. But this was a gross overreaction on the part of the general. He court-martialled me, without giving me a chance to defend myself!'

The chief pointed to a plaque. The adage 'The Boss is Always Right', was embossed over it.

Finally, Nipun smiled faintly. 'Yes, Sir! In fact, this is the mantra most commonly chanted by me,' he said.

The King of Fiascos • 35

Then, he walked out of the office, leaving the chief on a high.

The day before Gen. Himmat Singh's wife was to be operated on, Dr Ujjwal informed him, 'The surgery will begin at 8:30 a.m. sharp tomorrow.'

'Let us see,' the general replied sarcastically.

To play it safe, Dr Ujjwal asked the junior doctors to get the patient ready by 8 a.m. Thus, he kept a margin of half an hour to account for any delay.

But the surgery started at 8:45 a.m. The anaesthesiologist had gotten stuck in a traffic jam because a couple, along with their relatives and friends, had blocked the main road. They had been pressurizing the police to take action against a gang of girls who had been teasing their son.

Nipun was gleeful. 'Let the chief face the music now!' He expected the general to rustle up a mini tornado and direct it at the chief.

Pre-empting any hostile action, the chief apologized to the general for the delay.

The general replied, 'It's okay. Last night, I thought a lot about the lack of punctuality among the civilians. I have come to the conclusion that it is my mindset which needs to change! You can't fight a lone battle against more than a billion people!'

After his skirmish with Gen. Himmat Singh and the subsequent reprimand by the chief, Nipun was desperate to redeem himself. In fact, he hoped to become chief's blue-eyed boy through a judicious combination of hard work and sycophancy.

In the pre-operative room, Dr Ujjwal told Nipun to get an infant feeding tube for the six-month-old baby who was being operated on by a combined team consisting of the paediatric surgeon and the chief. As the feeding tube arrived, Nipun sensed an opportunity to show the chief that he always planned one step ahead. So, even before Dr Ujjwal had instructed him, he inserted the tube through the mouth into the stomach of the baby. After confirming that it was in the proper position, he eagerly waited for his boss to visit the bed and select him for the award of 'Doctor of the Year'.

Soon, Dr Ujjwal came to do his rounds. Upon looking at the child, however, he made one of the strangest expressions Nipun had ever seen. He was frowning and smiling at the same time.

'*Oye Ullu* (Idiot)! What is this? The infant feeding tube was supposed to drain his urine,' he howled. Then his facial expression turned decidedly wrathful.

'Sorry, Sir. It didn't occur to me that for the infants, the feeding tube could also be used as a catheter to drain their urine,' Nipun replied in a choked voice.

'Over-smartness is dangerous. Now take out this tube and get another one,' the chief said and left for the OT in a huff.

Nipun looked around. All the staff nurses were smiling. But he was not perturbed. Since the first-year resident doctor received no element of respect, there was no question of feeling insulted. He smiled back.

After reaching his room in the hostel, Nipun buried his head into the pillow. Ever since he had joined the department, he had been falling or failing. He could be typecast as a doctor who was more dangerous than the disease itself. Nipun thought of a few nicknames for himself—Jinxed, Wretched and Loser but he finally settled on The Fiasco King.

Consulting an astrologer seemed to be a way out. But he reasoned that even if his errant stars were determined, the cost of the corrective measures proposed by the astrologer would require him to take out a loan.

5

Some Consolation

> *Whenever a human being thinks that he has become equivalent to God, God intervenes so that the illusion is shattered soon.*

Nipun's next posting was in the surgical recovery unit, a vital area adjoining the OT where patients were shifted immediately after the completion of their surgeries. Melodramatic scenes were common here. The relatives of the patients often failed to hold back their emotions once they found their loved ones to be hale and hearty after the surgery. There were always some who feigned sentimentality to make their presence felt.

It was late in the afternoon. The last case had been shifted out of the OT at around 4 p.m. The chief had operated on a young girl named Piya. A part of her thyroid gland had been removed. Thyroidectomy was one of the few operations where Dr Ujjwal was utterly selfish—rarely did he give others a chance to conduct it.

The patient was comfortable. The monitors showed normal parameters. However, five minutes after her arrival, the normal bleeping sound of the monitor suddenly changed to an alarm tone. The doctors and the nurses were conditioned, through years of training, to become frantic once they heard it.

Everyone rushed to patient's bed. An oxygen mask was clamped to her face. But Piya's oxygen saturation fell further, and the alarm tone became shriller.

'Doctor, please... Save me!' Piya said, in between gasps. Nipun realized she was not responding to the oxygen supply because unusual blood collection in the operated area was pressing on the windpipe, thus obstructing it. He had to do something by himself, and promptly because waiting for the seniors could mean losing the patient.

'Get me the suture removal set. Fast!' Nipun shouted at the top of his voice.

Within a minute, he removed the stitches on her skin. This released the tension in the tissues and allowed the air to flow into the lungs. Piya's blue face turned pink.

'I feel much better now,' Piya said, after a moment. She was aware that she had escaped certain death.

Meanwhile, reinforcements arrived in the form of the senior doctors, well after the crisis had been taken care of. But just to throw their weight around, they provided some instructions.

Dr Ujjwal re-operated on the patient. As expected, a collection of blood was found. The offending, bleeding blood vessel was ligated.

Once the patient had been shifted back to the recovery unit, Dr Ujjwal patted Nipun on the back. 'But for your presence of mind, we may have lost this patient. You are not as useless as I had presumed!'

For Nipun, even the sarcasm laced appreciation was a big boost. After a long time, he had the courage to believe in himself. But there was an upsetting thought too. *Even a vastly experienced surgeon like Dr Ujjwal had erred in conducting his specialized procedure. This implied that anyone who called himself a perfect surgeon was a bluff master!*

Nipun opened up to Nakul, his senior. 'If some resident doctor had caused this complication, the chief would have told him to leave the course and join a butcher! But there is no one to take the chief to task.'

'And yet he converts donkeys like us into accomplished surgeons! For this, he has had to own up many complications that were caused by us. In fact, we shall never be able to repay the chief for his contribution to our professional life,' Nakul said.

Although he didn't show it, Dr Ujjwal felt remorseful. *When someone has illusions of being a God, God shows him his place!* he introspected.

He had many more opportunities for such reflections during the next few nights because even the sedatives failed to seduce sleep.

On the day that Piya was discharged from the hospital, she, along with her parents, met Nipun. When Piya touched Nipun's feet, he blessed her–like a saint with his hand on her head. A box of sweets was offered to him by Piya's father.

Nipun smiled. 'There was no need for this. Piya hasn't survived because of me. When the agents of death came to fetch her, she told them: "It is a case of mistaken identity. My name is Riya"!'

Although he was feigning his modesty, Nipun's chest swelled with pride.

The father of the girl said, 'She does owe her life to you. These sweets are from my own shop. As long as I am alive, I will personally present you with a box of sweets every year on her birthday.'

Nipun, who was fond of sweets, thanked him gleefully.

'Her wedding is in a month. You have to attend it. In fact, Piya is adamant about not taking her marriage vows without your presence.'

My fan club has been initiated, Nipun thought.

After everyone had gone away, Nipun opened the box and quickly introduced a piece of kalakand (a type of Indian sweetmeat) into his waiting mouth. It seemed to have been made just for him—a special batch. He kept on eating, delighting his taste buds till his stomach expressed helplessness. Then, he hid the box. The sweets were too heavenly to be shared with others. After a few hours, Nipun was drawn back to it again. He looked at the box longingly. But the thought of the weighing scale stopped him from opening it.

Suddenly, his hand moved towards the box.

'Fuck self-control!' he bellowed, and finished it all.

6

The Sweetest Surgeon

The nickname often describes a person more accurately than the proper name.

Nishtha was able to cope quite well with her duties. The previous year, when she had been just an intern, she had worked with so much zeal that even her boyfriend had been barred from distracting her during duty hours. As a result, unlike some other junior doctors, she didn't develop cold feet when asked to carry out basic procedures like putting intravenous lines and taking blood samples.

Nishtha was on her first night duty. She was mentally prepared to match the nocturnality of the owls.

The senior resident doctors were also posted for the night. But these highly educated bullies were often busy in the OT, conducting emergency surgeries. During these hours, the lowly junior doctor had a taste of power. But they also had to take on a lot of responsibility. Apart from looking after the patients, and keeping staff members on their toes, one had to troubleshoot any medical or non-medical issues that could crop up. The dark nooks and corners had to be watched for signs of any suspicious, amorous activity. Couples had been caught red-handed, in various stages of intimacy, in the unlikeliest of places. And sometimes, the moral police themselves indulged in these immoral acts.

Just after she had finished her *single* course dinner, Nishtha got a call from the private ward. She rushed to attend to the call. The patient, a fifty-year-old male, looked much older. *He has either manipulated his date of birth or has a strong ageing gene*, Nishtha reasoned.

Two days ago, Dr Anuroop, alias Candy, the second-in-command of the unit, had operated on him to remove his gall bladder through a keyhole surgery. Presently, he was feeling uneasy.

Nishtha examined the patient. He had prominent frown lines on his forehead. When he strained his features further, they converted into deep crevasses. With his Type-A personality, the patient was bound to keep the doctors and nurses busy. Nishtha assumed that he must also be annoying his family, who had no choice but to put up with him and his friends, if he had any left. His blood pressure, pulse rate and breathing were normal, and the abdomen was also soft. She came back to the nursing counter with the look of a student who had just read an out-of-syllabus question in an exam.

'Staff, this patient seems to be on edge due to the hospital environment. He must be thinking of us as witches! What do I do?' Nishtha asked Angela, the staff nurse on duty.

'Doctor, this patient actually requires candy!' Angela replied. 'I mean you should sit with him for a while, and reassure him in a sweet, gentle way. That will work better than an injection.'

Nishtha did as advised. Soon, the patient was as comfortable as he could be in a hospital.

'Thanks, Angela. I am much wiser.'

Both of them returned to the nursing station. Even though it was past midnight, Angela looked as fresh as morning dew. After initial resistance, her biological clock had synchronized with her waking hours.

'Come,' Angela gestured. 'Let us have tea. Work will never end. Us medicos have no choice but to resort to stolen moments of relaxation!'

'You used the word "candy". I have heard that's what Dr Anuroop is also called,' Nishtha said with a wink.

'To understand the workings of this surgical unit, you need to know quite a few facts—especially about Dr Anuroop. To avoid being overshadowed by a big shot like Dr Ujjwal, he has developed a smart strategy. While Dr Ujjwal is a surgical artist, Dr Anuroop is adept at social skills. The charm manoeuvre begins as soon as the patient is admitted into the hospital. On the rounds, he tells the staff nurse, "This patient is well known to me. Take special care of him." After the patient has been discharged, Dr Anuroop pays them a surprise visit—the very next day. Ultimately, he develops such rapport with his patients that they start thinking of him as a family member and start addressing him as 'bade bhaiya'. In fact, Dr Ujjwal has personally coined his nickname. It has caught on so much that some doctors don't even know his real name!' Angela explained.

Nishtha added, 'I think his baby face also makes him seem like he has an adorable personality.'

'Have you noticed his butt? Doesn't it look like that of a lady?' Angela chuckled.

'Yes. If he walks on heels, I will surely get a complex!' Nishtha added.

Both of them laughed heartily. The relative of a patient passing by wondered what could be so funny at midnight.

They must be telling jokes to each other to stay awake! he thought.

Nishtha continued, 'Now I understand why Dr Anuroop does almost as many surgeries as Dr Ujjwal.'

'Dr Anuroop has many other tricks up his sleeve,' Angela added. 'He tells the patients, especially villagers—"I apply stitches with a machine!"'

'Cool! That is a good way to impress them. How does he actually do it? I am not aware of any machine which is used for applying stiches.'

'He simply applies the staples.'

'Very smart!'

'Dr Anuroop is known as a surgeon of the English language because he cuts and alters words. He also has a unique email address—theperfectsurgeon@gmail.com.'

'Wow! With so many freakish characters in the department, there will be lot of free entertainment!' Nishtha smiled.

But even Angela knew only a few of the details. Candy had undergone an English-speaking course thrice, but he had wasted his hard-earned money each time. The way he twisted the language amused many, but it also exasperated the purists. Candy's upbringing had a lot to do with it. He was born and brought up in a remote village where the only English word used was time, pronounced 'tem'.

That night, Nishtha realized she could learn many fundas from the staff nurses—they had lot of interaction with the patients. Of course, gossip-mongering sessions with them were vital too—to maintain a work-life balance.

All night, something or the other kept happening. Finally at 4 a.m., Nishtha was able to settle on the recliner in the doctor's duty room, which felt like a feather bed to her weary body. Before she knew it, she had dozed off.

But just half an hour later, she woke up abruptly. Two hands on her shoulder were shaking her rather harshly.

'Get up, Doctor! Cardiac arrest!'

Nishtha's sleepiness vanished in an instant. She started running behind Angela. They reached the bed of an old lady in the ward. 'The patient had been operated by Dr Candy three days ago for a hiatus hernia. She was absolutely fine until a few minutes back,' Angela panted.

A staff nurse had already started the cardiac massage. Although an ambubag with mask was available, an excess of adrenaline rush made Nishtha go straightaway for mouth-to-mouth resuscitation. She made an airtight lock of her lips with those of the patient. Then she exhaled with full force. After three puffs from Nishtha, the patient's own breathing started. Miraculously, the patient was revived.

The ECG indicated that patient had undergone a heart attack. She was shifted to the Intensive Coronary Care Unit.

In the morning, after finishing her exhausting duty, a dopey Nishtha was slowly walking back to her hostel. On the way, she bumped into Nipun.

'Hey, how was your first night?'

'Respectable! I attended to a lot of calls. In the morning, I revived a patient through mouth-to-mouth resuscitation,' Nishtha said with pride.

'Why didn't you use the ambubag?'

'I forgot to use it and realized my mistake later.'

'You are crazy! So many diseases can be transmitted by

mouth to mouth resuscitation.'

'I did it in the heat of the moment, and I don't regret it. But the bad breath of the patient did disturb me!' Nishtha chuckled.

Meanwhile, unknown to Nipun and Nishtha, the relatives of the patient were seething with rage. The family had a trait which had been passed down, from generation to generation. They looked for a scapegoat whenever anything went wrong. They assumed that some blunder during the surgery had led to the heart attack. A few brawny men, whose brains had shrunk because of years of disuse, entered Candy's office. They didn't care to go through his personal assistant.

'Bhai Sahib, please have a seat,' Candy said gently, realizing that a display of arrogance could add him to the list of battered doctors.

'Doctor, what went wrong during the surgery? She was hale and hearty at the time of admission. But now she is on her deathbed,' the oldest among the group said. He stared so menacingly at Candy that he nearly lost voluntary control of his bladder.

Candy recognized him to be the husband of the patient. He was the same person who had previously told Candy, 'You are like God for us'.

'See, I am one of the best surgeons in the country! The heart attack was not due to any complications during the surgery,' Candy explained. 'It might have been caused by stress or some unknown factor. In fact, we have done a video recording of her surgery. If you still have reason to doubt me, you can get the DVD from my office and show it to whoever you feel like.'

All of them looked at each other; they seemed disappointed to lose the opportunity of roughing up a doctor.

'All right, Doctor. There is no need of the DVD. We believe you,' the mellowed spokesman for the tough family said. All of them left the office.

'Once a surgeon uses the scalpel to cut up a patient, he becomes the culprit of anything that goes wrong with their body, or even life, later on!' Candy grumbled.

Luckily, the lady came out of the ICCU safe and sound.

The next day, Nishtha attended the OT with Candy. She noticed a portable stereo on one of the slabs.

'Who has brought this?' she asked Sanchi, the theatre-in-charge.

'Like some of the other surgeons, Dr Anuroop likes to listen to music, especially during long surgeries. It helps him concentrate better.'

As soon as the patient was shifted onto the operation table, Candy turned the stereo on. Devotional songs dedicated to Lord Krishna began to play. Sujay, the patient, was comforted that he was being treated by god-fearing doctors. But as soon as the patient was knocked off by the anaesthesia, Candy told the theatre staff to put on songs from Bollywood movies.

Sujay had a collection of pus in his right buttock. The

quack who had given him an injection a week ago to treat his fever had probably been miserly in the use of the spirit that was used for cleaning the skin.

'I love draining abscesses. The sight of pus gushing out really excites me!' a beaming Candy said.

'Blood, pus and urine are good company for the surgeons!' Nishtha added, smiling.

After cleaning and draping the patient, Candy made the incision. At least 100 ml of pus poured out.

The wound was left open. That was all Candy had to do. From that moment, Nishtha took over. She had to do the daily dressing, which took around fifteen minutes each day. When she cleaned the wound by irrigating it under pressure with a syringe, the saline solution would often land on her pretty toes.

But her efforts were not in vain. Within a few days, the wound healed completely.

Two weeks after the patient had been discharged, his wife came to the OPD. She touched Candy's feet. 'Doctor Sahib. You have transformed my life completely.'

Candy was puzzled. He had only treated her husband's abscess. How on earth could he have affected her life so profoundly? The only philosophical advice he used to give to others was, 'Be a hedonist. Take each day as it comes.'

She continued, 'Doctor, while discharging my husband, you warned him that if he continued to consume alcohol, the infection would recur in a more virulent form, and could even lead to impotence. He has followed your advice. As if it was a commandment from a messiah! I've been trying to make him quit drinking for so long. He's even taken my threat to commit suicide very lightly! But he hasn't consumed even a drop for the past two weeks, and has vowed never to touch alcohol again.'

'There is no need to thank me,' Candy replied, 'Your husband is like a younger brother,' making the lady so sentimental that tears began to stream down her cheeks.

Candy was delighted. *Ah! There is another addition to my family*! he thought.

Nishtha felt that there was no appreciation for the person who did the dirty work of repeated dressings. But she realized that the credit for success always went to the team leader. She would have to slog a lot before attaining that exalted status.

7

A Nation of Cricket Maniacs

The day an important cricket match occurs, the Indian economy suffers.

The day Nipun had been eagerly waiting for had finally arrived. He had gotten a chance to assist in a major surgery. Daksh, the patient, was a property dealer. Rumour was that he had lost many deals because of his addiction to cricket.

He was to be operated on because he had a tumour of the adrenal glands, known as pheochromocytoma. Daksh didn't need to ride a roller coaster for the adrenaline rush. The tumour was constantly pumping excess adrenaline into the bloodstream. On the flip side, it was causing high blood pressure, palpitations and other symptoms. The usually placid man had become hot-headed. A high-risk consent form had been filled. The patient's relatives had been told that there was a chance, although quite remote, that this might be his last day as an honoured inhabitant of planet earth.

Just before the patient was to be shifted inside the theatre, Nipun interacted with Daksh to purge his mind of apprehensions—with a combination of true and false assurances.

Just when Nipun was about to leave, Daksh said, 'Doctor, one last question. What is the Indian team's score? I wanted to bring my mobile to check out the live cricket action, but I was not allowed to do so by the security man at the entrance. He got worked up over it, as if I were trying to smuggle in a firearm!'

Nipun was aghast. The realtor was being absurd. He was behaving like someone who is on the edge of a precipice but focuses on the scenery instead of watching his step.

He was aware that India was playing a cricket match in Australia but had not been following it. As a boy, Nipun had played street cricket, and he had broken a sufficient number of windowpanes to qualify as a respectable player. Frequent chases by angry homeowners had also helped him become a good sprinter. But after his admission into a medical college, because of a number of women in his class, he had discovered more exciting pastimes.

'I don't care for cricket,' Nipun declared.

Daksh looked scornfully at Nipun, as if he were the disowned child of Mother India. Nipun realized that if he didn't henceforth follow the game, he could very well become the victim of a hate crime.

The preparations for the surgery had begun a day in advance. Doctors of the surgical as well as the anaesthesia teams had also been coping with the secretion of copious amounts of adrenaline in their blood. Like exam-taking students, they were frantically reading about the disease and its management until the very last moment.

The arrangement of instruments, by the theatre-in-charge, Sanchi, looked like a work of art. The scissors with the golden tips took pride of place. The chief's attachment to it could even put the most lovey-dovey couple to shame. When the scissors became blunt, it was sharpened, but never replaced.

When the anaesthesiologist started the induction of anaesthesia by putting a gas mask on his face, Daksh snatched the mask away. He spoke in a slurred voice, 'Sir, where is Dr Ujjwal?'

'He is in the surgeon's room. His juniors will finish cleaning the skin as well as the draping, and then he will take over.'

But Daksh was adamant. 'I refuse to be anaesthetized till I see Dr Ujjwal's face!'

Obviously, he was afraid that some junior surgeon would operate on him and send him off to heaven.

Daksh's demand was conceded to. Dr Ujjwal entered the OT.

'Hey, I'm here. Don't worry. Except for me, all the surgeons will refrain from operating on you!' he said to Daksh and began scrubbing up.

Daksh was anaesthetized. While the surgery was complex, the chief, too, had a highly convoluted cerebrum. He knew about the pitfalls and how to circumvent them. Finally, the tumour was removed. After the surgery had ended, Dr Srinivas, the anaesthesiologist, told the patient to show his tongue. He wanted to check whether he had woken up fully.

Daksh stuck out his tongue. Its orange colour was a

telltale sign of frequent rendezvous with supari.

Everyone was relieved. But the monitor suddenly blurted out the alarm tone—his blood pressure had suddenly shot up. The anti-hypertensive drug was promptly administered intravenously. Within two minutes, the blood pressure was normal again.

Dr Srinivas looked at the patient. He couldn't help but grin. Daksh's tongue was still protruding.

'Why are you teasing me?' Dr Srinivas asked, rather tongue-in-cheek.

'Doctor, you asked me to stick out my tongue. How could I put the tongue back into my mouth without your instructions?'

Dr Srinivas couldn't help laughing. 'You are right. It's my fault!'

After the extensive surgery was over, Nipun heaved a sigh of relief. As he had been assigned the most awkward position around the operation table, Nipun had developed a cramp in his right forearm. A gentle massage by a pair of lovely hands could have comforted him in no time. But he would have to make do with the balm on offer, which didn't even have an enchanting image on the label of the jar, not even one of the divas who mentioned it in their item songs.

As the patient was being shifted after the surgery, Nipun realized he had forgotten to update himself on the latest cricket score. What if the patient asked for it in the recovery room? He found it on his mobile immediately. India had lost the test match. That was worrisome. If the diehard fan found out, he could have wild fluctuations in his blood pressure, and could even go into cardiac arrest.

To his relief, the patient spoke out a '*Hai Ram*' instead.

The post-operative pain, which started as soon as he was shifted to recovery, had taken his attention off the match. An opiate injection was promptly administered to him. It zapped the pain and also put him to sleep. In his dreams he was likely to hear a newsreader announce that the Indian cricket team had *won* the match.

'Nipun, the patient is still not out of danger. His BP has to be monitored very closely. I am posting you here for the night, and Sehaj will cover the evening. You are not going to leave the recovery room at all, even if God orders you to!' the chief said with a straight face.

'Yes, Sir. If God calls for me, I will request that he wait till morning. I will plead that serving mankind is *as good* as serving God!' Nipun replied.

Immediately, he realized that he had breached the unofficial code of conduct with his chief.

But the chief had relished Nipun's witticism. He didn't recall any junior doctor daring to use humour as a medium of communication with him. However, Nipun had been funny without being disrespectful; he had sort of liked it.

The day before the next OT, the operation list was being prepared.

'Tomorrow, both of us are going to operate on a patient who has a stricture of the small intestine. He also suffers from AIDS,' Nakul told Nipun calmly, as if his white blood cells had special spikes which could stab all AIDS viruses to death.

Nipun had known that this had had to happen someday. Still, his immediate reaction was one would expect from any other human who had to have a brush with the don of the microbe mafia.

'Why does our unit have to take up the cases where there is such risk to the surgeons and OT staff?' Nipun couldn't help but say this to Nakul, although he risked coming across as a spineless doctor.

Nakul replied, 'Ours is the apex institute. So we can't pass on the buck. The Supreme Court doesn't refer its cases anywhere else! Don't worry. We'll be using double gloves, waterproof gowns and gumboots. If you are scared, you can put on an additional glove!'

'What if there is an accidental injury to our hand? From the suture needle? That can easily pierce through layers of gloves!'

'Yes. That is a major worry. But there is only 0.3 per cent chance of contracting AIDS after a needle injury, and the risk can be decreased even further by post exposure drug treatment.'

'And yet cases have been reported in literature, about the surgeons actually contracting an infection from the patients,' Nipun said.

He kept tossing in bed the whole night and even visualized magnified images of sadist virus particles moving in his blood vessels, annihilating his body cells at will.

The next day, the operation was carried out smoothly. However, throughout the surgery, Nipun's heartbeat had often crossed one hundred and twenty, especially whenever the suture needle had passed close to his gloved fingers. But by the end of the surgery, he had conquered his fears.

Nakul had relished the jittery look on Nipun's face in the morning and had wanted to scare the shit out of him once again. He told Nipun, 'In three days, we are operating on a patient who is Hepatitis C positive. Be prepared!'

'I am okay with it,' Nipun said, without even a semblance of a quiver in his voice. He had come to terms with it; a synonym of 'conducting surgery' was 'playing with fire'.

After he had left the OT, Nipun went into the doctors' duty room, where Nishtha was waiting for him. Nipun's eyes sparkled upon noticing her tiffin.

He had perfected the fine art of poaching the food brought by the staff nurses and female doctors. The women were happy to feed the sprightly guy who had been bringing cheer into their lives with his witticisms and humour.

'Come on, Nishtha. Show me what you have for lunch.'

'Something special. Veg pulao.'

As she opened the tiffin, the aroma of basmati rice, bay leaves and cloves triggered feverish activity in his olfactory nerves. He became nostalgic. His mom used to make a great pulao. It had often triggered fights among the siblings for a bigger share.

I have to eat this at any cost. If she refuses, I will snatch the tiffin and run away! Nipun thought.

He tried a soft approach first. 'Let me help you with finishing this. There are two benefits. You can earn brownie points from God by feeding a hungry mouth. And, there will be a lighter burden on your weighing scale!'

'Stop your *bak bak* (nonsense) and eat!' Nishtha replied.

Nipun tucked into the pulao. Before he knew it, he had emptied out more than half of the grub. The rest he handed over to Nishtha.

'Sorry for leaving so little. It was so scrumptious that I had to make a superhuman effort to stop.'

'Please wash the spoon because there is only one,' Nishtha said in a stern voice.

This was an unexpected complication. Nishtha was unequivocally giving him the red signal.

Nipun, however, was not the one to admit defeat easily. He began, 'See, even when people kiss passionately, there is some exchange of saliva. There is no medical study to substantiate any kind of harm in that. So why should you bother about us eating with the same spoon?'

Nishtha didn't say anything. She picked up the spoon, washed it and began eating with it.

'If your snubs were legal offences, you would have been sentenced to life imprisonment—in my custody!' Nipun grinned.

Nishtha smiled too. His comical advances never failed to amuse her.

Dr Ujjwal's conduct was a big surprise for Nishtha. Before her joining, Nishtha had been warned by all and sundry to not opt for his surgical unit. They had explained that it was full of depraved surgeons. But the best way to persuade Nishtha to do something was to dissuade her from it. However, the chief never made a pass at her. She had even been scolded by Dr Ujjwal a few times although in a gentler manner as compared to Nipun; probably because the chief had not wanted to make her cry.

Nipun went back to his hostel room to freshen up. On the way, he met Shishir, his old classmate who was studying for an MD in dermatology. He was sitting in the corridor outside his room, with a cup of coffee in one hand and a bestseller in the other. After he returned from his duty in the evening, Shishir rarely needed to go back to the department because there were so few emergencies in dermatology. Also, Shishir had no extra co-curricular agenda to visit the department.

Shishir got a chair for Nipun. 'Come, sit for a while.'

Openly admitting to feeling envious, Nipun said, 'I made a blunder by taking up surgery. Otherwise, I would also be leading the high life, much like you.'

'But I miss the excitement of the surgical branches! The aura surgeons have is unmatched,' Shishir replied.

Their subsequent discussion soon reached a dead end. They came to the conclusion that a neighbour's wife always looks prettier than your own wife. Each of them would remain unsatisfied—even if they were able to exchange branches.

8

The Bitter Experiences of Candy

A mismatch between aspirations and abilities often leads to funny situations.

After being released from his addiction of exploring topography, comprising two identical hills and a distant valley, Dr Ujjwal decided to widen his horizons by visiting other lands. But he was afraid that during his absence, Candy would cause havoc in the department.

Dr Ujjwal was also handicapped by the fact that he couldn't rely upon Dr Vishesh, the head of the second unit, who was his bête noire. Although, there was an uneasy truce for the past few months, previously, both of them had regaled the hospital staff with their fights, which often resembled those at cheap drinking taverns. During their last skirmish, a gaudily dressed, small-time crook, the relative of an admitted patient, had needed to intervene in order to separate them. He couldn't help but comment, 'Have some decency! Don't demean your white coat!'

Those doctors who had tried to mediate between them, without any success were of the opinion that both of them derived an uncanny pleasure out of the conflict. Thus, they kept it simmering, on one pretext or the other.

Since quite a few of Dr Ujjwal's classmates had settled in the US, many evenings of unrestrained revelry were guaranteed during his trip there. To lessen the guilt of taking such a long holiday, Dr Ujjwal tinged it with academia, by registering for the two-day-long International Conference of Surgery being held in New York.

As soon as he received confirmation of his visa, Dr Ujjwal called all the doctors of his surgical unit into his office.

'I am going to America for about a month. You have to work with the same zeal. Don't let me down!' he said, gesturing like a motivational speaker.

All the doctors chorused 'Yes, Sir', to please the chief. They were beaming. Without Dr Ujjwal, the work was likely to be a fraction of what it presently was. At least, for a little while, they could eat their meals unhurriedly, and not just gulp it down only to leave their taste buds disappointed. Their sleeplessness was also likely to disappear unless caused by a budding love affair. The married ones could make love without having to look at the clock frequently. Those who had been feeling down because of their inability to take advantage of discounts and sales could bounce back with the help of retail therapy. Dhairya and Vibhore, the two bookworms were excited too at the prospect of devouring more books.

Dr Ujjwal had a separate meeting with Candy. He had no choice but to put him in charge. 'Dear Anuroop, take up only those surgeries about which you feel absolutely confident.'

'Okay, Sir! Hand over all the departmental worries to me—and enjoy your trip!' Candy replied in his usual, overconfident manner.

After he had come out of Dr Ujjwal's office, Candy

murmured to himself, 'The chief thinks God stopped creating good surgeons after he came along!'

Candy wanted to make the most of his temporary leadership. But he also hoped for an even bigger windfall. During the trip, the chief could get entangled with a gorgeous lady and stay in the US for good. That could lead to a velvet revolution in the department, resulting in the coronation of Candy as the king.

Even on his last day in the department, Dr Ujjwal was in the OT. The operation list was quite long. His flight was supposed to leave at 10:30 in the night. But even past 6 p.m., Dr Ujjwal was seen clinging to the operation table like a leech. Candy, Nipun and other doctors were left to wonder what he was up to.

Nipun could not restrain himself. 'Sir, I am afraid the plane might take off without you on board.'

Dr Ujjwal was unruffled. 'I have the luggage in the boot of my car, and my driver, who drives at a supersonic speed, is just waiting to take off! I will leave for the airport straight from the hospital. I know the reason for your discomfort. If my trip is cancelled, your plans to freak out in my absence will not materialize!'

The chief finished his surgery a few minutes after that and headed straight to the airport.

Nipun was impressed. 'When I become a top surgeon, I shall also be the last passenger to board the flight, like Dr Ujjwal.'

Just three days after the chief left for the US, Candy examined a patient with cancer of the pancreas. The patient had actually been referred in the name of Dr Ujjwal. But sensing an opportunity to prove his mettle, Candy decided to take up the case himself.

He proceeded on to his favourite part—tackling the relatives. 'I am an *internationally renowned expert* in the surgical treatment of cancer of the pancreas!' he told them, 'Hopefully your patient will be discharged in around ten days.'

The relatives were put in a quandary. They couldn't have waited for Dr Ujjwal's return, considering the urgent requirement for treatment. Moreover, Candy seemed to be a competent and compassionate doctor.

The patient was admitted into the hospital and investigated. The Whipple procedure, a marathon surgery, was planned for the next day.

The resident doctors were all flustered. The same evening, the junior doctors held a secret meeting in Nipun's hostel room.

Nipun began, 'Even Dr Ujjwal gets a cold sweat while operating on the pancreas. Although Candy's intentions are good, he is no match for the chief when it comes to the Whipple procedure. We have to do something for the patient's sake!'

'For our sake too! If there is a complication, we will have to do the dressing and other sundry jobs. Candy will only pass orders with his sexy lips!' Saksham chipped in.

Everyone had a good laugh.

'If a close-up photo of Candy's face is cropped to reveal only his lips, they could be mistaken for those of a lipstick model!' Saksham continued.

'The only way out is to convince the patient to go to some other hospital,' Sehaj, the senior resident said.

Nipun volunteered. 'Leave it to me.'

He roped in Ejaz, one of his close friends. Ejaz had been working as a resident doctor in the second unit. They fine-tuned their plan together.

Ejaz went to the patient's room and called the relatives outside so that the patient couldn't hear the conversation.

He said with a poker face, 'I just wanted to inform you—out of the ten such cases that we have operated on in the last one year alone, five did survive the surgery! Out of five that survived, four had to be re-operated. Two out of these survived and two died. Please sign the consent form.'

'Doctor Sahib, please allow us some time to decide about the surgery,' one of the relatives replied immediately. All of them were shuddering with fear.

After Ejaz had moved away, the patient's father told his relatives, 'This unit seems to be staffed by butchers rather than surgeons! Let us get out of this place.'

They immediately got the patient discharged and shifted him into another hospital.

When Candy got to know about this, he was incensed. 'Nipun! I'm sure someone misguided the relatives.'

'Sir, I heard that a doctor employed in Noble Hospital visited them. He might have convinced the relatives to shift the patient to his hospital.'

'*Bluddy hell*! This profession is going down and down, down and down,' Candy fumed.

The standard of Candy's English also refuses to change direction! Nipun smiled.

Even after the disappearance of the patient, Candy

was undeterred. The next day, he admitted an even more complicated case, in which a part of the patient's liver had to be removed. The resident doctors were in a quandary again. But they were afraid to repeat their con. However, to their utter surprise, Candy discharged the patient that same evening.

A sustained investigation conducted by the junior doctors cleared the air. When Sanchi had read the operation list for the next day, she had been shocked to know about Candy's plan to conduct a liver resection. She visualized a major bloodbath in the OT. Sanchi swung into action and informed the chief of anaesthesia. He was so outraged that he complained directly to the director.

The director summoned Candy to his office. Unfortunately for Candy, a member of the management had just left the director's office after having levelled some false allegations onto him. Candy came in handy for the director to offload his exasperation expeditiously. He used adjectives that don't find mention in the mainstream dictionaries. Candy was also ordered to discharge the patient and refer him to a hospital where liver resections were done routinely.

The next day, an operation day, passed uneventfully because there were only straightforward cases, all of which were well within Candy's capability.

But all was not over for the junior doctors. Candy had a notion that to feel like a big boss, he had to intimidate the juniors. So he actively looked for flaws on the part of the resident doctors. During ward rounds, Candy noticed that Nipun had forgotten to put progress notes on a case sheet. This was just a minor oversight since it had no bearing on the treatment of the patient.

'Why haven't you completed the progress notes?' he shouted.

'Sir, I was busy with a dressing and I had planned to do it in the evening,' Nipun replied.

'I feel like throwing you out of the window!' Candy barked again. His baby face looked even funnier in its angry avatar. The staff nurses struggled to supress their laughter. Even Nipun wasn't intimidated.

He looked at the window and replied, 'Sir, there is a passage right underneath the window! If you throw me out, I might injure someone by falling on him!'

Candy's face underwent an immediate transformation. Arching his head backwards, he started laughing loudly. 'Want to see a combination of a comedian and a surgeon? Look no further,' Candy said while pointing his finger at Nipun.

The team had now been working for two weeks without the tyrannical presence of the chief. Everyone was happy with the exception of Nakul. As a consequence of the reduced burning of calories, coupled with binge-eating, he had put on four kilos.

When he entered the OPD complex in the morning, Nipun noticed that the waiting area outside Candy's chamber was crowded. 'What is the matter? I hope Candy has not announced a sale on surgeries! He can resort to any gimmick.'

A patient who had come for a follow-up visit, stood up. 'Sir, I have been waiting for half an hour. Dr Anuroop's meeting is taking too long.'

Nipun entered Candy's chamber after knocking at the door. Candy was alone in the room, playing Candy Crush on his mobile phone.

'Sir, has the meeting finished?' Nipun asked.

'Arrey buddhu (idiot), there is no meeting! This is just a tactic to create a respectable crowd outside my chamber! When you interrupted my game, I was about to exceed my last high score. All right! Start calling in the patients one by one,' Candy winked.

A middle-aged man showed up with complaints of a pain in the right lower abdomen.

'At last, we have a patient for admission!' Candy murmured. He told the patient to lie down on the examination couch. Then he put a hand on his right lower abdomen. Since it was tender at the place where the appendix is located, he jumped to the diagnosis of acute appendicitis.

The patient was told, 'You are suffering from an infection of the appendix. We will do an ultrasound, along with a few blood tests. Most likely, a minor surgery will be needed.'

'Doctor, my appendix has already been removed two years ago! Does it regenerate with time?' said the bewildered patient.

By having felt the abdomen without lifting the patient's shirt, Candy had missed the scar from the previous surgery. For the resident doctors, controlling their laughter was as difficult as retreating from the verge of ejaculation.

After the patient had left, Candy addressed all the doctors, 'You should have ensured the patient removed the shirt *before* the examination. Even a brilliant leader fails if he has such a bad team!'

During their lunch break in the mess, the resident doctors laughed their hearts out at Candy's antics.

The OPD started again. The next patient was called in. Muktesh's ailment had gotten complicated after he had relied on the unsafe hands and unknowledgeable mind of a village quack who had been the sole medical service provider in his remote village.

'Why did you seek treatment from a fraudster?' Candy shouted at the patient.

'When I have severe abdominal pain at midnight, it is the fake doctor who gives me the painkiller injection, not Dr Anuroop!' replied the patient, leaving Candy speechless.

After the patient had left, Candy addressed the junior doctors. 'With a single sentence, the patient has spoken volumes about the anomalies of the healthcare system in our country. In remote areas, qualified doctors are an endangered species. While in big cities, there are some localities with more clinics and hospitals than paan shops.'

A conference on infection control was being held at Nirog Hospital. Candy had always wished to shine at such events. Previously, he had been ignored since he was seen as a Lilliputian character in comparison to the chief. This was a god-sent opportunity. Candy shot off a series of emails to the organizing team, requesting them to make him chairperson. He reinforced this with phone calls, which were more annoying than those of telemarketers. The organizing secretary of the conference assigned Candy to chair a session, just to get him off his back.

As the session began, Candy took his seat proudly along with co-chairs. The first presentation began. But after a few minutes, the novelty wore off. He had to sit stiff and also had to desist from scratching his crotch or picking his nose. The delegates as well as the video cameras were keeping constant watch over him. Moreover, he needed to pay attention to the speakers because he was required to give his comments at the end of each talk.

After the first talk, the next speaker ascended the stage. The potent combination of monochrome slides and a monotonous voice caused an epidemic of sleepiness across the auditorium.

By the time the third presentation had started, Candy had begun to feel uneasy. It came from down below. His bladder gave him a gentle reminder that it had to be emptied. He became restless. He realized that the strong coffee he had consumed just before the session was the main culprit. He had chided the waiter manning the coffee machine for being so miserly with the instant coffee mix. The annoyed waiter had then used a whole teaspoon to make his cup. Even during the normal course of the day, his bladder was always so restless that he had had to mark his presence in the loo every hour or so.

There was no way he could leave the stage. To add to his misery, most of the speakers were overshooting their slotted time limits—in a bid to make an impact on the audience. He thanked the heavens when the last speaker did not turn up. But the question session with the audience was still to happen. To his chagrin, the doctors in the audience turned out to be an inquisitive lot. A number of them raised their hands to ask each of the speakers a question. Candy calculated—at least fifteen minutes would pass while doing this, and that was not all. At the end of the conference, mementoes were to be presented to all the speakers, followed by a group photo. By the time that came to pass, he was sure to lose control. His wet trousers would be duly captured, by the camera men and stared at by the delegates—a scenario in which he could then die of embarrassment.

In panic, Candy decided to act. He closed his eyes, leaned forward and let his head fall onto the table. Commotion followed. Many doctors rushed on to the stage. He was lifted up from the chair and made to lie down on the floor. His lower body was raised. All the while, Candy slowed down his breathing. After an auscultation of his heart with the stethoscope, a doctor announced that Candy was still clinging on to his life. But everyone wondered why he had not woken up quickly, like a typical case of blackout. Candy felt like laughing at the hullabaloo he had created, but he checked himself.

Since the conference was being held in the hospital auditorium, a trolley reached him in no time. Candy was lifted up, brought below the stage and shifted on to the trolley. The orderly rushed the trolley towards the emergency ward. A number of doctors were running behind it. Some of them started huffing and puffing and had to stop on their way. These doctors realized that they were over the hill.

After he had been shifted onto the bed in the emergency ward, Candy opened his eyes slowly.

'Where am I?' he said, putting all he had into his act.

'Dr Anuroop, you lost consciousness while you were chairing the session at the conference,' a doctor told him.

'I need to go to the loo immediately,' Candy said.

'It's not safe for you to walk right now. Staff, please bring the bedpan for him,' Dr Parakrit, the medical officer of the emergency ward said firmly.

After having relieved himself, Candy began to plot his escape from the emergency.

He told Parakrit, 'Doctor, I am feeling okay. Please discharge me immediately.'

But to his consternation, the director of the hospital entered the emergency ward.

'How do you feel?' he asked.

'I am okay. It was just a blackout.'

'But I've been told that you were unconscious for quite some time! We can't take a chance with such a valuable member of our organization! You must undergo some tests and remain under observation for at least twelve hours,' the director insisted.

There was no choice for Candy but to comply with the director's instructions, which included the administration of intravenous fluids. When the vein of his left hand was pricked for putting in an intravenous line, Candy's screams could be heard from outside the emergency ward.

There were more surprises. Just when he was considering informing Momita, his wife, she appeared in front of him. Nipun had called her. Candy was happy to find her in tears. It was obvious that she loved him, despite getting to know him fully over the years.

Next, he was sent for the CT angiography scan for his brain. By the time he came back, there were more visitors to call on him. Some had brought big bouquets and 'Get Well Soon' cards.

The report arrived after a few hours.

'Dr Anuroop, you have a 3 mm size aneurysm in the brain. I will consult the neurosurgeon regarding this,' Dr Parakrit said, with a frown.

Things were getting murkier. Now Candy was actually on the verge of a blackout!

Aneurysm! Neurosurgeon! Brain surgery! Complication! Paralysis! Hellish life!

A number of keywords flashed through his mind.

Dr Dr Bhanu, the neurosurgeon, came for the rounds. 'There is a small aneurysm in your brain, which was incidentally discovered in a CT scan. Did you have any symptoms previously?' he said.

'Does such an aneurysm enable a man to develop even better social skills than those of women?'

Dr Dr Bhanu smiled. 'Dr Anuroop, cast your social net even wider! You don't require any treatment for this aneurysm.'

'Thank you!'

Candy went back to the emergency ward and immediately got himself discharged, lest another fault was discovered in his body.

'I was much better off as Number Two!' He prayed that the chief would return and take over—as soon as possible.

9
The United States of Desis

Reputations are resistant to change. Even if a fox stops acting foxy, no animal trusts it.

Dr Ujjwal had boarded the flight to New York from the Delhi airport. At the departure terminal, he wondered why he had not bumped into an acquaintance, as that had happened quite often. Then, he noticed Parth, his old batchmate.

'Hey Limp Dick! What are you doing here?' Dr Ujjwal shouted.

In his excitement, he had become oblivious to the decent and the *pseudo-decent* people in his vicinity.

'*Abe luche lafange* (Rascal)!' Parth chuckled. 'Whatever reputation you may acquire, I'll never have any respect for you.'

Most of the eyebrows in the vicinity moved against gravity. Gentlemen in black suits were not supposed to mouth uncouth words, at least in public.

A bear hug followed. Although both of them had been batchmates in MBBS, the only interaction they had had in the past decade was via a few Facebook messages. Parth, who too was a surgeon, had only recently returned to India from the UAE. He was going to attend the same conference for which Dr Ujjwal had registered.

The conversation that followed was bereft of any sophistication. They started off by eulogizing the charms of the girls in their batch. Then they assassinated the character of their classmates, one by one. Finally, they disrespected their respected teachers. The flight had a layover at the Heathrow airport. But their conversation carried on. Their in-flight entertainment system was not even switched on.

However, at the conference, both of them became serious pupils, and listened to the speakers with rapt attention. This was unlike some other delegates, who had registered their names at the conference venue, and had attended the rest of it on the hop-on, hop-off tourist buses. The duo even resisted the temptation of gorging on delicacies during the lunch hour so as to be fully present during the post-lunch sessions, where many of the listeners could be found with their eyes shut and minds adrift. Dr Ujjwal was so excited by the newer techniques that he felt like returning to the OT right away.

He met Dr Rodney Taylor, his old friend, at the conference. Dr Taylor, from New York University Medical School, had visited his surgical unit in Delhi two years ago. Since then, both of them had been in constant touch. Standing over six feet and seven inches tall, Rodney made even six-footers look like pygmies. While he operated, the operation table had to be set at the maximum height. As a result, his assistants usually had to stand on foot stools. Successfully using his long fingers for dissection in the inaccessible areas, he would loudly proclaim—'size matters!'—much to the amusement of the female staff. The resident doctors in his unit often jested that if he opened up the stomach during surgery and put his hand there, his fingertips would show through the mouth of the patient.

'Presenting something, Ujjwal?' Rodney asked him.

'Not this time. I am just imbibing the clinical and academic inputs from the stalwarts. Of course, it doesn't hurt to have availed of some eating, drinking and socializing along with that!'

'I know you are doing good work, especially in bariatric surgery. You must write a scientific paper and present it at international conferences, so that others recognize you as a heavyweight in your field. In short, you have to blow your own trumpet!'

'I do have a flaw. People do less and show more, while it is the opposite with me! I promise to be ready with the paper within a year.'

'Let the first-year residents do the dirty work of gathering data and references. But don't feel guilty about it! When you were a junior doctor, you must have been exploited by your bosses!'

'Thanks for your practical advice!' Dr Ujjwal said.

After the conference, Dr Ujjwal indulged in the longest holiday of his life, covering the US from coast to coast. His network of old classmates vied with each other to host him. Dr Ujjwal had never realized that he was so popular among them. *I was always up to something or the other. So everyone has vivid memories of me. Nobody remembers the*

scholars who burnt the midnight oil! he reflected.

The grand finale was a reunion in Washington DC. All his batchmates who were staying in the US got together in the ballroom of the Arcadia Hotel. Here too Dr Ujjwal was the centre of attention.

Kulraj Singh, a burly Sikh man who was his batchmate, pressed his knees. 'Guruji. Please reveal your secret formula that entranced the ladies! We aren't your competitors any more!'

'A single key can't open all locks! And in any case, I am out of touch.'

'Look! A tiger claims to have turned vegetarian!' Kulraj laughed.

'Don't be fooled by the stripes. You are looking at a zebra!'

After testifying that he wasn't seeing anyone, Dr Ujjwal expected that he would be left alone, at least on the topic of his love life. But his batchmates opened another front. They began suggesting matches for him.

'I know an Indian doctor named Arunita. She is looking for a partner, preferably a desi,' Kulraj said.

A few other names were proposed.

'You guys seem to be desperate to find a match. I am afraid that I might even be abducted and married off at gun point! But I appreciate your concern.'

'Of course, all of us are your well-wishers. But the main reason for being so eager to get you married is that we are jealous of your freedom!' Kulraj said, making everyone break into peals of laughter.

As he boarded the return flight to India, Dr Ujjwal thought of his beloved surgical unit. Candy had painted a rosy picture about it in his emails.

However, his inner voice told him that with a laughable doctor like Candy as the acting head, there must have been at least a few, aberrant incidents in the department.

After exiting the arrival lounge of Delhi airport, he boarded a cab. The driver looked so emaciated that he could have been portrayed in an advertisement for a hunger-relief charity.

'What is your name?' Dr Ujjwal asked him.

'I am Dhan Singh.'

After navigating their way out of the traffic congestion at the airport arrival terminal, Dhan Singh said, 'Sir, I have a request. Please keep talking to me.'

'Why do you say so?'

'I have been at the wheel for the past eighteen hours—without a break. If you don't keep me engaged in conversation, I am quite likely to doze off while driving!'

Dr Ujjwal had thought of stealing a nap but the prospect of the car turning into a coffin made all his body hair rise in unison. He started conversing with Dhan Singh.

'Why are you working overtime?'

'There is a long story behind it. I had to undergo a surgery two months ago because my intestines had burst due to a prolonged typhoid fever. Subsequently, there was a long hospital stay. My insurance cover was exhausted in a few days. There was no choice for me but to take out a loan. Doctors nowadays have become money-minting machines!'

'I am also a doctor,' Dr Ujjwal interrupted him. If Dhan Singh had criticized the fraternity any longer, he was quite likely to be punched. That could have led to the inclusion of a couple more doctors in his memoirs.

Dhan Singh began trembling with embarrassment. 'Oh! Doctor Sahib! Please don't mind. I am a frustrated person; I may have been inappropriate.'

'Don't make doctors a scapegoat for the wrongs of the healthcare system. There are many reasons for the rising cost of healthcare. You are alive only because the surgeon operated on you promptly. But you still portray him as a villain.'

'I understand what you mean.'

Dr Ujjwal decided to close the topic; it was elevating his blood pressure.

During the rest of the journey, Dr Ujjwal kept Dhan Singh awake by conversing about his family.

As they were about to reach Dr Ujjwal's home, the cab stopped at a red light. Dr Ujjwal's attention was drawn to a line written on the back of a three-wheeler—'*Nazar lagayega, Nirog Hospital Jayega* (Whoever casts an evil eye over the three-wheeler or its driver, shall land up in Nirog Hospital)'.

Thank god, my name is not mentioned! he thought.

As soon as Dr Ujjwal returned to duty, Dr Lokhande, the director, summoned him to his office. The director, an avid fan of Ajit, the Bollywood villain, was attired in the same combination of a black shirt, white trousers and white shoes.

'Welcome back. You took a big risk by leaving the department in the hands of that haggard creature. We had to literally tie Candy's hands together to stop him from indulging in misadventures.'

'I will be careful in future, Sir,' Dr Ujjwal replied.

Back in his office, Dr Ujjwal called for Candy immediately. 'Oye Candy! I told you not to undertake complicated surgeries in my absence.'

'Sir, nothing like that happened. Dr Vishesh must have made false allegations to the director.'

'Usually, the Number Two in the department becomes the enemy of the Number One. Someday, they could surpass the HoD's popularity. But the way that you are working, I don't have a single insecurity!'

Candy felt that he had undergone enough bashing. He applied a solution that he may have used to tackle an adamant child; he tried to divert the attention of his wrathful boss. 'Sir, how was your trip? I have heard that the difference between the hospitals here and the US touches the sky!'

'I think you mean that there is a world of difference,' the chief replied. He alone could make sense of the neologisms, uttered by Candy.

'Yes!'

'If you compare it to our hospital, there isn't much of a gap. But their main strength is that inept doctors—like you—are filtered out early in the system!'

Sensing that the chief was in a mood to skin him alive, Candy moved out of the office, citing the excuse of attending to a patient.

Later, the ward rounds began. The patient on the first bed was suffering from acute appendicitis. Dr Ujjwal asked Candy for his opinion about the findings.

'Sir, this is a patient of appendicitis, but there is no lump.'

Dr Ujjwal palpated the abdomen. He gave Candy a dirty look. 'Anuroop, even a first-year resident doctor would be able to feel this lump. You need to be re-trained!'

Candy noticed malicious smiles on the faces of the resident doctors. Just a few hours ago, they had convinced him that there was no lump in the patient. He realized that they had ganged up to pull a fast one on him. Candy looked as bummed as a footballer who had just kicked the ball into his own goal.

10
So Near, Yet So Far

Some guys are poor finishers in romance like the football players who repeatedly fumble penalty kicks.

Within a few days of Dr Ujjwal's return, the surgical unit again turned into a madhouse.

The chief had not forgotten Rodney's taunt about his lack of research publications. He resolved to get a paper on his technique for the Roux-en-Y procedure for bariatric surgery, published as soon as possible. The first step was to retrieve the data for the last two years from the patient files. He zeroed in on Nipun and Nishtha, who as the junior-most resident doctors fully deserved such a boring and thankless job.

Dr Ujjwal called them into his office. 'Do you know about my special technique for Roux-en-Y anastomosis?'

'Yes, Sir,' both of them replied loudly, like courtiers at a king's durbar.

'Every afternoon, you will spend two hours in the medical records department, and note down the relevant data for the last two years, so that we can publish a research paper. The details will be explained by tomorrow morning,' Dr Ujjwal ordered.

'Sir, will we get some relief from ward work?' Nipun asked.

'No relaxation from your duties! A day can't be extended beyond twenty-four hours; the only option for you is to reduce your sleeping hours. Building up your stamina is also a part of the training!'

The medical records department was situated in the basement. Nishtha was not too enthused about working in such a drab and dusty environment. However, Nipun was ecstatic. *With Nishtha around, even the dungeon could become the Valley of Flowers,* he thought.

Soon, the other junior doctors found out about the formation of the research team. It was likely to give Nipun an unfair advantage, vis-à-vis the others. Nipun became the most hated person without having done any actual harm. He was gheraoed in the hostel.

'Hey, there are secret cameras installed all over that place. So don't even *think* of acting fresh.'

'Best of the worst luck!'

'Worst wishes!'

'Oh God! Why not Nishtha and me?'

Those were the voices of unabashed envy.

'Relax. The chief has chosen the least eligible guy in the department to partner with Nishtha. He understands that modern-day princesses don't lose their hearts to paupers,' Nipun said, in a bid to convince others that he was as harmless as an attenuated virus in a vaccine.

They started working the next day. For the compilation of data, the doctors had to make do with working on a very un-aesthetic table, and two chairs whose cushions had shrunk to one-third their original thickness. Nipun was relieved to find their table out of the sight of the staff of the department.

Taking the files out from the shelves was no mean task. The resting dust particles became airborne, and some of them made their way into their noses. Nishtha was also afraid of disturbing a sleeping lizard. If she saw one, she would scream. And her high-decibel screams would not only injure the eardrums of Nipun and the others in the vicinity, but also wake up other lizards, triggering more screams.

Both of them settled in their chairs to note down the relevant data. It was so quiet that Nipun could hear her breathing. Nishtha smelled nice.

Nipun decided to break the ice with a compliment. 'Your perfume is wonderful.'

'Silly. It's a moisturizer!'

Nishtha was wearing a simple salwar kurti. However, as always, she had put on lipstick and eyeliner—as if there were a decree that she couldn't appear in public sans make-up.

He moved to face her. Her breathing was more thoracic than abdominal, making her bosom move as if she was rehearsing the 'Dhak Dhak' song. Even though her kurti had a high neck, her cleavage was still visible.

'Probably, the only way she can conceal her cleavage is if she wears a scarf around her neck, or if she closes all the buttons of her shirt!' he thought.

Nipun's thigh inadvertently brushed against hers. She moved to recreate the gap that had previously existed.

'I'm sorry,' Nipun said.

'It's okay,' Nishtha replied calmly. She was unsure if this had been accidental or if Nipun was shaken by her sensuality.

The next day, she arrived before he did and took the opportunity to move the chairs a few inches apart. But there was some consolation for Nipun since she had not shifted to the opposite side of the table.

Henceforth, Nipun only gave compliments to Nishtha when he had composed and rehearsed them—well in advance. But Nishtha was unmoved.

'Neither hard work nor smart work seems to work!' he lamented.

However, there was nothing to stop him from fantasizing about her. Once he retired to his bed in his hostel room, all the other usual virtual consorts were relegated to the background. Just the thought of touching Nishtha was enough to trigger a quick release of the stress built up in his groin.

Amidst the atrocities that Nishtha committed on Nipun's emotions, the research paper slowly began to take form.

A few days later, both of them were surprised to find Candy in the basement.

'I am looking for a few files,' Candy said. But he seemed bent on catching them in a compromising position.

'May I help you, Sir?' Nipun asked.

'Thanks. You seem to have taken a liking to the underground life!' he whispered to Nipun.

The very same evening, Nipun was off-duty. Three of his old classmates and he were chilling out after a long time. Dipank's hostel room had been temporarily converted into a slipshod tavern. An old newspaper was being used as a tablecloth since spillage of liquid and food was expected, especially later on in the night. Vodka didn't look very aesthetic in stainless steel glasses, but all they cared for was that it let their emotions run riot. The spicy accompaniments like bhujia, papad and masala peanuts were known to be the close aides of alcohol.

'Hey, why are you drinking vodka and not whisky?' Nipun asked.

'It's just that all of us are on the rounds tomorrow in the wards. If we drink a lot of whisky, its smoky flavour wafting out of our mouths may be picked up by a patient or an attendant. Although it is common knowledge that doctors do drink, a doctor who smells of alcohol, while on duty, is not tolerated—even by a drunkard!' Dipank explained.

'And if someone among them turns out to be a connoisseur of whisky, he might judge that we imbibe cheap brands!' Nipun added. 'Out of the thirty-odd boys that had joined the first year MBBS in our medical college, only four used to booze. They were labelled the most despicable and characterless people on earth. However, by the end of the internship, the tables had turned completely. Only one teetotaller was left and he was thought to be a freak!'

If a layman had happened to listen to their small talk, his respect for doctors would have taken a big hit. However, after having downed a few pegs, the group seemed to be part of a special task force, constituted by a league of nations to find answers to the unsolved mysteries of life.

Just before they were about to disperse back to their individual hostels, the spotlight shifted to Nipun.

'Among all of us, you are the only one without a steady girlfriend. Why is that so?' Dipank taunted him.

'Yes, it is strange that somehow, below-average guys like

you have found love. This means either my luck is rotten, or women have no taste!' said Nipun

'You can say whatever you want. But follow my advice. Be proactive,' Dipank asserted.

Having been egged on by his peers, Nipun decided that he would convey his feelings to Nishtha explicitly. He chose to text her because a girl like Nishtha was quite likely to rebuff him explicitly as well. A digital smack was likely to be less painful.

He typed: 'We are already friends. Please promote me and let me into your heart.'

Nishtha replied, 'No chance. These days my heart is quite heartless!'

The next day, Nipun was apologetic. 'Please ignore yesterday's text. My emotions spilled over.'

'Chill, yaar. I was expecting this. If you had not proposed, I would have started doubting the effect I have on men!' Nishtha grinned.

Nipun relaxed and let go, just like a pizza delivery boy who gets attuned to ignoring the appetizing aroma. But he was seized by a sinister thought: *If things continued in this manner, Nishtha would set up with a hunk, and he would end up with chronic acidity.*

The data collection was over in a month. But this was just the first step.

Nipun and Nishtha were gradually imbibing clinical and surgical wisdom. The toddlers were being allowed to walk without support—they were being allowed to conduct some minor surgeries.

While scrubbing up in the OT, they were comparing the number of surgical operations done by them. Nishtha was much ahead of Nipun. He determined that the difference was statistically significant.

He cribbed, 'This can't be explained by luck or probability! Obviously, partiality is at work here.'

'Come on!' Nishtha said. 'I am not currying favours from anyone. Instead, I am utilizing a proactive approach; requesting the seniors to allow me to conduct certain surgeries. It has to be done. Even a mother forgets to feed her infant until it cries!'

'It isn't that simple. I'm sure some of the seniors have a soft spot for you.'

'Count some of your blessings too. Unlike you, I can't go alone at 3 a.m. to Khan Market to dig into the sumptuous aloo parathas of Puran Chand!'

Six months after their joining, the first-year residents were posted in different surgical specialities to broaden their experience. Nipun and Nishtha had to part ways. Nipun went to neurosurgery while Nishtha was posted in plastic surgery. However, both of them had gotten so habituated to each other that they had to meet at least once a day. When that was not feasible, they resorted to texting each other.

Nishtha confessed, 'I don't feel the need for a female friend because I can confide in you.'

'This implies that we can't live without each other!' Nipun said with excitement.

'No! It stands proven that even platonic relationships can be beautiful!' Nishtha replied, forcing Nipun to make a face at her.

Nishtha was posted with Dr Ambar, the plastic surgeon. Surgeons of other specialities were envious of him because quite a few of his patients were limited-edition specimens. What they didn't realize was that the prettier the lady, the more demanding she was about the results of any procedure.

Dr Ambar found more patients on a walk than in his outpatient chamber. While moving around in the hospital or at social gatherings, he would point at someone's broad nose or thin lips, and offer to fix the problem. One day, Nishtha and he were in the OPD when Dr Tarika, a gynaecologist, arrived to take his advice regarding the removal of a mole on her cheek.

Dr Ambar noticed that a substantial portion of her body was claimed by her buttocks. He couldn't restrain himself. 'The mole is a minor issue. Why don't you consider liposuction?'

'Doc, do you want my husband to leave me! He likes me as I am—big at the bottom,' Tarika fumed.

'Sorry, sorry.'

'It is okay. In the future, please mind your own business!'

For a few days, Dr Ambar stopped soliciting new patients. But he was back to his old ways in a while, just like a drunkard who had returned to drink, a few days after making a new year's resolution to quit alcohol.

In the next OPD, Dr Ambar received a middle-aged lady who was accompanied by her husband. As if her heavy jewellery was not enough to show off her affluence, she was also carrying a Vertu mobile phone and a Hidesign handbag. She wanted her rather convex abdomen to be turned flat. After examining her, Dr Ambar gave them his opinion. 'Since you have a lot of loose skin, a tummy-tuck surgery is the only solution.'

Her husband intervened, 'Doctor, she has a health insurance policy. Do we get coverage for this?'

'Since tummy tuck is a cosmetic surgery, it is not paid for by any health insurance company,' Dr Ambar said firmly.

The patient's husband gave him a crooked smile. 'You can report it as an intra-abdominal surgery for curing some disease. That way, we will be able to get the claim.'

A typical Indian who thinks nobody should indulge in corruption except him, Nishtha thought. She judged that the lady could well afford the tummy tuck, as well as the subsequent trip to a seven-star beach resort in Bali to showcase her flat tummy.

Nishtha couldn't control herself. 'You should be ashamed of yourself. False claims drain insurance companies, and as a result, a genuine claim may be denied to a poor, desperate patient!' she yelled.

The oversmart couple was so stunned by her verbal assault that they rushed out of the chamber immediately.

Ambar faced Nishtha. 'What you conveyed to them was absolutely right. But a punch was utilized when a gentle nudge would have been enough. You are a good worker but you might be bad for my practice!'

'I'm so sorry. I know you've lost the patient because of me. Sometimes I feel that instead of having joined the medical profession, I should have been an RTI activist.'

Nishtha enjoyed her stint in the plastic surgery department. But she had sulked when she had been denied a leave during Diwali. All doctors of the plastic surgery unit had to be in the hospital to attend to cases of burn injuries. There was no dearth of people who discarded safety precautions while bursting crackers, as if they would come across as cowards if they exercised caution. And there were bystanders whose luck could desert them, at the wrong place, and at the wrong time.

After 8 p.m., the cracker-injury victims started trickling in. Most of them had injured their hands, but some even had trauma to the eyes and the face. When asked about the cause of injury, even sensible-looking adults admitted to carrying out some of the dumbest acts imaginable, like holding a dangerous cracker in their hands, bringing it near the flame, and then throwing it away. Some had obviously exploded prematurely, causing the damage. Others admitted to transporting crackers in their pockets. The OTs remained busy the whole night.

Nishtha had always celebrated Diwali with a lot of crackers, including some high-decibel ones, which had once forced an elderly couple living in the neighbourhood to plug their ear canals with cotton. After having discovered the dark side of crackers, she decided to become an anti-cracker activist.

'Please don't fire crackers this year. They are extremely dangerous,' she told her mom.

Nishtha's relatives were astonished at her sudden change of heart. Many had gathered at her home just to enjoy the fireworks. The kids refused to budge.

Ultimately, they did fire all the crackers, but Nishtha's mother ensured that the pictures were not posted on any social media platform.

Dr Ambar had demonstrated the art of applying fine stitches to Nishtha. Later, he had even allowed her to operate on patients with injuries on their faces.

Once, while she was on emergency duty, a young woman had brought in her four-year-old son, Rian. He had a cut on his forehead.

'What happened?' Nishtha asked.

'He fell from the sofa. Although I was nearby, I couldn't do anything—he toppled over in a split second.'

'Where is his father?'

'He is rushing back from the factory.'

As they were talking, a young man entered in a hurry. After having observed the child's cut, he gave his wife a murderous look. Then he began to shout, 'You bitch! What is the use of having you at home all day if you can't look after Rian!'

The woman started crying.

Nishtha looked at him in the eye and calmly responded, 'If you don't quiet down, I will call up the women's cell, and also inform the local mahila mandal. I am sure had your wife not been in the hospital, you would have given her a black eye. Is it humanly possible to keep track of each and every movement of the child? If the child had been injured in your presence, would you have listened to the same abuses from your wife?'

The bully had a taste of his own medicine. Afraid that Nishtha would gather a crowd of women whose nails would have modified into claws, he slipped out of the emergency ward.

'After the stitching is over, you can take the child home. If your husband abuses you or hits you, just inform me. I warn only once! Next time, I will take concrete action,' Nishtha said to the lady.

'Thanks, Didi. I will not suffer in silence any more. Please keep in touch with me,' she said in a resolute voice.

'Whenever you call me, make sure your husband knows about it, so he realizes he is under my constant surveillance! I am your shield now!'

Nipun had gone into neurosurgery, the department which could easily beat cross-country trainers in building up endurance. Here, a surgery that lasted 4 to 6 hours was labelled a 'quickie'. Ones which were conducted past sunset were called respectable.

Nipun did develop an interest in the subject. However, during the surgeries, he had to scrub up as the second assistant. Only the surgeon, Dr Bhanu, and the first assistant, could view the field under the two eyepieces of the operating microscope. After standing in an odd position for long hours, he would feel like a palanquin bearer of the colonial era.

One day, just after a surgery which had taken longer than a transatlantic flight, Dr Bhanu told Nipun, 'Remember! Be quick at every job except when performing surgery or when performing in bed! One of my friends, Dr D.S. Somesh who is working in Mumbai, has been nicknamed Dead Slow Somesh by the anaesthesiologists in his hospital! That is unfair. A surgeon should be judged by his meticulous approach not his speed.'

'I agree, Sir. There are surgeons who boast about finishing major surgeries in 15 or 20 minutes, as if they were participating in the Formula One race,' Nipun commented.

'How do you like neurosurgery? Would you like to pursue it in the future?' Dr Bhanu asked expectantly.

'Sir, I like the branch but I wouldn't prefer to specialize in it.'

'Why not?' Dr Bhanu frowned.

'I'm not sure that I will be able to handle being married to both neurosurgery and to my wife. You rarely go home in time. Are you allowed to enter it easily?'

'Oh! The only thing my wife cares about is whether I am at home for dinner! In any case, I often reach home before my wife does. As an obstetrician, she has to conduct a lot of deliveries and caesareans. Babies love to exit their mothers' womb at odd hours!'

Even though they were posted in different units, Nipun and Nishtha had to work together on the research paper. So they had to meet quite often. One afternoon, as they were compiling the data, Nipun asked Nishtha about her stint at the plastic surgery unit.

'I received good exposure. The best part was that I was complimented quite often.'

'By whom?' a startled Nipun asked.

'Surprisingly, it was the female patients. During the consultations, the ladies kept pestering Dr Ambar to make them look like me, by all means. But things came to an impasse, when a man, planning a sex change surgery, too expressed a desire to look like me!'

'Even that may be possible after many surgeries. But it

will be difficult to match your attitude!' Nipun chuckled.

The next day, Nipun and Nishtha went to the chief's OPD to show him the text of the research paper. During these visits, the chief often made them sit in the OPD for a while. He wanted them to learn how to deal with the outdoor patients, especially those who made one feel like banging one's head into a wall.

Dr Ujjwal lectured, 'Some patients feel that it is a sacrilege to tell the doctors that they are perfectly alright! Often, the doctor feels that he has done an amazing job, and the patient should deify him. But the patient magnifies a minor problem. For them, a visit to the hospital is incomplete without flustering the doctor's grey matter, since he has been hired for a consultation!'

Inside Dr Ujjwal's chamber was a rustic old lady who seemed at peace with her uncountable wrinkles. She had been operated on three months ago for gall stones, and she had come for a follow-up examination. 'Doctor, ever since my surgery, I feel listless all the time. My daughter-in-law has to do all the house work,' she whined.

'So? Let her manage the house!' the chief winked.

'If I let her take over, the vixen will have total control over my son!'

Dr Ujjwal examined the patient thoroughly. There was no apparent cause to her complaints.

'I had prescribed a multivitamin tablet. How do you take it?' he asked.

'Doctor, I ingest the tablet every morning with water.'

To everyone's surprise, Dr Ujjwal made an angry face. 'This is wrong. The medicine is supposed to be taken with milk, and at night. Why haven't you followed my instructions?'

'You didn't tell me to do so,' she defended, and rightly so.

'Probably, I may have forgotten to explain it properly. But, in that case, you should have enquired.'

'Sorry, Doctor ji. I will do as you say from today.'

'I am changing your medicine. Take one capsule every night, with milk. Within a few days, your daughter-in-law will envy your energy!'

After the patient had left, Nipun and Nishtha couldn't help but smile at the subterfuge.

The chief explained, 'You must keep the mentality of the patient in mind while interacting with them. If an internet-savvy patient with a know-it-all attitude tries to teach you medical science, give them so much information that they repent challenging the sun with a just a torch! But arguing technically with a simpleton might confuse them further. It is common among the illiterate and semi-literate to demonize the surgery, and to blame all their subsequent health issues on it. Sometimes, a headache is said to have begun right after surgery has been done in the lower abdomen while others complain of sexual weakness after a surgery in the neck. Pregnancy is the only condition that is not attributed to an old surgery! Her baseless belief had to be tackled in a way that she could relate to.'

Just as his life had begun to settle into a pattern, Nipun was posted in the emergency ward, where the schedule was regularly irregular. Expectedly, most emergencies arrived during the odd hours. Rare was the night when the doctors could hit the couch. Nipun learnt to calm the attendants of the patients—some panicked as if the universe were about to collapse. The emergency complex had its own OT and anaesthesia team to take prompt action during surgical treatment to a new level.

Here, Nipun began to comprehend the darker side of alcohol. The life of a party was often its poison. Soon, just by keeping his nose in the line of the patient's breath, Nipun knew whether the patient had imbibed whisky, beer or country liquor.

One evening, his patient was a woman who had injured her face because she had failed to 'see' a glass door.

As he cleaned her forehead wound, Nipun sniffed an unusual smell. He brought his nose close to her mouth on the pretext of observing her wound more closely. She had definitely been drinking whisky and without any restraint.

He took her sister-in-law aside. 'She seems to have had one drink too many.'

'Doctor, to tell you the truth, she drinks alcohol daily although within certain limits. However, today she got carried away at a party.'

'Where is her husband?'

'As he was too drunk, there was no use in making him accompany us here. He is being escorted home by a few relatives. It is his fault since he instilled the habit in her.'

'That is quite surprising!'

'Not at all, Doctor. Nowadays, many men look for a wife who can raise their spirits by clinking glasses with them at home!'

'I am out of touch with the latest social mores!' Nipun murmured to himself.

Two days later, he treated an old man named Nathu Lal, who had sustained an injury to his scalp. His scooter had slipped. Nathu Lal's breath smelt of so much alcohol that the emergency ward seemed to be adjacent to a distillery.

Since his scalp was bleeding, Nipun applied a pressure bandage to prevent any further loss of blood.

'Sisterfucker! Leave me alone!' the man barked.

'Behave yourself. How dare you abuse a doctor?' Nipun shouted back.

'Don't try to fool me! You are just a ward boy—wearing a white coat!' Nathu Lal slurred and pushed Nipun's hand away.

Nipun called all the male paramedics present in the emergency room. They managed to restrain the old man strongly enough that Nipun could apply the bandage.

The next step was the application of stitches on the scalp to control the bleeding. Sedatives could not be given to the patient since he was intoxicated. Nipun had a battle on his hands.

At his wits' end, he decided to seek Nishtha's assistance, in the hope that one plus one would equal eleven.

'An abusive drunkard needs suturing. I need your help to calm him down,' Nipun told her.

'Am I a bouncer? Anyway, why do you want to spoil my day? What if he calls me a bitch?'

'You can reply with, "You swine, I will show you how ferocious a bitch can be!"'

'Nipun!'

'Okay. Let us focus on the task at hand. Nathu Lal seems to be the patriarch of a traditional family, where he lords over a number of children and grandchildren. In all probability, no woman in his house has ever dared to raise her voice in front of him. I think you can stun him by going on the offensive. Let us give it a shot. Please!'

'Just lip service will not do. You will have to take one of my night duties!'

'You are a tough negotiator! Okay, we have a deal,' Nipun said and both of them shook hands.

They went into the minor OT and they found Nathu Lal showing off his extensive vocabulary of swear words to the staff. Then, he tried to take off his intravenous line himself. Nipun shouted at the patient. Nathu Lal retaliated by pointing at his right hand which he had closed into a fist; the gesture was grossly obscene.

This infuriated Nishtha and she picked up the thickest dilator instrument she could find in the OT almirah.

Then she spoke in a rustic dialect. 'Enough is enough. Lie down quietly. Otherwise this instrument will be shoved up your ass, and that too without any lubrication!'

The patient became absolutely quiet, as if an anaesthesia drug had been administered. Nipun didn't let Nishtha move out of the OT until the procedure had been completed.

The academic year was about to come to an end. The seniors eagerly awaited the arrival of the new batch of resident doctors. The department had an unwritten rule: 'Do unto your juniors, what you received from your seniors'. At last, the names of Dr Mayur and Dr Ridhi had appeared on the noticeboard as the selected candidates for this year. Another girl was joining the department.

11
Newbies Create a Stir

Some patients are so witty, they leave the treating doctor speechless.

After their registration, the new entrants went directly to the chief's office where all the doctors of the unit had been waiting with dilated pupils.

As soon as Ridhi had entered the room, Nipun scanned her from top to toe. 'Girls like her make life worth living!' he mumbled.

From the corner of his eye, he noticed that Nishtha too was looking just intently at Ridhi. *It seems like she is doing a comparative study! Hopefully, from now, Nishtha will have a more realistic view of herself!*

Although Ridhi was not as voluptuous as Nishtha, she was more curvaceous, with a smaller waist-to-hip ratio. With her large eyes, arched eyebrows and oval face, she seemed to announce—'I am the most feminine of them all'.

The chief addressed Ridhi, 'Tell us something about yourself.'

'I am the first one in my business family to enter the medical profession. After I finished my MBBS degree, my mother said that she had had enough of my studying. She had wanted me to settle down. But Dad was firm. He said that I should concentrate on my career,' Ridhi replied in a sweet voice.

'Why did you prefer to undertake an MS in surgery?' Dr Ujjwal asked, surreptitiously hinting that she looked too delicate for a branch like surgery.

'Surgery is exciting and action-packed,' Ridhi smiled.

'But that comes at a price. There will be many occasions when you could be cursing yourself for having decided to become a surgeon!' the chief said.

Then he asked everyone to give their opinion on what they thought was the most important quality of a great surgeon.

'Perfect knowledge of anatomy.'

'Stamina and concentration.'

'Amazing dexterity.'

'Great technique.'

'Nerves of steel.'

There were a number of attempts to impress the chief, but he retained his vacant look.

'The correct answer is—"To know when not to operate!" And one requires a lot of experience to reach that stage,' the chief asserted.

The focus shifted to Mayur, the other newcomer. He too had excited a lot of curiosity because he could pass off as an old professor. Mayur had left his hair undyed to elicit more respect than he deserved.

It will be interesting to see how this geriatric fellow adjusts into the department. He will have to obey the orders of doctors who look like his offspring! Nishtha thought.

'Gentleman, you seem to have made quite a late entry into MS. But we'll make you feel young,' the chief said to Mayur. Dr Ujjwal implied that he wouldn't receive any concessions from hard work for his age and would be rebuked fairly regularly, along with the higher forms of scoldings when he committed a major mistake.

'Sir, I have enjoyed the security of a government job for too long. A postgraduate degree was outside my comfort zone. But there was a major upheaval in my life when my wife passed her MD in paediatrics two years ago and subsequently found a job in a corporate hospital. I confess, I couldn't digest the fact that my wife had become more educated than me, and that she had also started earning more than me! So I started preparing for the entrance exam for MS,' Mayur said.

Nishtha was unsettled by his chauvinistic mindset. She felt like asking Mayur, 'Has your wife's career progression led to a stoppage of testosterone production in your body and made you impotent?'

The next day, the chief began with the morning rounds in the general ward. Mayur was wearing a necktie. A tie was conventionally worn only by the senior doctors.

'Nice tie,' the chief said, giving him a half smile.

'Thank you, Sir,' Mayur replied. He thought that the chief had accorded some special status to him.

'Tell me the ways in which your tie can be of practical use in the hospital!'

Mayur realized he had rubbed Dr Ujjwal the wrong way. 'Sir, it can be used as a bandage in an emergency situation.'

'Good. Think of some other uses!'

'It can be used to hang a bottle of intravenous fluid if the plastic hook at the top of the bottle breaks away.'

'Okay. Take off your tie.'

Mayur did as he was ordered.

'Demonstrate the commonly used knots for stitches—the Reef Knot, the Granny Knot and the Surgeon's Knot.'

Mayur demonstrated the knots one by one. But he messed up the Reef Knot.

The chief sneered, 'Instead of showing off the double knot of your tie, pay attention to the knots used in suturing.'

'Right, Sir,' he replied, and put the crumpled tie in the pocket of his white coat.

Mayur looked around. The broad smiles of the onlookers indicated that his humiliation had been of a very high standard.

He felt like using the tie to strangulate someone.

During the night, Mayur had a dream. While operating, he was not able to tie a knot properly. There was massive bleeding at the operative site. The chief had to intervene. After the surgery was over, he was taken by the theatre staff to the recovery room, where the chief blackened his face with shoe polish. The junior doctors, including the girls, put a garland of shoes around his neck. Then he was walked through the wards, where patients and their relatives jeered at him. He looked down to see if he was being paraded naked.

At that moment, he woke up. His body was wet with sweat and he was panting.

Nipun and Ridhi were posted together. Nipun was content to be her secret admirer and nothing more. Nishtha was the main culprit for this display of low self-esteem. Nipun had tried a variety of methods to hook her, but they had been as ineffective as unsuccessful experiments carried out by alchemists in turning iron to gold.

One afternoon, after they had come out of the OT, Nipun told Ridhi, 'Go to the male ward. On bed number twelve, there is an old man, called Bhisham Singh, who is suffering from intestinal obstruction. Just enquire whether he has passed wind or not.'

Ridhi went to the bed and greeted the old farmer. His weather-beaten face could have been an interesting subject for a portrait painter.

Ridhi asked him, 'Babaji, have you passed wind today?'

Bhisham Singh was already on the edge because of the constant pain in his abdomen. The painkiller injection had also been proven to be a misnomer. But even more disturbing was the attitude of his three sons, who were constantly bickering over who would care for him. He fervently wished that he had a daughter. In addition, since the morning, the doctors had been nagging him with the same question that Ridhi had just put up to him.

'*Ae doctorni* (Hey, Doctor). Why don't you arrange a mike for me? Whenever I pass wind, I will announce it!' he said, with a sarcastic smile.

Although she was taken aback, Ridhi couldn't help but smile at the old man's witticism.

She rushed to meet Nipun.

'You played a prank on me!' Ridhi shouted. Then she narrated her conversation with Bhisham Singh.

'Be prepared for more one-liners from him!' Nipun smiled.

Later, Nipun briefed the chief about the deteriorating condition of the patient.

'Since he is not responding to conservative treatment,

we have to take him up for surgery. Get him shifted into the OT as soon as possible,' the chief said.

Nipun left for Bhisham Singh's bed immediately. He was surrounded by a number of relatives and he was signing some document.

'His sons are getting his signature on the will. They don't want to leave anything to chance!' the staff nurse, Tripti, revealed to Nipun.

'That is why these degenerates were running around during these past few hours. Instead of being by the side of their sick father, they had gone to get the documents ready,' Nipun said with distaste.

After they had finished the paperwork, Nipun addressed the patient and his sons, 'There is no alternative but to operate on him. Please sign the consent form.'

Khushal, the eldest son, immediately signed the form.

Shaking with anger, the patient lifted his head and bellowed, 'See, he has wasted no time in signing my death warrant! These bastards don't want me to live because I am more valuable to them when I am dead!'

Pallav, his youngest son, intervened, 'Doctor, when my dad was young, one of his brothers died on the operation table due to complications with the anaesthesia. Since then, he suffers from an irrational phobia of surgeries.'

Bhisham Singh was adamant. 'Doctor, you can give me the most expensive medicines. But I am not going to get operated on, even though my nalayak (useless) son has signed the consent form.'

Nipun asked all the relatives to move away, as he wanted to talk to Bhisham Singh in private. 'We are already giving you the best medicines and they haven't worked. Without surgery, your intestines will burst, and the resulting infection will spread all over your body through your bloodstream. I will not speak of what will happen after that!'

'I would speak out the word you are hesitating on! I would prefer to *die* rather than undergo your cheer phaad (surgery).'

'If you pass away, your sons will shed crocodile tears to show to the public that they miss their father. But after everyone has gone, they will gloat over the property they inherit. But imagine the look on their faces if you come out alive! After a successful operation!'

Nothing could have excited Bhisham Singh as much as the feeling of retribution. He raised his right index finger. 'That would serve them right! Doctor, please make preparations for surgery.'

The surgery was successful. The patient was discharged after a week.

'I'm going to change my will. Most of my possessions will go to an old age home. Let my greedy sons be content with crumbs!' he told Nipun and Ridhi, before leaving.

After he had left, Nipun said to Ridhi, 'I hope my children don't turn out to be so self-centred!'

'Fertility rates are going down, day by day. Don't be overconfident about fathering many children!' Ridhi chuckled.

Mayur too had begun working. Nipun, who had never shied away from extending a hand of friendship to anyone, invited him to have a cup of tea at the cafeteria.

Mayur made a disdainful face, as if Nipun had asked him to sniff a pair of dirty socks. 'I don't like the flavourless brown liquid they serve in the name of tea. In fact, I drink only Darjeeling Second Flush, sourced from just a few, specific tea gardens!'

'I like kadak chai, and I also make lot of slurping sounds while sipping it! In short, I don't have any table manners! But tea is just an excuse to indulge in a gossip session,' Nipun said.

'I do chat, but only with persons of my stature!'

Nipun felt like punching Mayur, but checked himself. As he walked away, he vowed to challenge him at the opportune time.

The next day, he instructed Mayur, 'Get the investigations mentioned by me in the file for the patient in room number 208. Dr Ujjwal is going to operate on him tomorrow, for hernia repair.'

Mayur went to the ward and examined the patient. 'This kid thinks he knows more than a veteran like me. I am going to skip these unnecessary tests,' he mumbled.

In the evening, Nipun returned to Room 208. He was shocked to find that a vital investigation had been omitted.

Nipun was furious. 'Why haven't you carried out my orders?'

Mayur replied in a condescending tone. 'Because I felt there that was no need for the liver function tests.'

'Listen, Mayur! You might look like my grandpa, but right now, I am your immediate senior and you have to carry out my orders. The evaluation of the patient won't be complete without all the tests that have been mentioned by me here. If you misbehave in the future, I will make sure you are rusticated,' Nipun thundered.

'Another instance of ward rage—this is a consequence of overwork,' a staff nurse, watching the tamasha, whispered to another.

Mayur felt offended but he didn't retaliate. He realized that to become a Master of Surgery, he needed to first master the art of docility.

Mayur visited the patient. 'Mr Maqbool, I'll have to take your blood sample again. We missed a test,' he said softly. He was hoping that the patient would be accommodating enough to not complain, the type who would not mind even if his wife had forgotten to put salt in the dal.

'So, you were about to take me to the operation theatre without having gotten the results of some vital tests. How dare you play with my life?' Maqbool scowled at Mayur, as if he was intended to roast him alive.

Mayur was surprised, but also awed by the sharp mind of the patient. 'Relax,' he said. 'There was just some miscommunication. Anyway, the anaesthesiologists would have made a final check.'

It was as if a lamb was scolding a tiger while the tiger was explaining himself, with folded paws. Still, Maqbool had not been fully assuaged. Later, he lodged a complaint with the chief.

Mayur was summoned by Dr Ujjwal. The chief remarked, 'The patient is sharp-tongued, but he has a point. Doctors have to shed their king-sized egos and come to terms with the reality that nowadays, with the exception of God, everyone has to be held accountable! The moral of the story is that an exceptionally intelligent patient is not good for a doctor's health!'

In contrast to Nipun and Mayur, the two girls, Nishtha and Ridhi were bonding well. This was contrary to the speculation that the two beauties would be frequently pulling each other by the hair. This happened once Ridhi realized that the only way they could be friends was if she let Nishtha have her way. Soon, Nishtha, Nipun and Ridhi began to hang out together and came to be known as the Gang of Three.

Nipun and Ridhi also got to know each other better. Nipun learnt that Ridhi was an emotional fool, that her favourite colour was violet and she rued the inability to paint her fingernails because of her profession.

Nipun also conveyed to Ridhi that his stinginess in the cafeteria wasn't endogenous by nature, but forced by circumstances. 'Once upon a time, I used to pay for myself, and often, even for my friends!'

Other doctors, who were already envious about Nipun's friendship with Nishtha, became more perturbed at the formation of the Gang of Three. Nipun was cornered by the male doctors in the auditorium of the department at the end of a seminar after both girls had left.

'The Gang of Three is a triangle with many interesting combinations,' Saksham commented.

'Actually, I've been employed by them,' Nipun replied.

'What!'

'Yes. It is one of those newer vocations. I've been appointed as their official flatterer, to keep them both in high spirits!'

'What about your emoluments?'

'All my canteen bills are on them!'

Saksham gave him a wry smile. 'But I feel as if you are with them to act as a foil for the other men. If you remain in the constant company of girls, and that too without being employed in some masculine activity, you will gradually see changes in yourself. Soon, you will only be able to pee in a sitting position. Then you'll have to entreat Dr Ambar to conduct a sex change surgery!'

Peals of laughter broke out.

'After that, Miss Nipun would be looking to date one of us!' Nakul added.

'That means right now he is in the transition phase,' Saksham continued.

'I will have the last laugh,' Nipun said, and ran away before they could poke any more fun at him.

12

Doctors in the Wilderness

When the chief took along his junior doctors on a departmental outdoor excursion, he left his attitude behind, but only for that day.

Rodney Taylor, Dr Ujjwal's American friend, had conveyed to him that periodic excursions worked better than motivational rhetoric to keep doctors in high spirits. It also had the effect of lessening petty fights in the department. The Jungle Calling Resort in the Alwar district of Rajasthan was chosen for the one-day departmental picnic because of its proximity to Delhi, and its owner's proximity to the chief. Param, the proprietor of the resort, was an old patient and a bhakt of the chief. He had wanted to pamper the chief and his group to the hilt.

Apart from the doctors, the senior nurses had also joined the trip. The happiest person in the group was Nipun, the nature lover, who had once even contemplated a career in wildlife, while he had been studying in higher secondary. However, that had been vetoed by his dad, who had been afraid that his son had been possessed by the spirit of Mowgli. When Nipun had insisted that he be allowed to pursue his passion, his dad had countered, 'When we get a marriage proposal for you, the first query will be about your profession. If I tell the parents of a prospective bride that your job is to watch birds and butterflies, they will immediately leave our house!'

'What if I am able to find a girl by myself?' Nipun had argued.

Unable to find a counter-argument, his dad had replied with a slap, which had reverberated so loud that it had made all the birds and butterflies in the vicinity fly away.

After Nipun had gotten admission into an MBBS programme, he had dropped the idea of becoming a jungle boy, and had resorted to watching nature for when he was stressed. In his batch, the ratio of girls to boys was 2:1. As a result, his attention had been diverted to the butterflies of the campus instead.

As soon as the bus had departed from the hospital, Dr Ujjwal stood up. He announced, 'Those who remain subdued during this trip may have to give an explanation in writing afterwards!' This triggered fun and frolic.

Sanchi, the theatre-in-charge, initiated the noise with a song and from then onwards, there was non-stop hungama (commotion) as everyone else joined in. Bathroom singers saw it as a golden opportunity.

'Apart from fooling me, these idiots have some other talents too!' Dr Ujjwal murmured.

Soon, they reached the resort. It was on the edge of a reserved forest area. After settling the demands of their tummies, by munching on the delectable spread that had been laid out by the resort, the group collected in the lawn.

Two teams were formed and a cricket match began. Nipun was not enthused by this as he was itching to go deep into the forest. He wished for a monkey to leap down a tree. He hoped it would take away the ball and make faces at the players.

The match was over in an hour. The exhausted players decided to skip a trip to their hotel rooms in favour of the soft grass. Suddenly, Nishtha shouted, 'Look at that bird! On the babul tree!'

The small-sized bird with its blue wings was a novel sight for everyone except Nipun. He focused his binoculars on the bird.

'That is an Indian roller,' Nipun said confidently and awed everyone by showing them the details through his binoculars. The lazy bird remained on the same branch for quite some time.

'This is a free show!' he smiled.

Sensing that a new window had been opened, he proposed, 'Let us trek inside the forest. I'll show you the most amazing sights. You will forget about malls and skyscrapers!'

The group accepted Nipun as their ringleader, and decided to follow him into the forest. But they also took along a local guide from the resort so they wouldn't lose their way only to end up as Sher Khan's dinner. Nipun was in his element. He spotted striking birds, including a small minivet, green pigeons and a coppersmith barbet.

As they reached a watering hole, Nishtha pointed out, 'Look! There is a large white bird. Is it a stork or a heron?'

Nipun focused his binoculars on the bird. 'Wow! Excellently spotted!'

Nishtha felt flattered. *I am a born genius*, she thought.

Nipun handed the binoculars to Nishtha. 'Take a closer look.'

Nishtha's face turned red. 'Oh, it is just a man wearing white! He has bent down to cut grass!'

'In our country, people can be seen in the remotest of all places. All of our land mass is reserved for a single species, the Homo sapiens!' Nipun cribbed. Mother Earth was no less dear to him, than his very own biological mother.

The shadows of the trees had become longer. Nipun wanted to turn back. But the others, especially Dr Ujjwal and Candy, were adamant about carrying on further. Both of them were so enchanted by the forest that they had begun to act like irresponsible teenagers. Nipun didn't want to confront the temperamental chief head-on. So while the others were a bit ahead, he whispered to the guide, 'Please devise some way to make them to turn around.'

The guide addressed everyone, 'I know this forest quite intimately. If we go any further, we won't be able to reach our resort till late in the evening. Past sunset, there is a risk of being attacked by sloth bears.'

Most of the doctors in the group had treated fresh as well as old wounds from a bear mauling. They had heard that the hairy beasts were quite cranky, and that they often attacked for no rhyme or reason. Everyone took a quick U-turn, without so much as a whimper.

Everyone was on the lookout for bears on the way back. But Candy seemed to be the most fearful among them. He kept moving his head like a pendulum.

A rustling of leaves on the right side of the path sent everyone into a tizzy except for Nipun and the guide, whose act seemed to be working well.

'Relax. It is just a chital,' the guide said.

'If a bear actually appeared in front of you, what would

you do?' the chief asked everyone.

'I would try to run away,' Candy replied.

Mayur offered a cliché. 'I would stop breathing and pretend to be dead.'

Nishtha too responded, 'I will say my last prayers.'

'Nipun, what about you?' the chief asked.

'I will simply tell the bear—"Don't kill me. I will help you get rid of your unwanted hair with the help of a laser treatment!"' Nipun replied, bringing some cheer to the sombre faces.

Throughout the trip, Ridhi had been keenly observing Nipun. She felt that Nipun deserved much more respect than he was being given. *Both by his colleagues and by me. He is a joker with substance*!

Ridhi was also a nature lover, but she had never had the opportunity to develop a hobby related to it.

After they had returned, Ridhi was explicit in her admiration. 'You know so much about nature. I am impressed!'

Nipun's face lit up. 'If I hadn't gotten admission into MBBS, I would have been researching a bird or a butterfly,' he added.

Ridhi let out a sigh. 'We have no time. It is the same story with most doctors. Ever since I joined MS, I haven't been able to paint, not even once!'

'We can take some solace in the fact that performing surgery also gets one's creative juices flowing,' Nipun said.

'And the risk involved in it; that provides the thrill of adventure!' Ridhi added.

On the return journey, Nipun boarded the bus before Ridhi. He was extremely pleased when she settled into the adjacent vacant seat. But the non-stop chorus singing continued throughout the journey. Nipun had no chance to converse with her. His shoulder kept waiting for Ridhi to rest her head on it. But she used the back of the seat as a headrest during her brief nap.

13

Teething Troubles

He saved her from a certain fall but still his graph didn't rise.

Nipun was summoned by the chief. 'Hey! Our scientific paper is quite likely to be accepted by the journal for publication. Take a look at this mail. We have to respond within two weeks.'

Nipun read the email. The editor, who seemed to be an aspirant for the title of 'The Most Meticulous', had asked for so many modifications that almost three-fourths of the text had to be rewritten.

The chief noticed Nipun's unease.

'Do you need help?' he asked Nipun.

'Yes, Sir.'

'You and Nishtha can work together again.'

'Thank you, Sir,' Nipun replied.

Work seems like play whenever Nishtha is in my team! he smiled to himself.

And Nishtha and Nipun were at it again. The Gang of Three had temporarily split. Ridhi felt left out. She didn't like Nishtha and Nipun spending their hours in each other's company. Ridhi couldn't fathom the reason for her envy because she hadn't lost her mind over Nipun.

But the ground reality remained the same. Nipun again failed to take advantage of having Nishtha's company exclusively. He called himself 'the worst finisher in history'.

While Nipun and Nishtha had laughed away their travails during their first year of MS, the going was not as easy for Ridhi. Even a rebuke from a senior would leave her on the verge of tears. Her upbringing had a lot to do with that. The pampered princess had always been dropped to school by her dad, even though a school bus was available. Her tears had always been enough to put her home in a state of emergency. However with time, Ridhi's sentiments were blunted, and she became reasonably better at putting up a facade.

But her taste buds remained inflexible. 'Yuck' became one of her most common expressions because often the meals were cold and insipid.

In the next OT, Ridhi was to assist Nipun. He was operating on a case of fibroadenoma, a benign tumour of the breast. Nipun made a small incision since the patient had indicated that if she was stuck with a long, or even a broad scar line, she would fret over it all her life. During the closure, Ridhi's fatigued hand moved clumsily. In a split second, the tip of her left thumb was pricked by the needle with which Nipun had been making a stitch.

'Oh, I'm so sorry,' Nipun said.

'No, it was my fault. I lost my concentration,' Ridhi insisted.

Ridhi immediately removed the gloves, squeezed the blood out of the tip of the thumb and applied the Povidone Iodine solution.

'I hope there is no risk to me,' Ridhi said shakily, afraid that the opportunistic AIDS and hepatitis viruses had discovered an entry gate to invade her body.

'You know very well that the patient has been tested pre-operatively for viral markers, and they are negative.'

'What if she is in the window period when blood tests can miss HIV and hepatitis infections?'

'You can do nothing but pray!'

Nipun looked at Ridhi. Even though her face was partly covered by the mask, he could see that she was on the edge, like a passenger on a sinking ship.

Nipun continued, 'Relax. Surgeons are always at risk. I have also been pricked many times. In fact, if I die due to AIDS contracted from a patient, I will consider it martyrdom. Of course, it is not as great as being martyred in a war. I won't get any awards posthumously or make it to the headlines.'

'Nipun, this is not funny!' Ridhi fumed. She appreciated dark humour in novels, not in real life.

After completion of the surgery, Ridhi went to the ward to finish the pending work. While she was moving around, an old man who seemed to be the attendant of a patient, started walking by her side.

'Yes,' she said, expecting him to begin with—'Please, could you take a look at my patient?'.

'Doctorji, I have noticed that you have been working continuously since early morning. Do doctors drink some secret elixir which makes them tireless?'

'We don't take any magic potion. Imagine that my duty is over at 5 p.m. and I get an injured patient five minutes prior to that, I would have to start treating the patient, even if I had to miss a coffee session with my friends! Our meal timings and resting hours are so uncertain, that ultimately, our bodies reconcile to the fact that they will not be treated decently!' Ridhi replied.

'I was thinking of having a doctor as my daughter-in-law. But after watching the doctors work here, I have changed my mind!' he declared.

'Okay. See you some other time,' Ridhi said, realizing that the chatty geriatric was in the mood to have a long conversation with her.

The man took Ridhi's hint and retraced his route to his relative's bed.

Monday mornings were the harbingers of hectic weeks. But the weekends too didn't excite the junior doctors because they were usually just as hectic as weekdays. Ridhi snubbed the alarm, as if it were an aimlessly barking stray dog. As a consequence, she had to cut her breakfast short.

It was the chief's operation day, and body aches were guaranteed. In the first surgery, Dr Ujjwal was to be assisted by Nipun and Ridhi.

'Scalpel please,' the chief said to Sanchi.

With his experienced hands, he opened the abdomen quickly. Ridhi and Nipun were given retractors to make a comfortable operating field for the chief. Just as he was about to start the dissection, Dr Ujjwal noticed that Ridhi was retracting with excessive force.

'Ridhi! Are you lost?' he shouted.

There was no response from Ridhi. When he looked at

her, he was utterly surprised. Her eyes were closed.

Impossible! How can someone sleep in a standing position, and that too while assisting in a surgery! Dr Ujjwal thought.

Meanwhile, Nipun had become aware that there was something wrong with Ridhi.

The retractor slipped from Ridhi's hand and she started to fall backwards, like an axed tree. Nipun instinctively moved to his left. He was able to support her head just in the nick of time, although, he had to make a lot of effort to maintain his own balance. Everyone realized then that Ridhi had blacked out. The anaesthesia team moved into action. They put her on a bed and lowered her head. In a few moments, she woke up, absolutely dazed.

Ridhi was sent to the surgeon's room to rest. The chief continued with the surgery after having called another resident doctor from the ward. After all, it was below the dignity of his highness to operate with just one resident as his assistant.

After the surgery had finished, Sanchi narrated the sequence of events to Ridhi. She highlighted Nipun's acrobatic save.

'The khota sikka (bad coin) worked today!' Ridhi said.

'Come on. Dr Nipun deserves some respect. He showed great presence of mind.'

'I know. I was just joking.'

Ridhi rang up her father. 'Dad, I had a blackout in the OT. But right now, I am okay. Please don't tell Mom because she might react with a fainting fit stronger than mine!'

'My brave girl is not going to give up. These are initial hiccups and you will get over them soon. Don't think about your weight all the time! Eat well, and always keep some energy bars with you.'

'Thanks Dad. I will surely fulfil your dream of having a daughter who is equally adept at using a surgeon's knife and a kitchen knife.'

'Yes, an all-rounder, just like your dad!'

Ridhi was told to rest for a few hours in her hostel room, to recuperate. She felt that the incident had given Nipun an advantage in the game of hearts. 'This isn't just a coincidence. A divine force is conspiring to bring both of us together,' she philosophized.

Later in the evening, she met Nipun back at the hospital.

'If it wasn't for you, I would have been listening to the jarring sounds of monitors in an intensive care unit!' she said, fluttering her eyelashes and putting on a coquettish smile.

'Today we can list yet another advantage of being slim. If you had been heavy, both of us would have fallen to the ground.'

Ridhi thought, *This buffoon will never learn how to court a lady, not even when she is receptive.* She had been expecting that Nipun would have come up with something mushy to say, and as usual, he was frivolous.

Nipun saw Ridhi's warmth as a token of her gratitude, a squall, which would go away as dramatically as it had appeared. Moreover, his mind was preoccupied by the trip he was to take to his hometown, Jaipur, in a few days. Although his parents had indicated that things were looking up on the home front, he was not sure that his dad had actually turned around his failed business. It could just have been a ploy to make him feel better.

A few days ago, his mother had called him up. 'Beta, it feels as if you are living in a foreign land. If your boss doesn't grant you leave, I will personally request him.'

'Mom, tackling my boss is not your cup of tea. An interaction with him might just leave you with a bad taste in your mouth. I will manage.'

As expected, Dr Ujjwal granted him a leave with a deep frown.

'As a resident doctor, you are in a war zone. When there is action on the front line, soldiers are not supposed to go home, just to do lip service to their loved ones.'

On the other hand, Dr Ujjwal saw Ridhi as a dainty doll, aiming for an 8,000-metre summit. He posted her in emergency so that a change in environment could help her adapt to the life of a surgeon. But the emergency ward too had nasty surprises for the uninitiated.

The day Ridhi joined for her duty in the emergency ward, Nipun left for his home. There were no surgical emergencies till the afternoon. But the chaos of the other specialities maintained the decorum of the emergency ward.

A middle-aged housewife arrived; she was suffering from gastroenteritis. She was severely dehydrated and had low blood pressure. The only way to save her was to push intravenous fluids rapidly into her bloodstream. However, neither Dr Kirti, the resident doctor in medicine, nor any of the nurses, could put in the intravenous line since all her veins had collapsed because of the low blood pressure. Moreover, because of the panic, their dexterity had regressed to the level of novices.

Ridhi was called for help. She went ahead with a cut-down procedure, where she canulated the vein under direct vision, after having made a cut on the forearm under local anaesthesia. Everyone appreciated her for having salvaged the difficult situation, and it made Ridhi feel on top of the world.

As the nurses' hands cramped while squeezing the plastic bottles to deliver the intravenous fluid, they had to take turns.

After fifteen minutes, the staff nurse, Revati, called everyone to the patient's bed.

'Look!' she said, pointing towards the urinary catheter.

It was a scenario which could have only taken place in a hospital. At least six people were longingly gazing at the patient's urinary catheter, and they were excited by the light, yellow-coloured fluid which had started to flow into the catheter. For once, urine was worth its weight in gold.

The patient's term on earth had been extended, while Ridhi had taken her first step towards reserving a seat in heaven.

The next day, she typed the words 'missing you' after having opened the message box on Nipun's Facebook profile. But she couldn't bring herself to press the enter button. There was a lack of clear-cut signals from Nipun. Ridhi dreaded rejection. She ended up deleting the text.

'Why blame Nipun? I am no better,' she lamented.

Two days later, a twenty-year-old girl named Ela landed up in the emergency with a cut on her right palm. While driving a scooter, she had taken the quote, 'Devise your own path', too seriously and had tried to take a short cut through a vacant plot. The scooter had hit a large stone concealed in the grass. She had ended up in the emergency ward of Nirog Hospital, as a patient of Dr Ridhi.

Ridhi explained to her, 'I'll have to stitch up your wound.'

'Doctor, I can't tolerate pain at all,' Ela interrupted.

'I understand. Pretty girls are so pampered that they have a low tolerance for any hardship! I will give you some local anaesthesia to numb the area.'

After having administering the local anaesthesia injection, Ridhi started on the stitches. To distract Ela, she asked her about her education, family, blah blah. Just when around 70 per cent of the stitching had been completed, Ela screamed, 'Ouch! That hurt.'

Ridhi was in a fix. A safe dose of local anaesthesia had already been administered.

'What are your hobbies?' she asked.

'Doctor, I will tell you about them after I receive another injection of local anaesthesia. I know you have been keeping me occupied with constant conversation! But that is no longer working,' Ela said.

What do I do now? Ridhi thought.

Suddenly, she had an idea. 'Do you have a boyfriend?' she asked.

'Yeah! A pretty cute one,' Ela said, revealing her beautiful smile for the first time.

'Why don't you tell me something about him?'

'Oh! I could talk about my jaan for hours. Doctor, finish the stitches and keep on conversing with me, or rather, keep listening to me!' Ela said. She cooperated fully during the rest of the procedure.

Ridhi made a mental note—love is the most potent intoxicant for a young lady.

'What is stopping me from reaching that exalted state?' she asked herself, but drew a blank.

14

Unkempt Becomes Polished

Looks do matter even in the case of men.

Nipun boarded the *Shatabdi Express* for his hometown, Jaipur, at the New Delhi Railway Station. He was pleased to have a window seat, which was usually so coveted by him that he had indulged in fights with his cousins over it, well into his adolescence. A charming young lady requested him to help her with her luggage and then she settled into the adjoining seat.

He remembered his medical college days when he often used to carry the luggage of the girls of his class, and had been called a 'coolie' by his classmates.

Nipun covertly introduced himself. He opened his textbook on laparoscopic surgery, and tilted it slightly, so that the contents were visible to her.

'Are you a surgeon?' she asked him.

Nipun couldn't believe his luck.

It seems she idolizes surgeons. She must be overjoyed to have stumbled upon one by chance, Nipun thought, and visualized scenes from movies where strangers travelling on adjacent seats became co-passengers on the journey of life.

'Actually, I am a trainee surgeon, presently in my second

year of MS. But, being the boss's favourite student, I have already been allowed to conduct quite a few extra major surgeries,' Nipun said. He looked at her to check if her jaw had dropped.

She gave him a half smile.

'What a coincidence! I am also a surgeon!' she said. 'Dr Suparna, I'm a senior resident at the National Medical Institute. I cleared my MS last year. My husband is a paediatrician in the same hospital.'

'Oh. It will be good to have your company on this journey,' Nipun smiled, hiding his colossal disappointment.

It should be mandatory for all married women to wear symbols of marriage! he thought. Suparna had not been wearing a mangalsutra, sindoor, or jewellery.

'I am quite surprised that you have been allowed to do major surgeries in your second year of MS!' she taunted.

'As I have said, my boss has lot of confidence in me,' Nipun replied. He couldn't look Suparna in the eye, since he was not an accomplished liar.

Suparna wasn't unduly surprised. She knew bragging came as naturally to surgeons as it did to war veterans. Nipun had been in the mood to take a break from his profession, but Suparna felt a moral obligation to provide tips and tricks for various surgeries. He regretted taking out his book on surgery; had he opened the bestseller he had brought along with him, the journey would have been more relaxing.

Upon reaching home, he received yet another surprise. The rooms had been freshly painted and furnished. Before he could react, his mouth was stuffed with a besan ladoo. Jagriti, his mom, had already prepared his favourite delicacies.

'Oh my child! You have become so weak.'

'Mom, from which angle do I look weak? I have gained four kilos since my last visit.'

'Is the quality of food in your hostel mess better now?'

'No. But that doesn't matter to me. I have become a seasoned parasite. I eat the food brought to the hospital by nurses and female doctors!'

'Do you like any of the female doctors?'

'Mom, I love two of them!'

'But one is enough!'

'The love is not reciprocated!'

Sarwan intervened and brought this inane conversation between mother and son to an end. 'You must be surprised by the facelift of our house. My business has turned around,' he told Nipun.

'How?' Nipun asked. He was certain that his dad couldn't have done so by himself. It was either a divine miracle because of his mom's prayers, or someone had joined him to provide the 'checks and balances'.

'My cousin, Nagendra and I, are partners in this business. Our team has clicked. Don't worry about us. Keep your entire stipend to yourself.'

'Dad...the stipend is merely peanuts. But since I am a simple person, I will manage somehow! However, you will have to buy my books.'

'No way! Purchasing medical books makes one financially sick!'

In the evening, a few relatives and family friends got together for dinner. For Nipun's mom, this was an opportunity to showcase her ace of spades. 'My son can operate equally well with both hands! He does surgeries so cleanly that sometimes the patient doesn't even lose a single drop of blood!'

Nipun felt embarrassed. However, he had no choice but to keep mum.

If I start a private practice, I can employ Mom as a patient counsellor! he thought.

A guest commented, 'That is amazing. You are blessed to have such a brilliant son.'

Egged on, she bragged further, 'Nipun has become such an expert in operating on the appendix that he could remove it even if he were blindfolded!'

Nipun could read between the lines. His mom was trying to spread the word that an unbelievably talented bachelor was up for grabs.

After everyone had left, Manhar, his neighbour, stayed behind. He requested that Nipun examine his son, who had a lipoma on his back.

Nipun opined, 'He requires surgery. There is no other option.'

'Doctor, please do me a favour. Get it done in your department.'

Nipun pondered this over. He wanted to help his neighbour. But what if Manhar discovered that Nipun was just a *keeda makoda* (nobody) in the department?

'We have a long waiting list. This surgery can be easily

done in Jaipur. I will help you out,' Nipun replied. Thus, he had managed to wriggle out of a tricky situation.

He spent the last day with his old pal, Suraj, who believed that the intensity of any friendship was directly proportional to the unsolicited advice given. Initially, Nipun had followed all his suggestions. But after a few disasters, he had realized that Suraj grossly overestimated his own wisdom.

Their first visit was to the 'world-famus', Super Deluxe Chaat Bhandaar—which was actually a cart, although its fan following could put big eateries to shame. Their paani-puri had helped them both build their immunities against gastrointestinal infections. As teenagers, Nipun and Suraj would get a kick out of coming here without having informed their parents.

Suraj gave him a cold stare. 'Doctors usually don't keep beards in this fashion. And your moustache makes you look funny!'

'I went through a bad patch and stopped shaving. Anyway, my identity is because of my profession,' Nipun defended.

'But a polished appearance will create a better impression for your patients, seniors and potential girlfriends,' Suraj argued.

'You are giving me ideas.'

Suraj closed the fingers of his right hand to make a fist. 'I am serious. You are going with me to the Scissors Salon. Saaley, if you say no, I will punch you!'

'Okay yaar. This is one of the rare occasions where you seem to speak sense!'

Parting with his moustache and his beard was difficult as he had been emotionally attached to them. The unruly growth on his scalp was also trimmed, to a gentlemanly length.

When Nipun looked in the mirror, he felt that it had become friendly after a long time. He exclaimed, 'You look great, Nipun!'

Nipun realized that his odd-looking moustache, with its extra wide gap above the centre of his lip, had been the worst feature of his face.

His attire no longer matched his look. On the way home, Nipun picked up designer clothes and shoes.

His parents were delighted to witness his transformation.

'Jagriti, take a look at Nipun! Our boy is all set to woo a lady.'

'Dad, in cities like Delhi, sometimes the opposite may also happen,' Nipun chuckled.

Nipun returned to the hospital. Straightaway, he was buried under an avalanche of compliments. Even Nishtha and Ridhi couldn't believe their eyes. They also noticed his branded clothes with a sense of relief. For too long, he had been proving the emptiness of his pockets by showing them inside out. That was not likely to happen again.

'Hi, Handsome,' Ridhi said to his utter delight.

'You've changed for the better,' Nishtha commented.

Nipun sensed that Nishtha and Ridhi had no alternative but to consider him again. He concluded that looks did matter in the end.

During his morning rounds, Nipun eagerly awaited more compliments, especially from the chief.

Dr Ujjwal took a good look at him. 'What a contrast! A good-looking doctor, with miniscule brainpower. Previously you had depicted a truer picture of yourself!'

Dr Ujjwal's creativity seemed to increase while operating and while scolding Nipun.

15

Yet Another Goof-up

The first date should be kept simple, otherwise complications can occur.

The next day, the whole team was on the grand round. While climbing down the stairs behind Ridhi, Nipun began to compose an ode dedicated to her curves. He missed the last step and twisted his ankle. In pain, he was unable to walk and a wheelchair was requisitioned.

'Consult an orthopaedic surgeon and get an X-ray, if required. Should I accompany you?' Dr Ujjwal asked.

'Sir, please carry on with the rounds. There seems to be a sprain. I will show my ankle to the senior resident in orthopaedics in the emergency ward.'

Ridhi wished she could be with Nipun. Her presence would have obviated the need for painkillers.

Nipun was relieved to find Dr Kabir, his old friend, on duty in the emergency ward.

'What happened?'

'I slipped on the stairs.'

'Reason?'

'Distraction!'

'I get it. This is a common cause of injury for lecherous

people! I will get an X-ray done. Let's hope you don't turn out to be the centre piece of our OT today!'

After having taken a look at the X-ray, Kabir told Nipun, 'You are a lucky bloke! Got away with just a mild sprain. I would suggest that you apply a crepe bandage.'

'Listen, put on the plaster. I will get it removed in three weeks. Mention "major sprain" as the diagnosis.'

'Ah! You want to hoodwink your chief, and watch movies in your room!'

'No, I will attend my duties. Actually, this would be the best way to impress my female colleagues because all the other methods have failed! You know that girls like sincere, hardworking guys; guys who are likely to take good care of them and the kids! Even the chief will see me as an angel in the garb of a human!'

Nipun returned to the ward with a plaster around his right ankle, a stick in his left hand and a huge wave of sympathy around him. Whenever Ridhi was around, he grimaced and feigned pain.

As he had expected, Ridhi was distraught. 'Why don't you take complete bed rest for a few days? I'm sure the chief will grant you the leaves necessary. I'll even do your share of the work,' she told him.

'For me, taking care of the patient takes precedence over everything else,' Nipun said, mimicking the resoluteness of freedom fighters.

'I admire your dedication. Our country needs more doctors like you!' Ridhi replied.

Nipun passed a sleepless night because of the discomfort of wearing a plaster. But nothing could have been done about it.

Ridhi also lay awake. She couldn't get Nipun off her mind.

For the next three weeks that his plaster was on, Ridhi was mostly by his side. She didn't let him exert himself. Nipun loved the way that she held his hand to support him. Often, he felt guilty about playing with her emotions.

'But all this is for a noble cause!' he rationalized.

Both of them felt in their gut that they were heading towards a relationship. Ridhi decided to ignore the conventional 'no first move' policy that women typically followed. There was a distinct possibility that he would get tongue-tied. She planned to take charge.

Just two days after his plaster was removed, Nipun was with Ridhi in the cafeteria.

Ridhi said, 'Hey. Let us plan an outing to a place away from the hospital. You need a change!'

Nipun couldn't believe his luck. He reckoned that he should go for a birdwatching trip with her because he would be in his element in such an environment, and was likely to find all the right words. He asked, 'Hey, you have been asking me to show you how birdwatching is done. Let's go for a short trip to the Okhla Bird Sanctuary?'

'Are you sure that your ankle will be able to take the strain of walking on uneven ground? Your plaster has just been taken off just two days back.'

'For a birdwatching trip, I can rise from my grave! Don't worry. I will wear a crepe bandage.'

The next day, by the crack of dawn, they had reached the sanctuary, a wetland abutting the river Yamuna.

Upon sighting a flock of migratory birds, Nipun went ballistic. 'Hey! Look. We have guests from Siberia and Central Asia.'

'While flying from Siberia, do these birds rest on the way?' Ridhi asked, like an inquisitive little girl.

'Next time, I will fly with them, and then let you know!' Nipun chuckled.

'Shut up!'

Nipun took out his SLR camera, with a foot-long, zoom lens. Soon, he was crouched on the ground just to get the right angle for his shot. He was least bothered about getting his clothes dirty or crushing innocent insects. Ridhi could have never imagined that Nipun would act so maniacal over winged creatures.

They kept walking. Ridhi was hesitant to jump over a swampy patch. A wrong step could result in a fall, followed by a complimentary mud-therapy session.

'Come on. You are a surgeon and surgeons aren't too calculative!' Nipun said.

He held Ridhi's hand and helped her cross. But Ridhi held onto his hand. She looked at him longingly. Nipun decided to build on the momentum by pulling her closer to him.

A sarus crane suddenly appeared out of the blue. Nipun took away his hand. The bird had moved behind the elephant grass.

'I absolutely have to photograph it by all means! Just wait for a while,' Nipun said. He was panting with excitement.

Nipun disappeared out of her sight. After a few minutes, Ridhi started feeling uneasy, although the bird song provided some respite. Then she heard male voices. As she turned around, she found two young men leering at her. They had the typical look of small-time crooks—oiled hair, gaudy clothes and thick chains on their necks.

Ridhi's breathing became laboured. 'Nipun!' she shouted at the top of her voice.

The men were now aware that she had a male companion. Still, they refused to budge.

Although Nipun had gone a considerable distance, he heard Ridhi's scream. He scampered back. It still took him two minutes to reach her. From a distance, the long lens of Nipun's camera appeared like a firearm to the rowdies. They mistook him to be a hunter. More at home with punches, kicks and knives, they disappeared.

Ridhi's face was red with anger. 'It was so mean of you to leave me alone for that stupid bird. These guys had bad intentions.'

'I admit, I am at fault. Sorry,' Nipun said, folding his hands for an added effect.

'Let us go back. I am not in the mood to stay here any more.'

'I promise I will never do this again,' Nipun pleaded. He held onto both of his earlobes and pulled them down; a more dramatic show of apology.

Ridhi replied with stony silence.

The melodious magpie robin had joined the orchestra. Nipun mumbled, 'Just shut up. You guys screwed everything up.'

While they were returning, a group of crows began to crowd above them, irritating them with calls. Suddenly, a dropping fell on Ridhi's shoulder, narrowly missing her face.

Nipun was sure that this was a deliberate act of mischief.

'Oh! I am so sorry,' Nipun said, as he wiped her shoulder clean with a handkerchief.

On the way back, Ridhi didn't utter a single word.

This guy prefers birds to humans. He is not for me, she had decided there and then.

Daisy, her cousin, had recently left her husband because of his fetish of spending endless hours watching the battle of bat and ball on sports channels. All her tactics, from pleading to screaming, had failed to dissuade him from his addiction to cricket. Ridhi had been forewarned to keep a safe distance from hobbyists.

Nipun realized that the way in which he had messed up, the odds of Ridhi changing her mind were low. If he had been able to take a picture of the sarus crane, there would have been some consolation at least.

Upon entering his room, Nipun stood in the front of the mirror. He gave himself a stinging slap.

Then, he shouted, '*Saley chutiye* (You pussy)! You should jump into the Yamuna.'

Later, he posted on the Facebook page of his birdwatching group—'Beware birders—birding sites are no good for dates'. But his tip about the presence of Sarus cranes in Okhla Bird Sanctuary had created quite a stir. The next morning, hordes of birdwatchers made a beeline to the area. However, the sarus cranes couldn't be sighted. They had flown further south; the avian crowd at Okhla wasn't hep enough for them.

Nipun lost face among birdwatchers too. One of them commented, 'Nipun deserves an award for the hoax of the year.'

The same night, Nipun drowned his sorrows in another drinking session with his old friends. He told them all about his ill-fated birdwatching trip.

'You people pushed me into it.'

'We never suggested that you take her to a bird sanctuary. Even a child knows that a nice restaurant is the best choice for the first date!' Jivan said.

Kshitij interrupted, 'I have an idea. Next time, the both of you could go to a much better place.'

Nipun said, 'Tell me fast!'

'The Delhi zoo!' Kshitij said, precipitating raucous laughter.

But Nipun wasn't amused. 'Stop it. There have been reports of people dying because of excessive laughing! If you don't believe me, google it.'

16

The Angry Old Man

Anger management courses should be mandatory for all heads of department because the headship invariably goes to their head.

For the junior doctors, the day had started on an ominous note. Whoever took a look at the chief's face, prayed—'God, please mark me safe today.' Whenever Dr Ujjwal was seen with a pursed upper lip and flared nostrils, it was a given that he would behave like the one-eyed pirates of yore. Last evening, he had found out from a relative that Apoorv, had gotten engaged a day ago, without his knowledge. Meenal, seemed to be the fountainhead of the conspiracy; she had hit him where it hurt the most. She obviously felt that Dr Ujjwal's wrongs were too loathsome to deserve a pardon.

The chief had started with the rounds. As he came around to the first bed, he took a good look at the treatment chart. The previous evening, Mayur had added the drug Pantoprazole.

'Tell me the potential adverse effects of Pantoprazole,' the chief said.

Mayur was speechless. He only knew about the good effects of the drug.

'How could you start the patient on a medicine without knowing about it in detail? Medical books aren't bulky just to make them look impressive! Take your old head to the library and don't return to this ward until you have filled it with some knowledge.'

Dr Ujjwal's hawkish stance sent shivers down the spines of Ridhi and Nipun. On the next bed, the chief looked at the case file. There were no progress notes for the previous day.

Why does the chief check only the incomplete files? Ridhi wondered. She had completed all the files, but for the last two.

'Ridhi, what is wrong with you? I had the impression that you were different from these rascals!'

'Sir, I couldn't find the time,' she replied meekly.

Dr Ujjwal reacted to this explanation as if someone had showered him with *ma behen ki gaali* (expletives). 'My delicate princess, leave the ward and take the incomplete files with you. After completing them, stand in front of the mirror and ask yourself whether you have it in you to complete the MS in surgery.'

Finally, only Nipun was left unhurt, along with a few staff nurses. He braced himself for the inevitable.

They had reached the bed of a patient who had to have a blood transfusion. Nipun told the chief, 'Sir, a technical snag has delayed the issuing of the blood bottle from the blood bank by an hour. The relatives have been told about it.'

However, the patient's relatives were sceptical of each and every action of the doctors and nursing staff. (They had recently watched a movie whose main theme had been doctor bashing.) Umang, the brother of the patient, had donated the blood. Umang said, 'Doctor, we were wondering why the blood has not been transfused yet?' The chief was incensed by the tone he took.

'Actually, it is because all the doctors enjoy a drink of blood after the end of their rounds,' the chief thundered. The bewildered relative ducked at the sudden barrage of Kalashnikov fire. He apologized profusely.

The team then reached a patient suffering from Buerger's disease, a condition where smoking had shrunk the blood vessels of the lower limbs. The middle-aged man was a chronic smoker and had non-healing wounds on both his feet.

'How will you manage this case? All the investigations have already been done,' Dr Ujjwal said.

'Sir, I would take him to surgery. A lumbar sympathectomy would be my procedure of choice,' said Nipun.

'Oh God! Save me from these duds!' the chief ranted. 'Wouldn't you ensure complete cessation of smoking before operating on him? Get out of my sight!'

Meanwhile, Candy had also reached the ward to ask Dr Ujjwal's advice about a patient. One of the staff nurses stopped him on his way. 'Sir, the chief has turned into a hooded cobra! You'd better stay away for some time.'

Candy retreated hastily.

After Nipun had left, the chief realized that he was only left with a few staff nurses. There was no doctor left to take notes or to carry out his orders. Calling back the three resident doctors would have been like licking saliva that had been spat out. He moved ahead. A boy had pulled off his nasogastric tube. It had to be put back urgently.

'Staff, give me a new tube and some glycerine.'

The chief tried to insert the tube but it wouldn't go in; the boy was not cooperating. He gave up after two attempts. Actually, the chief had not done this procedure for more than a decade, since he felt that routine ward procedures shortened his tall stature.

The staff nurses, who had observed the fumble, were startled by the fact that a surgeon who could do complex operations became a novice during a minor procedure. The ward-in-charge, Mary, finished the job in the first attempt. Dr Ujjwal was left red-faced.

'Should I order myself out of the ward rounds? It seems like I need to work as a resident doctor for a few days, to regain the skills that I have lost,' he finally said, faintly smiling.

'But womanizing will not be allowed!' Mary whispered to him. She knew the chief inside out, as she had followed all the phases of his life.

As usual, the chief worked till late in the evening. While driving back to his home, he reflected that for the last few years, he had been using it like a bed-and-breakfast inn. Achhey Lal, his domestic help, was the only human with whom he interacted at his place.

The wives of Dr Ujjwal's contemporaries were reluctant to have them maintain social contact with a man who could have a bad influence on them. Although they didn't admit to it, the men were afraid that he would have no qualms about stealing the affections of their wives.

Realizing that Dr Ujjwal was not his usual, exuberant self, Achhey Lal said, 'Sahib, this house badly needs a memsahib.'

Dr Ujjwal smiled, 'I know. But as a groom, I am not in demand! By the way, why are you single?'

The Angry Old Man • 143

'Not by choice, I am compelled to be single. The system of bride price is prevalent in my district. I am saving up for it!'

To divert his mind, Dr Ujjwal looked at his Facebook account. But the pictures of happy families on vacations dispirited him even more.

A few days later, Candy visited the chief in the OPD while he was examining a patient.

'Do you recognize me?' the patient asked Dr Ujjwal.

The chief recalled that a few years ago, Nirav, a banker, had been operated on because of a tear in his liver following a road accident. Nirav had literally cheated death because of the extraordinary effort on the part of the chief and his team.

'Yes! Good to see you, Nirav. Where have you been all these years?'

'For the past four years, I have been in Kolkata, my hometown. I have managed to stall a transfer with many deft manipulations.'

'Why do you like Kolkata so much? Is it the sandesh, rosogolla or mishti doi?' said the surgeon with the sweet tooth.

'All of those. I also get a lot of food for thought since people rarely indulge in small talk back in Kolkata. Instead, they passionately discuss various issues. A Delhiite would simply say, "saanu ki (how does it matter to us)?"'

'What brings you here?'

'Please hazard a guess!'

'Something is wrong with your body. What else? You couldn't have come so far to say namaste to me!'

'It's true that I am here to show you the swelling on my neck. But I think of you a lot, almost every day. If you had not treated me, I would have been consecrated to the flames long ago, and my wife wouldn't have had the fortune of spending her life in the company of a genius!'

The chief examined him. 'It is a small lipoma, a collection of fat. It requires a minor surgery under local anaesthesia. Even a dud surgeon should be able to tackle this problem comfortably. Are you sure that you have come all the way from Kolkata just for this? It is as odd as a person from Kolkata flying to Delhi for groceries!'

'I know, Sir. Actually, I have a phobia when it comes to surgical procedures. But I feel secure in your hands.'

'Oh dear, this is the height of trust! Anyway, I will personally operate on you tomorrow. But the doctors under me aren't used to seeing me at minor surgeries!'

'Just tell them that I am your devotee!'

Candy had been following the whole conversation as if he were an attentive student. After the patient had left the office, he said, 'Sir, a thought is harassing me. Travelling so much, just for a minor procedure is an injustice to Mother Earth. It leaves a huge carbon footprint.'

'Since when have you become earth's bodyguard?'

'I can't tolerate hot weather. So I am scared of global warming!'

'Have you made any personal contribution towards saving the environment?'

'Yes boss! The battery of my watch is recharged by solar power!'

'What an effort!'
'Most beginnings are humble!'
'You should install a solar water heater.'
'Oh! That is very costly.'
'I should have expected such an excuse from a kamina (rascal) like you! You should also stop flying abroad, that adds to carbon dioxide emissions!'

Candy was nonplussed. 'Sir, I shall plant a tree after returning from every foreign trip instead!'

Dr Ujjwal often had fun at his expense, but Candy never took offence. Under the chief, he was as well protected as a joey in a mother kangaroo's pouch. Dr Ujjwal bailed him out whenever he got stuck in a surgery, and that happened quite often. However, Candy had unique talents, which compensated for his inadequacies and idiosyncrasies.

Just a month ago, Dr Ujjwal had operated on the son of a minister of the ruling party. The spoilt brat was intoxicated with power 24×7. He had made his presence felt by misbehaving with the doctors as well as the paramedical staff. However, when he had tried to act smart with the chief, there was an equal and opposite reaction. The boy had poisoned his father's mind by telling him a concocted story. The politician, blinded by love for his son, found fault with the chief. In turn, the chief countered with a potent weapon—Candy's offbeat wisdom.

'Anuroop, take care of Netaji. He thinks his son is the axis around which the whole universe revolves. I too can show him the power of my connections but let's not waste our time and energy on senseless duels.'

Candy befriended the politician in no time. He told him, 'Please don't take Dr Ujjwal's actions to heart. Many doctors, including me, curse their luck when they are at the receiving end of his crankiness. To tell you the truth, his pretty wife left him for another man and that has made him a frustrated person!'

The politician, who had often utilized the 'sympathy factor', was swayed by it too. He pacified his son. The duo made a low-key exit from the hospital and threw their weight around elsewhere.

When the next patient entered. Dr Ujjwal greeted him with a wide smile.

'Here is another bhakt of mine,' he murmured. The chief had operated on him twice.

'Satyavan, how do you do?'

'I look okay, but there is a blood clot inside my skull. The accident occurred three weeks back. My motorcycle slipped.'

'How?'

'A truck was bent on overtaking me. The reflection of the sun in its rearview mirror blinded me temporarily and I lost my balance,' Satyavan replied with a wry smile.

'Don't waste my time! Tell me what exactly happened.' The chief's tone had turned stern.

'To tell you the truth, I had been drinking beer.'

'But when I discharged you the last time, you promised to abstain from drinking.'

'I have never touched hard drinks since then. I take only beer!'

'Super-strong beer?'

'Yes, Doctor.'

'How many at a time?'

'Two or three!'

Dr Ujjwal smiled. 'Okay. What happened next?'

'I fell on the road but I felt okay. However, two weeks after the accident, I started to feel dizzy. A CT scan of the head shows that there is a blood clot around my brain. You gave me a new lease on life the last time around. I request you to cure me this time too.'

Dr Ujjwal took a look at the scan.

'You should consult Dr Bhanu, our neurosurgeon. He is the right person to treat you.'

'I am not going anywhere. You have to do it yourself,' the patient insisted.

Dr Ujjwal was in a bind.

With some quick thinking, he found a way out. 'Dear Satyavan. I will be able to open your skull and remove the clot. But I don't know how to close a skull! Imagine moving around without a part of your skull? In such a scenario, even if someone mildly punches you in the area, you've had it.'

That worked. 'Okay, let Dr Bhanu do it. But you have to stay by my side in the operating room for the full duration of the surgery.'

Ujjwal readily agreed.

Anything for bhakts! he thought.

17

Coming of Age

> *Buttering the external examiners is a sure-fire way of obtaining a good result in the practical exam.*

Nipun and Ridhi didn't break up in the conventional manner, where the boy tells the girl—'I will never set foot in your lane again.'

As colleagues, their paths crossed multiple times a day. They had no choice but to interact with each other. Both of them displayed the acumen of seasoned diplomats, and forged a truce based on a few principles.

The first—there would be a mutual non-interference in each other's internal affairs. (They wouldn't ask each other—'Are you dating someone?')

There would be no provocative statements made by either side. (They could poke fun at each other, but not with respect to their soured relationship.)

They would leave communication channels open. (They decided not to remain slaves to history—a future alliance wasn't ruled out.)

Overwork also played its part in helping Nipun get over Ridhi. There was no time for brooding and sulking. And tiredness acted as an excellent sedative at night.

As second-year residents, Nipun and Nishtha had the added responsibility of taking classes to instil clinical sensibilities into the third-year MBBS students. Most of these greenhorns were hungry for knowledge. But there were a few who just kept their eyes open while their distracted minds wandered far and wide. However, when the teacher happened to be a rare female, the boys often concentrated on her.

The first class was taken by Nipun. The batch of students comprised six girls and four boys. As soon as he entered the demonstration room, the students chanted a 'Good morning.' Some even bowed their heads. The veneration charged Nipun and he even tried to copy the chief's mannerisms, with modest success.

The patient for the clinical demonstration was suffering from hydrocele. His testicles had become unusually large because of the collection of fluid. Ramasray, the young, unmarried, migrant worker, had shifted recently, from his village in Bihar. His innocence was largely intact. But soon he would learn the tactics one needed to survive in the urban jungle, full of wily creatures, ready to go to the extent of selling someone—if it served their purpose.

'Ramasray, the student doctors will examine you one by one,' Nipun told him to prepare him against the impending invasion of his privacy.

Being shy, Ramasray had concealed the problem from his family members until the swelling had become so prominent that it had showed through his baggy trousers. The idea of being unclothed in front of so many people, including women, was so dreadful to him that he prayed to his isht devta to make him invisible.

Sensing his unease, Nipun told Ramasray, 'Relax. Even bigwigs like ministers and officers have to remove their clothes in front of doctors!'

'We're all in the same boat!' Ramasray realized. He agreed to the examination.

But he was not prepared for what was about to come. Nipun placed a torch underneath his balls. Then, he made all the students, feel his lesion. To Ramasray's dismay, there were some slow learners. He was trapped and all he could do was close his eyes.

The students went back, much wiser. The reluctant patient had contributed his bit to the field of medical education.

Nishtha too had an eventful class. She was to demonstrate the clinical findings of fibroadenoma, a benign tumour of the breast, to the medical students. Phoolwati, the patient, was a forty-three-year-old lady from a village in Haryana. Nishtha began with the theory. As soon as she had started her lecture, she noticed that two boys sitting in the front row were leering at her, specifically at her breasts.

Maybe I should have worn a thicker dupatta for the class, she thought.

After she had been lecturing for about ten minutes, Nishtha asked the two boys to stand up. Then, she asked one of them, Shobhit, a question from the topic she had just covered. As she had expected, he was blank. Rasik, the other offender, didn't fare any better.

Nishtha grinned maliciously. 'Now I am going to start with the clinical presentation. Both of you can stare at me to your heart's content so that you can keep concentrating on the subject in the same manner!'

Shobhit and Rasik turned red.

After a while, Shobhit spoke, 'Madam, actually both of us are a little disoriented because we studied late into the night.'

'Does disorientation make one look in a particular direction? Even if you have to lie, make it plausible,' Nishtha sneered.

'I'm sorry. This will not happen again,' Shobhit said.

Nishtha explained the steps for the examination of the breast, and made all the students feel the lump. The lady cooperated initially, but she lost her patience towards the end. But she kept mum, out of respect for the doctors.

Just before Nishtha was about to leave the class, a student, Girish, entered the room in a hurry.

'Sorry. I am late because of a punctured tyre. Could I still have a look at the case?'

'Sure, I will accompany you,' Nishtha said.

Girish went up to the lady, 'Bibi ji, please let me feel your lump.'

Phoolwati was under the impression that the whole session was over and that she would finally be left in peace.

'Come, come. Molest me!' she fumed.

'It is okay. We'll not disturb you,' Nishtha said immediately. Girish and Nishtha retreated hastily.

After the class, there was still more trouble for Shobhit and Rasik. Their classmates, who had witnessed their licentious conduct, teased them with the nicknames, Shameless Shobhit and Raunchy Rasik.

The biggest status symbol for the second-year residents was conducting major surgical cases independently. Following Nishtha's dictum, Nipun decided to shed all his inhibitions and ask the chief in plain language to let him conduct a cholecystectomy to remove the gall bladder.

The next morning, he waited for the right moment. After the first surgery had finished, Nipun moved towards the Surgeon's Lounge to gauge the situation. He overheard the chief humming, *Sama hai suhana suhana, nashe mein jahaan hai* (It is a pleasant moment. Everyone seems to be intoxicated).

The chief is in a good mood right now. I must talk to him before some nincompoop gets in the way of his cheer, Nipun thought.

He went inside. 'Sir, I have a humble request. Please allow me to conduct the cholecystectomy all by myself in the next OT.'

The chief replied, 'So you want to impress the girls with your prowess as a surgeon! Okay, if you can convince me by tomorrow morning that you know all about a cholecystectomy, you'll get it.'

'Thank you, Sir. You are a devta (God)!' Nipun said, making the chief smile at his melodrama.

Nipun studied late into the night. But he also found the time to visit a temple. Although he wasn't a religious person, he wanted to cover all his bases. The next morning, the chief gave him the go-ahead after having taken a mini exam. However, Nipun wasn't exactly bubbling with enthusiasm; he had read about the potential complications in detail.

Depth of knowledge also has its drawbacks though not as many as too little knowledge, he thought.

Nipun started the surgery with Mayur as his assistant. Initially, the dissection had been proceeding smoothly. However, when he was about to clip what he thought was the cystic artery, he developed cold feet. *I'm not sure about this step. Should I call the chief?*

The dilemma resolved itself. Miraculously, the chief appeared in the OT. Upon observing the operative field, he told Nipun to wait. Dr Ujjwal scrubbed up, took the instruments in his hands and demonstrated his mastery. He then removed his gloves and let Nipun take over once again. The only hitch during the rest of the surgery was that Nipun had an urge to scratch his nose but there was nothing he could do about that.

After he was done with the operation, Nipun went to the Surgeon's Lounge and touched the chief's feet.

'Well done!' the chief said. 'Don't be disheartened that I spoiled your show.'

'Sir, I am still puzzled as to how you came by yourself, just when I was thinking of calling for you! Are you a mind reader?'

'There wasn't any mind reading or even divine intervention! After having spent so many years in the OT, I have a fair idea about the surgical steps where the youngsters are prone to err.'

Candy, who was nearby, couldn't help himself, 'Nipun, there is a tradition in the department to celebrate a resident doctor's first major case.'

Nipun got the hint. 'Sir, I will arrange for Tara Chand's bread pakoras.'

'Get them with extra chutney,' Dr Ujjwal added.

Nipun tried to find a person who could fetch the grub

but he couldn't, as no one was in a purposeless state. In the recovery room, he noticed Mayur. He was wearing a pair of baggy trousers, which were even more ill-fitting than the OT uniform. It seemed like his priority had been all-round ventilation when he was buying them.

'Dr Ujjwal wants you to go to Munirka to fetch bread pakoras from Tara Chand,' he told Mayur firmly.

'Okay, I will do it. Even if the chief says the day is actually night; I will have to nod in agreement!' Mayur replied.

He had swallowed his pride so often after joining the department that it had all but vanished. However, Nipun made a couple of concessions for him. He forewarned Mayur about the canine bully, the open manholes and the waiting period during which one could finish a novel.

Nipun went back to OT. He joined a group of junior doctors who were recuperating, with the help of gossip therapy. Soon, he felt uneasy because he sensed something wet. Nipun discovered that blood, mixed with saline from the operative field, had stained his OT uniform and had even seeped into his undergarments. Probably, the protective plastic gown had an imperceptible crack, which he had failed to notice in his excitement.

'Look. I played holi with blood,' he said.

'This is nothing compared to what I had to go through when I was just a first-year resident,' Sehaj interjected. 'I was suctioning a tracheostomy tube. The patient had coughed so violently, that his sputum had landed all over my handsome face!'

Ridhi too chipped in. 'A few days ago, I was examining a four-year-old. As soon as his pants were lowered, he shot off a stream of piss which drenched my clothes. I think the kid did it on purpose! Luckily, my face narrowly escaped.'

'I must go to my hostel room and take a bath,' Nipun said.

'Actually, you need to be autoclaved!' Sehaj chuckled.

A few days later, Nipun was reminded of the song, *'Zindagi har kadam ik nayi jang hai'* (In the journey of life one has to fight many battles on one's own). He had to face a novel challenge. Sumitra, his aunt, who had been staying in Delhi, had developed an intestinal obstruction due to umbilical hernia. As expected, she had landed up in the hospital where her nephew was known to work. Nipun had a premonition about Sumitra giving the doctors and the staff a hard time because of her fixed notions about modern medicine. But the bigger fear was that his bluff, of being a big shot, would be caught.

Sumitra had always relied on homeopathy and ayurveda. She thought of allopathic medicines as poisons in disguise, causing more harm than good. Once it was clear her that her surgical problem warranted admission in a modern hospital, her son tried to convince her.

'No way! I would prefer to die at home rather than go to a hospital.'

Her son was thirty-two years old, but he had the wisdom of a septuagenarian. He told her, 'In that case, our family will be shunned because the relatives will think we neglected you on purpose.'

Sumitra buckled under the emotional blackmail, and agreed to be admitted into Nirog Hospital. After examining her, Dr Ujjwal pronounced, 'She needs to be operated on as soon as possible.'

'Doctor Sahib, I have been told that in big hospitals experiments are done on the patients,' Sumitra said.

'That is true!' Dr Ujjwal replied, with a poker face.

Sumitra froze in horror.

The chief smiled. 'Relax. What I mean by this is that every case presents new challenges, and we have to be inventive. Don't worry. Since you are related to Nipun, you will be treated like a VIP.'

'Doctor, please don't give me any allopathic medicines. They cause lot of side effects.'

'Okay,' said Dr Ujjwal. He followed the funda—don't waste your time and effort trying to change the beliefs of those who have crossed the age of seventy.

During the surgery, while she was under the effect of anaesthesia, a heavy dose of a long-lasting antibiotic was administered, so that subsequent doses would not be required. Before she regained consciousness, all the injections and medicines were moved out of her sight.

'Even a con act acquires respectability if it justifies the end!' Dr Ujjwal said to Nipun.

On the second post-operative day, she was shifted to a private room.

Dr Ujjwal came for the rounds. 'Dr Nipun, how are her vitals?'

Nipun was pleasantly surprised. The chief had prefixed a doctor to his name for the first time. It was as if a king had addressed a commoner as 'His Excellency'. The chief had consciously kept Nipun's spurious aura intact in front of his aunt.

'Every parameter is normal, Sir,' Nipun replied.

Dr Ujjwal looked at Sumitra, 'What is your present opinion about allopathy?'

'It is quite efficacious and side effects are rare!'

'You should become a brand ambassador for allopathy!'

The trio of Nipun, Nishtha and Ridhi were together after a hectic day in the doctors' duty room.

'Life is becoming tougher day by day. The chief sticks around the department till late in the evening and keeps giving us one task after the other. I am afraid that one day he may begin to live in the hospital!' Nipun grumbled.

'If we can get him married, he might look forward to leaving the hospital in time,' Ridhi proposed.

'But how?' Nishtha frowned. 'Nipun, what do you say?'

'Let me think over it,' Nipun said.

After a while, he rose up from the chair, his eyes wide open with excitement.

'I've got a brilliant idea!'

'Tell us—fast!'

'One of you could get married to him! He is handsome, rich and famous. What more could you ask for in a man?'

The girls jabbed him simultaneously. But he kept on laughing.

Nishtha's long-overdue visit to her home in Ghaziabad finally materialized. She settled into her favourite spot, the bench beneath the mango tree. It was her childhood friend, although it had nevertheless overgrown her, by a wide margin. Her mother had prepared so many delicacies that she couldn't help remarking, 'Mom, I am being pampered as much as a son-in-law on his first visit to his in-laws' house. Her mom replied, 'The food in the hostel mess is like a medicine-you have to eat it whether you like it or not! So you have earned this feast.'

But later in the evening, Nishtha learnt that she was being mollycoddled so that she wouldn't react in an impolite manner. Her younger sister's marriage had been fixed up without her participation in the selection process of the groom.

Her dad tried to cover up with a laughable excuse. 'Both families took a quick decision. We couldn't contact you since it was your OT day.'

Nishtha realized that they had deliberately avoided her, fearing that if she had taken the interview of the prospective groom, he would have run away from their home. For a change, she decided to suppress her anger.

It was a break from the usual routine. Nishtha was not nagged by her parents about a marriage proposal—from a handsome boy, who was a teetotaller, earned seven figures and was as unstained as a slab of Makrana white marble. She had never believed in these declarations. 'Would anyone have revealed in the matrimonial ad, or even in a meeting, that the boy has had affairs in double figures, or that he has passed most of his exams by cheating?'

Previously, she had been irritated by her parents' pestering her. But now, she was disturbed by the lack of it. They seemed to have given up on her.

Nishtha wondered, 'Am I being considered a lesser child? The rebellious daughters look cool on television serials, but the darlings are the obedient ones.'

She felt jealous of her sister for the first time.

The practical exam in the subject of surgery, for the students of final year MBBS, was only a day away. Usually, the cheerfulness of the examiners had a direct correlation with good results. So the responsibility of receiving the examiners from the railway station was assigned to Candy, the foremost exponent in the art of flattery.

The first examiner to be picked up was Dr Manav. Candy had wanted to welcome him with a garland of marigold flowers, but the chief had vetoed his plan, reasoning that this would be overkill.

As soon as they had settled into his car, Candy said, 'Sir, I am a big fan of yours. I regret the fact that I've never had the chance to work under you, Sir!'

Dr Manav's chest swelled with pride.

'No problem. I will tell Dr Ujjwal to send you over for some time.'

'Thanks a lot for your kind offer, Sir.'

Candy hoped Dr Manav would forget this conversation, just like tourists who became friends after staying in the same resort during the holidays, and promised to keep in touch but never bothered to call.

After leaving Dr Manav in the company of Dr Ujjwal, Candy went back to the railway station to receive Dr Vidyut.

He began all over again. 'Sir, I have heard that at the onset of surgery, you predict the expected duration, and the surgery usually finishes within a margin of a minute or so.'

Dr Vidyut's face brightened. 'You are right,' he replied.

'Sir, how I wish I could attain the same level of precision!' Candy added.

In fact, Candy had even managed to find out about the favourite food of the examiners by ringing up the doctors working at their parent institutions. (Dr Manav was pleasantly surprised to find mutton biryani for dinner.)

The next morning, the final-year medical students began to assemble for their exams. They had undergone a quick 'cultural revolution', where they had cast away their individual style statements so as to appear to be studious, docile creatures, deserving the mercy of the examiners. All the girls had styled their hair in buns or braids. The boys had shaved so closely that two of them had cuts on their chin.

All the examinees looked on the edge except for two. One was Vansh, the topper, who called himself—'I the great'. The other was Astitva; he had already flunked thrice. He seemed to be more afraid of passing than failing because if he got through the exam, he would have to leave the medical college, and also forego partying, skirt-chasing and aimless driving on geri routes with his lackeys. Of course, his rich, indulgent dad was the key facilitator in his crimes against sobriety.

The candidates were told to examine the patients and then present their findings.

Soon, the viva began. The experienced examiners noticed a pattern. All students had done well in a short case where the patient had multiple nodules all over the body due to neurofibromatosis.

Dr Manav went to the patient, looked at him in the eye and said sternly, 'Have you told the findings to the students?'

The patient cracked. 'Yes, Sir. Actually, I know about my problem in great detail. I have been reading about it on the internet. I felt like helping the students; some of them were trembling with fear.'

'You are only helping them become bad doctors.'

'Sorry, Sir. I will never repeat this mistake in the future.'

The examiners unanimously decided that they needed to assign another patient to be able to give grades for the short case.

'Sir, it will be difficult to find a patient with good clinical findings at such short notice,' Candy asserted.

Only moments later, Manav came up with a solution. 'Bring any normal, healthy person!'

Candy called his domestic help, Bhanwar. The devious plan was revealed to him. He was to pretend to have a pain in the lower abdomen.

'Don't worry, Sir. I will act so well that the students will be convinced I am sick.'

The students examined Bhanwar one by one. Then they were called to present their findings to the examiners.

Most students described one clinical finding or the other

like an enlarged liver, an enlarged spleen and an abdominal lump. Throughout this, the examiners struggled to hold back their laughter.

After the viva had ended, the candidates were called back in.

Vidyut smiled. 'Actually, this patient has neither a lump nor an enlarged organ in the abdomen. He is absolutely normal!'

'Ooh!' the students chanted in chorus.

Even Vansh, the topper of the batch, had been fooled despite having the head of a professor on his young shoulders.

He said, sheepishly, 'Sir, I thought there must be some finding, since the case appeared in the exam.'

'This case should serve as a lesson to all the budding doctors! Every person with a symptom is not suffering from a serious disease,' Vidyut emphasized.

Dr Ujjwal added, 'I am reminded of the early days of my MS. One day, I had a pain in my abdomen. Coincidentally, I had been reading about lymphoma and everything seemed to fit. I thought that I had only a few days left to live! I rushed to my chief. But to my utter surprise, he started laughing at me! He examined me and diagnosed the problem as acidity.'

The results were out in a few days. The biggest surprise was the success of Astitva, the chronic examinee. He seemed to have gotten bored of his decadent lifestyle. Four students whose performance was much below par would have to cool their heels in the medical college for another six months.

18
The Serious Comic

Most of the comedians are not so jolly in real life.

When Dr Ujjwal announced that Harshil, the zany comedian, was to be admitted for the operative correction of his inguinal hernia, Nipun was in awe. He had often laughed his heart out while watching Harshil's performances on YouTube.

The doctors in the surgical unit had treated saints, murderers and every type of human in-between. But they had never come across a stand-up comedian. However, at the hospital, comedy was the last thing on Harshil's mind. He was basically a wuss; he couldn't even stand the sight of blood.

While Harshil was walking towards the private ward for admission, he saw a trolley shifting a dead body. He began to feel dizzy and lost his balance. He would have fallen to the ground had his brother not supported him. A wheelchair was requisitioned.

From that moment onwards, the comedian remained under the spell of horror.

The chief had deputed the jokester of the surgical unit, Nipun, to look after him.

'In the television serials, "Mash" and "Scrubs", most surgeons come across as colourful characters who love cutting as well as flirting!' Harshil taunted Nipun.

'In reality, all surgeons aren't skirt-chasers. Your views will change once you observe us working,' Nipun replied.

A day prior to the surgery, Nipun started with the pre-operative work. He requested Harshil to sign the consent form.

'What does it imply?' Harshil asked.

'Basically, it absolves us of any responsibility for complications due to the surgery!'

Harshil was scared and his face showed it.

'Relax, even after taking a patient's consent, the surgeons are accountable,' Nipun clarified.

'To tell you the truth, I am quite scared of undergoing the surgery.'

'Why? Nowadays, undergoing a surgical operation is less of a risk than driving on a highway, especially amidst the maniacs who drive as if they are on a racetrack.'

'Actually, I've come to know that surgeons can remove a kidney, during the abdominal operation, and sell it to a person who needs it!'

Nipun couldn't help but grin. He explained, 'That is an absolutely baseless fear. In a kidney transplant, elaborate pre-operative testing is required to match the blood and tissue type of the donor to the recipient. Moreover, the kidney can't be stored for too long. Anyway, if you want, we can get a post-operative ultrasound scan, to confirm the presence of both kidneys.'

'Got it, Doctor!'

The next morning, Harshil was shifted into the pre-operative room. Used to theatrical performances, he started chanting his prayers loudly. Soon, other patients too folded their hands and joined him. They were followed by the staff nurses and the junior doctors. Candy happened to pass by. Harshil was late for surgery, but Candy didn't dare interrupt the mass prayer. He was well aware that even the most docile Indian turned into Godzilla if he perceived even a minor disrespect to his religion. Finally, Harshil finished his prayer. He was shifted into the OT where spinal anaesthesia was administered to him.

Candy started the surgery. He was being assisted by Nipun.

'So, is Harshil entertaining everyone?' Candy asked Nipun.

'He has left his sense of humour at home! But Harshil is still amusing everyone by suspecting foul play at every step of his treatment!' Nipun replied.

'Shh...the patient is not being operated under general anaesthesia. He might have heard,' Candy whispered to Nipun, after having realized that both of them had committed a faux pas. Nipun was also stupefied.

Dr Ketan, the anaesthesiologist, observed their discomfiture. 'Relax. The patient didn't overhear anything. He is in a deep sleep because I have given him a heavy dose of the sedative,' he said.

Nipun and Candy heaved a sigh of relief.

Candy dissected the hernial sac and repaired the defect with a mesh. After that, it was just a matter of stitching up the different layers. At the closure stage, the surgeon and the assistants often loosened up a bit and indulged in casual conversation. However, Candy and Nipun were careful not to talk about Harshil.

'Has anyone visited the Gourmet Food Point recently?' Candy said.

'Yes. I was there last weekend,' Ketan replied.

'What is their signature dish?.

By then, Harshil had woken up. He was scared when he heard this conversation between them.

The surgeons don't seem to be taking my surgery seriously. I hope they are not operating on the wrong side! Harshil thought.

'Doctor, could you please focus on my surgery!' he said, to everyone's astonishment.

'We are almost through. While applying the skin sutures, all surgeons tend to relax,' Candy said.

'Sorry. I just panicked. In any case, do try out the lasooni kebab at the Gourmet Food Point!'

After a brief stint in the recovery, Harshil was shifted to a private room. Despite the heavy medication, he felt pain in his operated site. To divert his mind, he switched on the television. On the Supersonic News Channel, there was a heated discussion among a group of pseudo-intellectuals over the demand made by animal rights activists; they had insisted that staring at a mating pair of stray dogs be declared an offence.

Just as he was about to switch channels, Breaking News flashed on the television screen. In the visual, a patient was seen lying on a hospital bed. This was followed by an image of an X-ray, which showed an artery forceps lying inside the abdomen of the patient. The newsreader announced, 'This patient was operated on one month ago. But now he needs another surgery, to remove the artery forceps.'

The Supersonic News Channel, like many other channels,

subscribed to the view that news would make an impact on the viewers only if it were presented in such a way that they were unsettled. So the picture of the X-ray kept flashing.

'It is not uncommon for surgeons to forget an artery forceps, or scissors in the abdomen. Last year, in the US alone, there were about four thousand such cases,' the presenter emphasized.

In India, the incident is more likely to occur. Could my pain be due to an instrument left in me? Harshil thought. To divert his mind, he switched off the television and closed his eyes. But the image of a surgical instrument inside his body refused to go away.

He called the staff nurse on duty. 'I need to talk to Dr Nipun immediately.'

Nipun was summoned.

'Yes, dear,' Nipun said.

'Are you sure there is no instrument left inside my body?'

'I will go to the OT and check in the almirah if some instrument is missing!' Nipun said with a straight face.

'Doctor, please do so quickly!' Harshil said.

Harshil's petrified face was precisely what he had wanted to see. But Nipun realized that he had gone too far with his prank because Harshil could die of fright. He decided to do some damage control.

'Come on, this is just not possible. Have you seen a news item about such an incident on television?'

'Yes. And I, too, have pain in the operated area.'

'Our surgeons aren't so forgetful! The staff nurses do a thorough counting of sponges and instruments at the end of every surgery. So there has never been such an incident here.'

'Thanks, Doctor. Sorry for troubling you again and again.

You must not have come across such a serious comedian before!'

'Yes, you are amongst the most wary persons I have ever met. On an unmanned railway crossing, you probably look around at least ten times before daring to cross!' Nipun grinned.

'I don't even take that risk. I avoid unmanned crossings altogether, even if I have to take a long detour!' Harshil said, finally coming into his own.

After two more days in the hospital, Harshil was discharged.

Nipun handed over the discharge card to him and told him to visit the OPD after a week.

However, Harshil came back just three days later. An operated patient showing up earlier than the appointment date wasn't a pretty sight for the doctor. It was a sign that something had gone wrong. Rarely, this also happened when a patient of the opposite sex was infatuated with the treating doctor.

Harshil looked off colour. 'Doctor, I feel dizzy and weak most of the time.'

Nipun examined him thoroughly. Unable to point to any cause, he assumed that as a comedian, Harshil had a fetish for exaggeration.

'Don't worry. You just have some weakness. Take the vitamin-B complex pills I have prescribed. Within a few days, you will be even more energetic than a politician during an election campaign!'

However, Harshil turned up at the hospital again after a few days, with the same symptoms.

'Doctor, I haven't been able to do any shows. My friends suspect that I have become a drug addict. My wife has gone one step further. She told me—"Your brain, which was already deranged, has been permanently damaged because of some drug injected during the anaesthesia."'

Nipun asked Harshil to wait outside the OPD. Was he missing something? He thought so hard that his head began to spin. But there was no eureka moment. Accepting his defeat, Nipun decided to ask the chief for advice.

Even Dr Ujjwal was puzzled. But the problem had to be solved for the patient's sake, and for the sake of his own king-sized ego. So he got into the mode of a medical detective and questioned Harshil for fifteen minutes. Finally, he asked him to get the packs of the medicines that he was taking. The next day, Harshil was in the OPD again. Dr Ujjwal checked his medicines—a smile crossed his face. The mystery had been solved.

He told Harshil, 'Stop these tablets and you will be all right within a day. Your body is reacting to them.'

'As you say, Doctor.'

Nipun was clueless about what was going on. After Harshil left, he asked the chief, 'Sir, did I miss anything?'

'Yes. You are unaware that you are a first rate idiot! The crux of the problem is your handwriting, which is bad even by a doctor's standards! You prescribed the antibiotic so illegibly in the prescription that the chemist misread it, and handed over an anti-diabetic to the patient. Actually, the chemist should have called you to clarify. So the two idiots, the chemist and you, came together well to cause

170 • *Lights! Scalpel! Romance!*

havoc in the life of the patient! I am the third idiot, who relies so much on a careless doctor like you! Since Harshil is not a diabetic, the drug caused his blood glucose levels to fall. The poor chap was feeling dizzy because of low blood glucose! But all the while, you assumed that he was just malingering! You should be thankful to me for not revealing all this to the patient. Otherwise, the comedian would have taken away your smile!'

'Sir, I'm so sorry. While I was preparing for the MBBS entrance exam, my relatives would tell me—"If you want to become a doctor, start spoiling your handwriting!" I promise that in the future, I shall write all my prescriptions in capital letters, or else get them typed.'

Nipun walked out of the chief's office slowly with downcast eyes. He opened up to Ridhi to let off steam. 'Whatever I have related to you is between you and me,' Nipun whispered to her.

'Don't worry. Even if I tell someone, I'll make sure that it is not passed on further!'

Anyway, Ridhi had liked that he had confided in her.

But the chief acted like an ancient town crier and made sure that all the doctors in the hospital found out about the episode.

Even Nishtha taunted Nipun. 'Hey, I've heard that your handwriting looks just like an ECG with low voltage. Soon, you may require an assistant—just to write out your prescriptions!'

'Dr Nipun, the chief wants you in his office, right now,' a peon interrupted them.

'What now? Has he organized a press conference to officially declare that I am the most inept doctor in town?'

Nipun grumbled.

'Sir, you called for me,' he said to the chief, bracing himself for more scolding.

But the chief spoke as if he were Nipun's defendant. 'I might have acted like a tabloid journalist! But it was for the common good. From now on, all the doctors in our hospital will write readable prescriptions. So there will be minimal chance of the patients receiving the wrong medication.'

'Yes, Sir. I understand.'

Harshil came for his follow-up after two days, blissfully unaware that he was the cause of the upheaval in the department. As expected, he was fit and fine.

'From my experiences at Nirog hospital, I've gotten many ideas for lampooning the doctors in my shows!' he laughed.

19

A Matter of Life and Death

Some of the most unromantic places are often a fertile breeding ground for romance.

The chief was all smiles as he entered the outpatient department. In the morning, he had received a long-awaited email from the editorial office of the *International Gastrosurgery Journal*. The picky editor seemed to be in an unusually joyous state of mind. Their paper had been accepted without any further instructions for modifications. Nipun and Nishtha, the beasts of burden employed in the project, received a rare pat on the back from the chief.

As the HoD, Dr Ujjwal always had to multitask. Still, there were times when he could take a breather or two. The arrival of an old friend or colleague would often lead to chatting sessions during which time the waiting patients were told that he was in an administrative meeting. They believed it too.

Since it was a Monday, the OPD was chock-a-bloc with patients. Just when he was about to instruct the receptionist to start sending in the patients, she informed him, 'Sir, Dr Prateek wants to see you.'

'Send him in immediately,' Dr Ujjwal said. Prateek, who

too was a surgeon, had been his classmate during MBBS and both of them enjoyed mocking the other.

'I was just passing by. Felt like talking to you. But after noticing the rush outside your chamber, I feel that I have disturbed you,' Prateek said. He looked subdued.

'Not at all. I can talk with you while I attend to the patients. I socialize like this. There is no time to go to the clubs and I am not welcome at family gatherings! So, how are you doing?' Dr Ujjwal said.

'For the past six months, I am working as a property dealer!'

'What!'

'Yes. I am not joking. I have given my hospital on lease to another surgeon.'

'But why?'

'You probably know about the incident that took place at my hospital. Six months ago, an eighty-five-year-old lady, with multiple preexisting medical problems, died on the operation table. However, the relatives of the patient concluded that I had been negligent. The whole set-up was vandalized. Quick thinking on the part of one of my employees helped me escape the roughing up I was to receive from the relatives. He locked me up in the storeroom in the basement! Just one complication can negate thousands of good deeds, done over the years. The day is not far off when arms training and self-defence will need to be included in the MBBS curriculum!' Prateek elaborated.

'You have overreacted. Every profession has its hazards. If you want to be absolutely safe, get incarcerated. You can start working again. Just hire the services of a good security agency.'

'I'll think about it,' Prateek said.

After Prateek had left, the chief instructed the receptionist to send in the next patient. A lady entered and seated herself on the examination stool, next to Dr Ujjwal's chair.

'Tell me your problem,' Dr Ujjwal said, without looking up at her. He was reading an official file.

'You are the problem!' she shouted.

The chief was badly shaken. Nobody dared speak to him like this. However, the voice seemed familiar. Was it a disgruntled ex-girlfriend?

He was relieved to find Riya, his cousin.

'For you, patients are just like objects in the factory assembly line! Isn't it?' Riya cribbed.

'Not at all. I live for my patients. Actually, my mind is preoccupied because a team from the Medical Council of India is about to grill me during the annual inspection of our department, which is just two days away. On top of that, a bizarre situation has developed in the ward. A fourteen-year-old boy has developed a massive crush on Nishtha, one of the resident doctors. He is insisting that all procedures be undertaken by her alone!'

'This boy is going to grow up into someone like you!' Riya chuckled.

'Ha, ha...'

'I called you last night. But you didn't pick up the phone,' Riya said.

'I was busy.'

'Doing what?'

'An emergency surgery. What else?'

Riya came to the point. 'Actually, I have brought a patient. Ayana, my close friend, wants to get her dad treated by you. Three months ago, he was operated on for the removal of his gall bladder by Dr Mantav, who as you know, is a renowned surgeon. But the surgery went horribly wrong. Corrective surgery was done elsewhere but that too failed. Ayana has been feeling so helpless. I reassured her. I told her that my cousin is eccentric, but he is one of the few surgeons in the country who could save your dad.'

'What a way to introduce me! You could have used a better adjective! Okay, let me have a look at the patient.'

'Listen carefully. After taking a look at Ayana, you are likely to have a strong urge to make her yours. But don't try to entice her. She hates skirt-chasers. In fact, she has separated from her husband because she caught him cheating on her. I am still puzzled as to why a guy with a wife as gorgeous as Ayana would have gone off-course.'

Dr Ujjal had a ready explanation. 'That's what is left over of the caveman's promiscuity! The saying, "Men will be men", has existed since the Neanderthal age! But what kind of a cousin are you? You should be scouring the city to find a suitable match for me.'

'For that, I need to be convinced that you have started believing in "soul to soul" rather than "body to body"!'

'I am all for a long-term relationship. But the only way for me to prove that is if I'm allowed to give a practical demonstration! Anyway, I give an undertaking—I will not make the first move! But if she takes the initiative, the game changes. Then you can't poke your long nose in our internal affairs!'

Riya had already taken care of that possibility. She had warned Ayana that Dr Ujjwal had treated many ladies just like the disposable gloves that he wore during surgery.

'I think we are losing track here. Treating her dad is the real issue,' Riya said.

'Send the patient,' Dr Ujjwal instructed the receptionist.

As Riya had expected, Ayana caught the chief's eye. Even without make-up, she was a head-turner. Her cheekbones didn't need any assistance from the blusher to stand out, her succulent lips were naturally pink and her large eyes had the power to cause pile-ups on the road. But there wasn't even a semblance of a smile on her face. Dr Ujjwal quickly shifted his gaze to her dad.

Because of jaundice, Sampat's eyes looked as if they were displaying the deepest yellow that could have been seen on a shade card. Loss of fat had left his cheeks sunken.

'Doctor, my dad used to be a jovial person. But I haven't seen him smile in ages. How long will it take for him to be perfectly fine?'

Dr Ujjwal replied, 'I can't say. God steadfastly refuses to hand over the power of the cure to the doctors! But, I will try to cure him, as hard as I would for my own father!'

Sampat was admitted. It was planned that the surgery would be done after his general condition improved.

Ayana observed Dr Ujjwal with the eyes of a sceptic. However, to her dismay, she couldn't help feeling weak in the knees whenever she listened to his husky voice. Her gaze hovered on his face for longer than the officially permitted time. His handsomeness was enhanced by the fine wrinkles.

Dr Ujjwal seemed to offer a ready example for why women fell for older men.

Ayana actively looked for the streak of licentiousness in him so that her inappropriate admiration could be aborted in the nick of time. During her first visit to Dr Ujjwal's office to discuss her dad's condition, she did catch him in a compromising position, but only with a medical journal. It was the same story every other time. In the wards too, she never noticed him trying to work his magic on women, whether doctors or nurses. Rather, it was Candy who tried to charm her by striking up a conversation with her on one pretext or the other. Candy had been taking his wife's trust for granted. He used to tell his friends that blind faith often proves costly for spouses, voters and devotees.

Dr Ujjwal instructed Nishtha to personally ensure the best care for Sampat. Despite that, just four days after his admission, Sampat was breathless in the middle of the night. Dr Ujjwal rushed to the hospital from his home, in his own car, without waiting for the official hospital vehicle.

'Don't worry. We will overcome this,' he said, while laying a hand on Ayana's shoulder.

Tears, which were bigger than the size of drops falling in the drip chamber of an intravenous set, trickled down her cheeks. He would have hugged her had other people not been around.

Sampat was examined by the chief. An emergency X-ray chest examination confirmed that he had developed pneumonia. This warranted admission to the ICU.

In the ICU, the status of a patient was defined by the number of tubes inserted in the body. Initially, Sampat had an intravenous drip and a urinary catheter.

The ICU had a high turnover. Some of the patients were shifted out after an improvement in their general condition. The unfortunate ones, whose term on earth had expired, had to leave for the mortuary. Sampat noticed that even after declaring a patient dead, the doctors and the nursing staff went about their work without even a tinge of grief on their face. He understood that death had ceased to shock them.

If a demon lives in the same house, you gradually start thinking of it as one of your kin, he thought.

The next day, Sampat's immediate neighbour in the ICU lost his life, making him lose his nerve. The infection was taking too long to clear. But Sampat was desperate to escape. When Dr Ujjwal came in for the rounds, he hoped he would be shifted to his room.

Dr Ujjwal asked him, 'Are you feeling better?'

'Actually, I'm feeling jealous of the patients who are leaving the ICU, dead or alive!'

Everyone was stunned. Patients on their death bed rarely jested.

'Just give me a few days. Please,' the chief said.

'So, you want to be sure if I go this way or that way!'

'Shh… Don't say ominous words, Mr Sampat,' the staff nurse accompanying the chief interjected.

When the tubes that had been inserted into his body were removed one by one, Sampat realized that he had given the mortuary a slip. Five days later, he was shifted back into his private room. The first thing he did there was sit in the balcony. Even the adjacent vacant plot, which was overgrown with weeds, seemed like a scenic place to him.

After another week, Sampat underwent the marathon

surgery. Four units of blood had to be transfused.

Late in the evening, Sampat was fully alert. When Dr Ujjwal came in for rounds in the surgical recovery unit, Sampat asked him, 'Doctor, how did my surgery go?'

'Very well.'

'When will I be able to go home?'

'In about five days hopefully. But a lot depends upon your clinical progress.'

'Doctors are very smart. The maximum they commit is 99 per cent. But the remaining 1 per cent is the tricky part!' Sampat said, finally revealing his toothy smile.

Later, Nipun asked Dr Ujjwal, 'Sir, it will take a minimum of about two weeks for his jaundice to clear. Wouldn't it be risky to discharge him earlier?'

'Yes. We are likely to keep him for about three weeks. I gave him false assurance so he would be able to tide over the crucial initial period in a positive frame of mind. We do have to lie sometimes for the patient's sake!' the chief replied with a wink.

Post-operatively, the yellow hue in Sampat's eye was gradually becoming milder with each passing day, while Ayana had started smiling, off and on, albeit faintly.

During this period, Ayana and Nishtha had initially become friends for purely self-serving motives. Nishtha wanted to be in Ananya's good books, so that she would speak to the chief in glowing terms about her. On the other hand, Ayana wanted to be able to approach Nishtha if her dad had a problem, especially during odd hours. However, once they revealed classified information about their exes to each other, they developed a genuine intimacy.

One day, Nishtha and Ayana were having gupshup (gossip session) at the cafeteria. Ayana had put on make-up after a long gap. Nishtha couldn't help staring at her.

'Dr Ujjwal is like a God for me. I had lost all hope of Dad's recovery,' Ayana said, lowering her long eyelashes. Her flushed face gave away her adoration for Dr Ujjwal.

This got Nishtha thinking. The conditions were ripe for both, Ayana and Dr Ujjwal to bond so strongly that even elephants could not pull them apart. And once they started living together as man and wife, the chief was unlikely to stay in the department past his duty hours. Then the junior doctors could have some respite from his bossing.

Later, she texted Ridhi and Nipun—'Would you care to help me in getting the chief tamed by a beauty? If yes, let's meet at 6 p.m. in the cafeteria.'

All of them were there on the dot. Nishtha explained her plan to the gang.

'Although our motives are selfish, successfully executing our plan will also transform his life. At last, the chief will understand that being in a steady relationship has its own charm,' Nipun remarked.

Nishtha instructed, 'Whenever you go to examine Sampat, praise the chief in front of Ayana, so that within a few days, she knows his best qualities. But you should talk in such a way that she doesn't suspect that she is being set up. Leave the rest to me!'

The first one was Nipun. 'Dr Ujjwal lives for his patients. It is said that the chief would even part with his shirt if a needy patient asked for it!'

When it was her turn, Ridhi went a step further. 'I have never seen a more generous person! He is not only a regular blood donor, but has also willed to donate his body.'

After Ayana had been primed for a week, Nishtha decided to execute the next step of her plan. She met Ayana at Karma Café situated near the hospital.

Nishtha knew that the easiest way to pep up a lady was to compliment her on her looks. She told Ayana, 'I am not going to take a selfie with you today.'

'Why not?'

'I look so *"feeki feeki"* (pale) in comparison to you!'

After some more casual talk, Nishtha came to the point. 'I strongly feel that chief and you would make a nice couple.'

'I have seen for myself that Dr Ujjwal is a compassionate person. But there is a catch. He is said to not follow any ethics when it comes to pretty women,' Ayana replied.

Nishtha was quick to come to Dr Ujjwal's rescue. 'That phase is history. Ever since I have been in the department, I've noticed that surgery is his only passion. In fact, sometimes I feel bad because he doesn't even compliment me when I look fabulous! Historically speaking, he may have been so irresistible to some ladies that they took the initiative themselves.'

Ayana's face flushed again. 'He is so handsome even now, and he's a genius to boot.'

'Very true,' Nishtha replied, pleased that she had hit the bull's eye.

The theatrics of the Gang of Three were not in vain. The same night, Ayana dreamt that Dr Ujjwal and she were enjoying a romantic evening at his home. While he was taking an important call from the hospital, she began to arouse him. He could neither cut the call, nor resist her warm touch. He gave in completely to her charms.

She had to convey her feelings to him. But there was no point in talking to Dr Ujjwal while he was on his rounds. Someone or the other always hovered around him. So Ayana went to his office. She was mightily pleased to find him alone. All the lackeys seemed to have gone away to attend a seminar on 'Recent Advances in Chamchagiri'.

'Please have a seat,' Dr Ujjwal said.

'Doctor, you are the real hero for me. I've become an avid fan,' Ayana said, with a bewitching smile.

'People like you motivate us to go that extra mile to take care of the patients. Some people feel that saving the lives of our patients is no big deal for us, since it is just our job,' Dr Ujjwal replied.

Ayana was disappointed by this sterile response. She had expected that he would return the compliment by telling her that he too had become a fan of her charm and beauty.

For the next few minutes, Dr Ujjwal discussed Sampat's case history. Then he began to look at the office file in his hands.

'Thank you, Doctor,' Ayana said. She left with a glum face. 'Even a geek would have done better! And this man is supposed to take only a few minutes to sweep a woman off her feet?'

After she had left, Dr Ujjwal repented having become

tongue-tied in her presence, even though she had given him enough to discern her affection. The only consolation was that Ayana was likely to meet him again, at the time of her father's discharge.

The next day, Dr Ujjwal noticed that Sampat's jaundice had all but disappeared.

'You are not a "yellow man" any more!' the chief said.

'I have become so averse to yellow that I am not likely to wear it again!'

'Maximum credit for your recovery goes to your daughter; she persisted with the treatment against all odds.'

'Yes. The little girl has grown up, and now holds her dad by her hand. She even put her career on hold for the sake of my treatment.'

'Now, another moribund person needs her urgent attention!' Dr Ujjwal mumbled to himself.

20

Experience Matters

Love amplified by lust is amongst the strongest forces on our planet.

On the day Ayana's dad was to be discharged, she was delirious with joy. She would also get to meet the chief. But she was afraid that forcing him to come out with his feelings would prove to be as tough as firing up damp wood.

On the other hand, Dr Ujjwal was determined to act drastically less dumb than the last time.

'I have to give her important instructions regarding her dad. Don't send anybody in until I say so,' Dr Ujjwal told Chintan, his personal assistant, after she had entered his office.

Chintan smiled; he knew that it was the job of the junior doctors to explain everything to the discharged patient.

After a few minutes, Candy came to the chief's office to get his leave sanctioned.

'Sir, please wait. Dr Ujjwal has an important visitor,' Chintan told him.

'Should I come tomorrow?'

'You are applying for a long leave and that too, to go abroad, for a fellowship. It is better to get it sanctioned today itself because the chief is likely to be in a good mood.'

'Why so?'

'You will come to know soon!'

Candy decided to wait in the PA's room.

Initially, Dr Ujjwal and Ayana talked about her dad's condition. Then Ayana decided to take charge.

'Doctor, I have a small request. I hope you don't mind,' Ayana said.

'Just tell me.'

'Could we be friends on Facebook?'

'Why just Facebook, we can also meet face to face,' Dr Ujjwal replied, smiling.

'Okay. I would love to chat with you, but in a place that isn't surrounded by sickness and misery!' she said. Both of them were replying to each other promptly, it was as if they had rehearsed their lines together.

'How about dining together this coming Saturday?'

'Saturday is fine with me.'

'I will book a table at a nice restaurant and let you know.'

Ayana looked into his eyes, as if she were to trying to decipher their intent. Then, she bade him goodbye.

Candy saw Ayana come out of the office. He looked at Chintan. Both of them grinned.

'Lady Luck is going to smile upon the chief soon!' Candy said.

'You guessed it right, Sir,' Chintan added

Candy entered the chief's office. Dr Ujjwal was humming, '*Tu meri zindagi hai* (You are my life).' True to Chintan's prediction, Dr Ujjwal sanctioned Candy's leave without batting an eyelid. Last year, the leave had been denied.

Plus, he had to listen to Ujjwal's lengthy lecture on his lack of work ethic.

After Candy had left his office, Dr Ujjwal called up the front desk of the rooftop restaurant in the Purple Orchid hotel. 'Please reserve a table for two for Saturday at 8 p.m.'

'Sir, it is done. If it is a special occasion, a cake can also be arranged.'

'Do you have any cakes for a first date?'

'I am sorry, Sir!' the puzzled receptionist replied.

On Saturday, Dr Ujjwal talked sparingly with everyone, including a talkative aunt. He also postponed all his non-priority jobs. So he was able to leave the hospital at 5 p.m., the official time. However, some of the sharp minds of the department noticed his early exit and speculations were rife. Candy was almost certain as to where the chief had headed but decided to keep the secret, for the time being. However, this was a burdensome task because the secret was yearning to escape his mind, just like the fizz out of a soda bottle.

Meanwhile, Ayana had been preparing for the long-awaited date all afternoon.

'Today, I will show him how gorgeous a lady can look!' Ayana had muttered.

The beauty salon that she had visited that day did very good business. Unable to refuse, she agreed to all the treatments and make-up suggested by the beautician, who was also a seasoned salesperson. Ayana wanted to destroy all the remnants of resistance in Dr Ujjwal. The final touch was her saree, with a noodle-strap blouse, which too, was draped by the beautician.

At home, Dr Ujjwal too was trying to look as presentable as possible. Then, his mobile rang. Nakul's name flashed on the screen.

He picked up the phone gingerly, hoping that the call was only for his 'valuable' advice.

'Sir, Nakul here.'

'Tell me.'

'We have admitted an accident victim. The CT scan shows injury to the pancreas.'

It was obvious that the patient had to be operated on as soon as possible. Dr Ujjwal thought of instructing Candy to do the surgery, but he was aware that the surgery of the pancreas was beyond Candy's capability and it was almost certain he would mess up. It made sense to go right away. However, he didn't want to miss his date with Ayana either.

Saving lives is your raison d'être. Everything else is secondary, his inner voice slapped him.

But when he put himself in Ayana's shoes, Dr Ujjwal concluded that she would be pretty dejected. Worse, she could sense a pattern in this, and refuse to see him again.

He called Ayana. 'I'm so sorry, dear. I have to rush to the hospital for an urgent surgery.'

'It is okay. While performing the surgery, don't keep thinking about me! I don't want to be responsible for any complication!' Ayana replied, and then hung up.

Ayana was feeling bad, as horrible as a mountaineer who had had to turn back just before the summit because of an unexpected event—a blizzard, or the appearance of a Yeti. But after a while, she felt more understanding. In fact, she appreciated Dr Ujjwal for having the mental strength to resist a date with a beauty for the sake of his duty. But she was convinced that in the future he would not neglect his duty towards the beauty. Ayana also recalled that Dr Ujjwal had often visited the hospital at odd hours when her dad had been critical.

She took a selfie and posted it on Facebook. Every few minutes, she checked her Facebook account for comments with the words 'beautiful', 'stunning', 'gorgeous', and their synonyms and found them aplenty. Some guys and girls used more complex adjectives. Now that her mood had been elevated, she resorted to cooking some yellow daal. Shahi paneer could wait.

Dr Ujjwal finished the surgery past midnight. A look at Ayana's picture on Facebook triggered a crazy urge to go to her house and jump into her room through a window. Her dad was too weak to run after him with a gun in his hand.

The next morning, he called her. 'Hi, I hope you aren't annoyed with me.'

'It's okay. I have come to realize that if one is with a doctor, one should expect an interruption at any moment!'

'You are so understanding,' Dr Ujjwal said.

'I guess my only recourse is to stalk and then kidnap you, whenever I find you free!' Ayana laughed.

'Since I head the department, my juniors attend the calls. But I had to go yesterday because the problem was beyond the competence of Dr Anuroop, my deputy.'

'Thanks "Mr Head of the Department", for putting me in my place!'

'It's nothing like that. In fact, you are quite likely to lord over the HoD! We must meet today.'

'Call me after you finish your morning rounds. We'll work out where to meet,' she said.

'See you.'

Since it was a Sunday, Dr Ujjwal reached home early. He rang Candy up, 'Look after the emergency calls and contact me only if you can't handle a case by yourself. Also, to avoid missing a call from the hospital, keep your mobile with you at all times, even when you are in the washroom!'

The experienced clinician had judged the severity of Ayana's lovesickness. He felt that he could bypass the traditional facilitators like flowers, candlelight dinners and love letters.

So he called Ayana. 'Hi. Why don't you come over to my house? That would be the best place for us to get to know each other better.'

He is moving too fast! Wants to have the first date in bed! she thought.

She told him, 'Won't it be better if we go to some restaurant?'

'What if we are interrupted again? In my house, at least you can wait comfortably.'

Ayana couldn't say no. She didn't want to lose him.

'Okay. Reaching within half an hour,' she said.

Dr Ujjwal sent his domestic help on multiple errands so that he would be out of the picture for a few hours.

As soon as the door bell rang, Dr Ujjwal rushed out eagerly, only to find Narain Dass, his geriatric neighbour.

'Dear, I wanted to show you my blood pressure.'

'Sorry, Uncle. Right now, I am in the middle of a conference which is being broadcast through the internet,' he said.

For Narain Dass, getting his blood pressure checked was more of an excuse to discuss his son and daughter-in-law, who had rebelled against his autocracy. Once that was over, he would go on a never-ending comparison of the golden old days and the rotten, present era.

'All right. I will come in the evening,' Narain Dass said.

Ayana had little problem locating Ujjwal's bungalow. Whomsoever she asked for the directions, guided her properly. She wondered whether everyone in the colony knew that the surgeon was likely to be visited by a lady with a dimpled chin.

Instead of the chief's name, the words, 'Surgeon's Den' were embossed on the name plate.

And here I am entering the den despite knowing that there is the risk of being preyed upon! Ayana thought.

The double-storey house was impressive only in its dimensions. Some of the exterior paint had abandoned the concrete, and the rest was in the process of weathering away too. The chairs in the veranda seemed to be supporting their own weight with great difficulty, and if one sat on them by mistake, the services of an orthopaedician were quite likely to be required. The large open space in the front was occupied by a garden of weeds.

By leaving the exterior of the house so ill-maintained, Dr Ujjwal seems to be protesting his lonesome existence, Ayana philosophized.

There was no need to ring the bell. Dr Ujjwal had been

keeping an eye on the front gate through a window. He rushed out to receive her. She had never looked lovelier, daintier or sexier.

'Please come in.'

'Thanks.'

He bolted the door and turned around. She was waiting for him to escort her into the house.

They looked at each other intently. While her large eyes opened wider, his eyes narrowed even further. Neither of them blinked for a full minute, as if they were playing a game. Then, they moved towards each other with a sudden thrust, provided by one of the strongest forces in the universe—lust. They hugged each other tightly, and soon their lips met. Then he put his arms around her slender waist and guided her into the bedroom. She was so turned on that she forgot to put up the customary resistance.

'I had never imagined that a doctor could be so passionate. Rather, I was under the impression that surgeons might not have much curiosity about the female body,' Ayana whispered.

'On the contrary, a surgeon has thorough knowledge of a woman's erogenous zones and also knows how to reach them! Plus, we have very flexible wrists and fingers, which are always aching for action!' he said, with a mischievous smile.

After opening the buttons of her blouse, he halted for a moment as he was mesmerized by the black lacy bra.

It seems she already knows what turns me on. I hope she is not in touch with one of my exes! he thought.

Then he unhooked the bra and worked the magic of his fingers and tongue on the goodies he had freed.

Although her moans were enough to show that she was

in raptures, he asked her if she liked it, just to inflame her passion further.

'Of course! The pleasurable impulses from here pass straight downwards!'

'There's no direct neural connection between the two hotspots! First, the impulses have to go to the brain and then they travel down.'

'Hey! I am not here to listen to your medical jargon. Concentrate on action!'

He continued.

'Good boy!' she said sensuously.

'You have to be compensated for yesterday,' Dr Ujjwal replied, feeling even more turned on.

He proceeded to caress and kiss her all over. Then he used a combination of index and middle fingers on her valley of love with such finesse that just a few minutes later, she was forced to say, 'Stop it! I can't take it any more.'

It was her turn to return the favour. She too was no novice at lovemaking.

Finally, both of them got to the moment they had been secretly wishing for over the last few days. Dr Ujjwal gave a virtuoso performance.

'You made me so happy. I am afraid I might get addicted to you,' Ayana said as both of them lay embracing, exhausted but also ethereally at peace.

'Who is complaining?' Dr Ujjwal exclaimed as he pulled a sheet over them. It was time for some lovey-dovey talk, which, for a change, was happening after the lovemaking.

After a few days, Ayana met her friend Riya at Mahurat Sweets, their favourite haunt for enjoying tangy chaat and spicy chit-chat.

'How is your dad?'

'Absolutely fine. He has taken up gardening.'

'And how are you doing?'

'For the past few days, I have been itching to tell you something. Although it's been a week since Dad has been discharged from the hospital, your cousin refuses to get off my mind!' Ayana confessed, omitting the details.

'I warned you in the beginning. Everything is not lost yet. Divert your mind. Prostrate yourself at the feet of a swami in Rishikesh or start a painting that would take six months to complete!'

'It's too late now!'

'Oh! So, the fucking sessions are already on! All right. I am out of this!' Riya shouted.

'Cool down. Actually I am thankful to you for introducing me to Dr Ujjwal, even if it was for the treatment of my dad.'

'I don't know. Despite having suffered in life because of a philanderer, you are messing around with another one.'

'Mind your language! After all, he is your cousin,' Ayana roared, surprising Riya.

Their raised voices drew the attention of a group of ladies having a kitty party at the adjoining table. 'Both of them seem to be in love with the same man!' one of them commented.

Another lady had a solution. 'Why don't they decide with the toss of a coin?'

Meanwhile, Riya hollered, 'Are you sure you like him or his joystick, you bitch!'

Ayana walked away in a huff.

A few days later, Riya and Dr Ujjwal bumped into each other at a relative's wedding. She greeted him with a shout. 'Don't spoil my friend's life!'

'She started it all by visiting my office to talk about matters which could have been discussed on the ward rounds! Don't worry. Ayana will never blame you; rather, she will be grateful to you for helping her find a doting husband.'

'As you were talking, you were blinking rapidly. I wish I conduct a lie detector test and expose you right away!'

'You are impossible. I swear I want to spend my life with her.'

The gossip mongers of the hospital, having suffered a long-standing drought, finally had something to babble about as more and more witnesses testified that Ayana and Dr Ujjwal were a couple.

Lately, the chief had developed a phobia when it came to his exes. He was afraid that some old flame would make a sudden appearance, with a child, in Ayana's presence, and say, 'Bunty, touch your father's feet'. He reckoned that the earliest he slipped an engagement ring on Ayana, the better it would be.

Meanwhile, Ayana and Nishtha had their long-overdue meeting.

Ayana began, 'I have gone bonkers. I'm hopelessly in love with your boss.'

'That is stale news! The whole world knows about it

already. The best cure for your ailment is to make the doctor call on you 24x7!'

'You know very well why I have become wary of men.'

'But if there were no men, who would go crazy over just a hint of your cleavage?'

'Okay. Let's get to the burning topic. It seems that your boss wants me to be his wife.'

'That is awesome!'

'Of course, what more could a lady want from a man,' Ayana said, sighing. 'But, what if he fools around again?'

'I've already told you, I've never noticed the chief trying to act fresh with *any* lady. I've played the role of the private detective and have been keeping an eye on him. Reputations otherwise are usually very resistant to change.'

'Thanks, Nishtha. You are a true friend.'

The next day, Ayana reached out to Riya and made up with her like she had done so many times in the past. In the meantime, Riya had also accepted the inevitable.

The resident doctors, meanwhile, had never had it so good. Dhairya, the nerdiest among them, presented statistical proof of the decrease in the frequency of the chief's scolding. Even when Dr Ujjwal shouted, it seemed as if he had recently got a silencer fitted in his throat. Dhairya also felt that his hypothesis, about sexual deprivation as the cause for most of the anger in the world, had been substantiated.

Dr Ujjwal went to the jewellery market, and entered Glitterers, the biggest shop there.

'May I take a look at diamond engagement rings?' he said, looking as baffled as a villager entering a metropolitan city for the first time.

The experienced salesman was delighted to have an ignorant customer. He helped his showroom avail one of the most profitable sales they'd had in a while.

The next day, Dr Ujjwal booked a secluded table at the Capri Restaurant for a candlelight dinner. He had wanted to create the right environment, to transform her into a total emotional fool, which *he* had already become.

Just a few minutes after they were seated, he looked into Ayana's eyes and tilted his face slightly. 'Darling! I want you to be mine forever,' he said softly.

Then, he put the right hand into the pocket of his blazer, and took out the engagement ring.

Ayana rose up from her chair.

He was alarmed. *I hope she is not going to smooch me in public?*

But Ayana didn't budge from the spot. Raising her right hand, she said, 'Please hold it, I am not ready yet.'

The words were spoken sweetly, but they seemed vicious in their essence.

'How do I prove my love? If I weren't a professor, I would have climbed a water tank!' he said, resting his chin on his hand like a chess player who had been checkmated.

'Please, don't get me wrong. When it comes to taking decisions of any sort, I am quite the sloth. In fact, my relatives have stopped asking for my advice because I confuse them even further. And my friends don't take me along when they shop!' she said. Then she held his hand to defrost him quickly.

When he dropped her home, she even gave him a parting kiss.

The next day, Dr Ujjwal called Ayana in the evening, after having reached home. But she didn't take the call. Subsequent calls too didn't elicit any response. She didn't call him back. Finally, he received a reply to his text message—'Occupied in a family issue. I shall call you back in a day or two.'

Even official communications are warmer! Dr Ujjwal thought. He sensed an emergency in his relationship with Ayana.

He called up Riya. 'Ayana has been avoiding me since yesterday evening. Can you meet her as soon as possible and find out the reason?'

'I am quite occupied tomorrow.'

'Please, Riya. Try to understand. I can't live without Ayana,' Dr Ujjwal pleaded. Riya heard sobs.

Impossible! The cold-hearted scoundrel has learnt to cry! Riya thought.

She told him, 'Just chill, Ujjwal. I will bring Ayana back to you, by hook or by crook.'

The next day, Riya reached Ayana's house unannounced. Ayana greeted her warmly.

'What is going on? My brother is on the verge of a nervous breakdown.'

'Really?' Ayana asked, pleased that Dr Ujjwal was so crazy about her.

'Of course. Ayana, you are a dumbo! Can't you even judge the intensity of a man's love?'

'This letter has made a psycho out of me. Just read it.'

Ayana had preserved the envelope too. It was a non-registered letter, posted from the Janakpuri post office.

It read:

Miss Ayana,

You are warned—do not meet Dr Ujjwal again. I have been going steady with him for the last year, and we are planning to get married soon. Just get out of my beloved's life. Otherwise, be prepared for the worst.

Krutika.

'I think you were right when you warned me about your cousin,' Ayana said.

'First you were blind in your love for him, and now you blindly believe this shit.'

'What do you mean?'

'Come on, Ayana. I am sure he hasn't been seeing any woman for the last couple of years. This is a conspiracy, probably by one of his enemies.'

'I think we should have kept our meetings secret.'

'I don't know. But what you need to do right now is to burn this letter and resuscitate my brother.'

'Thanks yaar. You care about me so much.'

'Hey. No need to be that senty! Let's go.'

'What do we tell him?'

'A lie! What else?'

Both of them went to Dr Ujjwal's place, where they skipped any mention of the letter. Ayana gave him a sham explanation—she had had to go out of station to attend on her uncle who had met with an accident.

Two days later, Dr Ujjwal and Ayana again snatched an opportunity to get physical at the chief's home. The domestic help was now in the know about their friendly wrestling. He slipped out voluntarily. This time too their lovemaking was top-class. But Dr Ujjwal made no mention of the engagement ring.

It seems like he has put the ring in his bank's locker for safekeeping, just in case it may be needed sometime in the future! It is my fault. Since I told him the last time that I am undecided, he is not likely to propose to me anytime soon, Ayana thought.

But the urge was unstoppable, almost like an impending orgasm. While they were locked in an embrace, Ayana crooned, 'I don't feel like leaving your home.'

'It is our home now,' Dr Ujjwal said, precipitating an emotional surge in Ayana. They kissed for a full minute.

Suddenly, he spoke with an air of urgency, 'Let's get dressed.'

'Where are you taking me?' Ayana was puzzled.

'Nowhere. Do you want me to propose to you in my birthday suit?'

'Got it.'

Both of them looked for their clothes, which had been thrown off in the heat of the moment.

Dr Ujjwal brought out the ring, and asked for her hand in classic, timeless style. She was only too happy to hold out her ring finger.

The next day, both of them felt more grounded.

Dr Ujjwal asked, 'Have you spoken to your parents?'

'Mom's reminders for me to get married are as regular as her instructions to Dad to not miss his medication. So she should be relieved. As for my Dad, how can he refuse his saviour?'

'People will say behind my back that I misused my position to entice a patient's daughter!'

'But I wasn't taking any kind of treatment from you! So you have not violated the medical ethics.'

'I was ready even to break a few rules to have you!'

Ayana's confidence was not misplaced. Her parents readily agreed. To her amazement, they didn't express any surprise at the development, as if they had been already given daily updates about her life.

Parents are smarter than one expects them to be, especially when it comes to keeping track of their offspring's activities! she concluded.

Both of them decided to have a small wedding, with only close family members in attendance. *Their previous weddings had failed despite them being grand affairs*. They had lost faith in the efficacy of blessings from wedding guests, who commonly pronounced—'*Aapki jodi hamesha salamaat rahe* (May you always remain a couple).' In any case, the hefty hospital bills over the last few months had severely dented the finances of Ayana's family.

Later, Ayana called up Nishtha. 'Hey, things are moving pretty quickly. The engagement ring looks good on me.'

'I am jealous!'

'We are to get the seal of societal approval, next Sunday! Only close relatives have been invited for the ceremony.

You are the special invitee!'

'Won't that look awkward?' Nishtha asked.

'You were the key conspirator in bringing us together! So I can't imagine going through these marriage nuptials without your presence.'

'If I attend the wedding, my colleagues will get to know that I am your bosom pal. In the future, I may be accused of pulling strings in the department through you! Even the chief might find himself in an odd situation.'

'Since when have you bothered so much about other people? Am I talking to Nishtha, or her double?' Ayana said.

Once Dr Ujjwal found out about Ayana's invite to Nishtha, he told Ayana, 'Nishtha and you seem to have signed an agreement to share your secrets! So in all likelihood, the department will receive regular updates of all that happens in our home!'

'Don't worry. The news will be censored!' Ayana said.

At the wedding venue, Dr Ujjwal and Ayana looked at each other coyly, as if they had met for the first time. While taking the marriage vows around the sacred fire, Dr Ujjwal prayed, '*God, please grant me a boon so I may be faithful.*'

Even though they had made love several times, their wedding night was special. Both of them had reserved some of their love making skills for it.

The next day, Ayana said, 'Darling, when are you taking me out to the hills? I want to be in a meadow where I can embarrass the professor by rolling around with him in the grass!'

'Candy has managed to get his overseas fellowship extended, by a month. Until that trickster comes back, it won't be possible for me to leave the station. Anyway, I'll make sure that every evening is special.'

The chief had helped Candy get a fellowship on oesophageal surgery in Australia with Dr Frederick. Before leaving, Candy had gathered information about Frederick from an Indian doctor working in Australia. Once he learned about Frederick's keen interest in Buddhism, Candy scoured the Janpath market for a full day in order to buy vividly painted thangkas.

Upon reaching the Holy Cross Hospital in Melbourne, he surprised Frederick with the gifts.

Frederick said, 'Many thanks. I had been considering asking you to get the same, but my hesitation got the best of me.'

'You are extremely welcome, Sir,' Candy replied.

Frederick was startled by Candy's English but he presumed that Indian English had its discrepancies.

'What surgeries do you perform?' Frederick asked.

'I do lots of Whipple's, hepatico-jejunostomies and liver resections,' Candy replied so confidently that Frederick instantly admired the highly accomplished surgeon.

Actually, most of these cases had been undertaken by Dr Ujjwal, and Candy had only assisted in them. But Frederick was easy meat for Candy, as he was well qualified to teach a course in People Management—What Books Will Never Tell You!

'You can extend your stay for another month, if you like.'

'Thanks, Dr Frederick. I am obliged.'

Candy made friends with the staff. He kept them entertained with his wisecracks. Once he realized that they were amused by his English, he twisted it deliberately. Although the visiting fellows were not supposed to assist directly, he managed to scrub up in many cases.

Dr Ujjwal had to compensate for Candy's absence from the department, by working extra hard. But Ayana was quite supportive. Whenever he planned to take up a tough case, she would soothe his frayed nerves with comforting words and caresses.

Ayana went back to her teaching job in the same school that she had left six months ago because of her dad's illness. Upon reaching home in the evening, Dr Ujjwal often found her working on her lessons.

'I thought teachers had the easiest job in the world!' he teased.

'It is a misconception that teachers take a few classes and pass rest of their time bitching about other teachers and the principal. Nothing could be further from the truth. A smart school needs smart teachers! We have to prepare the lectures ourselves. If our students fare poorly in their exams, the principal makes sure we feel as bad as the failed student!'

A few days later, Ayana was promoted to teach higher secondary classes.

Eager to share the good news with Dr Ujjwal, she called him on his mobile.

'The number you are calling is either switched off or out of the coverage area', was the automated network reply.

Dr Ujjwal never switched off his phone. If it was not possible for him to attend to a call, like in the operation theatre, he kept his mobile on silent. She called again after five minutes, but there was no response.

She began to panic. *Is he cheating on me?*

The next moment, she chided herself for having jumped to the worst conclusion.

She called up the office landline number. The chief's personal assistant said, 'Dr Ujjwal left the office thirty minutes ago, without informing me.'

Ayana contacted the OT, but she still couldn't trace him. She concluded that he must be with some girlfriend, to whom he has told: 'You are the only one in my life!'

She called Nishtha. Again, there was no reply. Ayana decided to drive to the hospital straight from the school. Just as she was about to leave, she received Nishtha's call. 'Ayana! You rarely call me at this time. Is everything okay?'

'My hubby is untraceable. I am going crazy!'

'Relax. He isn't screwing a hottie! Actually, Dr Ujjwal and I had rushed to the orthopaedics department to examine the abdomen of a patient who happens to be the son of a trustee of this hospital. He's been injured in a roadside accident.'

'Now I understand. In his haste, Dr Ujjwal must have forgotten to inform his personal assistant.'

As soon as Dr Ujjwal returned to the department, his personal assistant told him that Ayana had called.

'What was it about?'

'Sir, if I had asked her the reason for calling, she would

have thought of me as nosy! But from her tone, I could make out that she was quite tense.'

Dr Ujjwal took out his mobile from his pocket. The battery had gotten fully discharged. He rang Ayana from the landline.

'Hi, I just learned that you were about to file a police complaint about your missing husband!'

Ayana became red-faced. 'Sorry for overreacting. I panicked as your mobile was not reachable. I found out about your whereabouts once I contacted Nishtha. I just wanted to tell you that I have been promoted.'

'Congrats! I am so happy for you!'

'Thanks.'

'You are no different from some of my junior doctors. They diagnose everything as a rare ailment without thinking of the common problems first!'

'I made the diagnosis by the logic of exclusion, just like you sometimes do!' Ayana replied.

'I've gotten rid of satyriasis long back,' Dr Ujjwal said.

'I have repeatedly told you not to use complicated medical terms when talking to me,' Ayana said, furrowing her brows.

'Satyriasis means an urge to bed every female with a hotness index equal to yours!' he laughed.

'So you admit you were like that once upon a time!'

'The whole world knows this! But as I have already said, I have had a full and final cure for this problem!'

From that day onwards, Dr Ujjwal kept a portable charger with him and made sure that it, too, remained charged.

Candy returned from Australia in a few days.

'Sir, congratulations on your latest wedding. I wish I had attended it.'

'What do you mean by latest? I don't marry every year! Anyway, thanks. So, how was Australia?'

'Dr Frederick is doing good work. But our unit is no less because of a stalwart like you!'

'Thanks for the compliment. I know you are doing makhanbaazi (oiling), but I like being praised! Were there any interesting developments during the trip?'

'Dr Frederick has become a close friend. He has also accepted my invitation to visit India.'

'Great. Your candy works all around the world!'

'If someone has a unique talent, he should utilize it fully!'

'All right. You had a good time. Now slog for a week because Ayana and I are going to Munnar for our honeymoon which has been delayed because you overstayed in Australia.'

'No problem, Sir. You can compensate by having another holiday soon. And I assure you that whenever you go out of station, I will return the surgical unit to you as it is when you return!'

'Let us see. The last time you promised the same but went berserk instead!'

21

Crowd Management is No Joke

Some people are so manipulative, they can even get the better of a crowd.

This time, Candy resolved to refrain from going off course. Two days after Dr Ujjwal had left, a young man named Teja was admitted with an injury he sustained to his intestines after an accident. Candy operated on him promptly. The patient, who was kept in the ICU post-operatively, made slow but steady progress.

However, the chap seemed to know half the city. Throughout the day, and even into the night, there was a crowd of well-wishers and relatives outside the ICU. They were managing to get past the security staff at the main entrance, by throwing names around.

The chief of security asked for Candy's help in dealing with the situation.

'Leave it to me,' Candy bragged. The security officer wondered whether Candy was going to hire a gang of musclemen.

Candy went outside the ICU and called out loudly, 'Who is with Teja?'

Almost all the visitors, who were present in the waiting

hall, crowded around him.

He talked in a sombre tone. 'The patient's condition is critical. He requires four units of blood. Please come forward to donate.'

Actually, only two units were required. They could have been easily arranged from the blood bank since critically ill patients were issued blood by the hospital and didn't need immediate blood donation by relatives.

Candy was utilizing his unique, time-tested method of dispersing crowds in the hospital. Usually, after hearing about the need for blood donation, the faltoo visitors trickled out because they were afraid of the vampires in white coats. Candy visited the area after half an hour to gauge the situation. To his utter amazement, the crowd had swelled further. His plan seemed to be in the category of hare-brained schemes.

A khadi clad elderly man, who looked like a hard core social worker, said, 'Sir, Mr Teja is an active member of the Blood Donors Society. These boys are ready to donate any number of blood units for him.'

Candy did some quick thinking and came up with an out-of-the-box solution, as only he could. 'Okay. Right now he needs only four units, but I request you to donate liberally for the blood bank of our hospital because that will help save many more lives.'

Candy called up the doctor-in-charge of the blood bank and got thirty-eight bottles of donated blood.

However, the main issue remained unresolved. The valiant donors couldn't be told bluntly to decongest the waiting area.

Turning to Plan B, Candy caught hold of Gopesh, the

leanest ward boy, and briefed him about his role. After putting a mask on his face, Gopesh sat in the waiting area. Periodically, he would take out the mask and cough violently, spitting out some saliva on his handkerchief.

A few men, who were a part of the crowd, went near him and asked what was wrong with him.

'I have drug-resistant tuberculosis of the lungs. I am just waiting to meet Dr Anuroop, who is treating me. But even the medicines prescribed by him are failing,' he replied.

The visitors talked in hushed voices and gradually trickled out.

When Candy came for reconnaissance, he was surprised that the bluff had worked so well.

'Good job, Gopesh. But I am worried about your future. You are likely to be avoided by potential brides! Do put on some weight.'

'I agree, Sir. In fact, three months ago, I proposed to a girl. She said, "I like you but I am afraid of losing you in the event of a storm!"'

'I am writing you a nutritional supplement. Also, improve your diet.'

'Sure. I won't keep three fasts in a week any more. To appease the Gods, I will rely on good deeds instead!'

Later, Candy was complimented by the director for making the blood bank awash with blood. It was also decided that he would be honoured with an award of appreciation at the annual convocation.

As soon as Dr Ujjwal joined duty, Candy entered his office. He told the chief about his feat of blood donation and eagerly waited to be bombarded with praise.

Dr Ujjwal said, 'Brilliant! So this cancels out all the blunders you have committed in the past one year!'

But the chief did take note of Candy's contribution to the department. He started making Candy do difficult surgeries and often assisted him to demonstrate the finer points. One day, he asked Candy, 'Do you know why I am trying to enhance your surgical skills?'

'So that I can hold the fort in your absence and you can be on a hammock in a beach resort for days at a stretch!'

'Also, I want to ensure that you aren't a danger to our society!' the chief laughed. Candy also put up a sham smile.

After his honeymoon, the chief continued to stick to the hospital timings. But the glee of the resident doctors was short-lived. After a few days, Nakul and Saksham, the senior residents, left the job. They had been poached by a corporate hospital that had offered them a massive increase in salary.

The chief tried to take the route of emotional blackmail to hold them back.

'I never thought you guys would leave me in the lurch midway through the session.'

'Sir, we are leaving with a heavy heart. But there is no other choice. We are not able to afford even basic necessities with the emoluments we get here.'

'I guess nowadays the list of basic necessities includes SUVs, Swiss jewellery watches and at least one foreign trip every year!'

'What to do, Sir. Social media is the main culprit for making life so complicated.'

'I would love to increase your pay, but that is not in my hands. The management decides.'

So there were fewer hands to do the same work. Consequently, each resident doctor had to put in more hours.

'We are already stretched to the limit. How will we manage?' Ridhi said.

'I think we will be worse off than pack animals. Even they get proper rest,' Nishtha added.

'Why don't you look at the positive? All of us get to do more surgery. Till the new senior residents join, make the most of it,' Nipun reasoned.

Nishtha made the thumbs up sign. 'So no grumbling except when we cross the boiling point! Get, set, go!'

Nipun was able to cope with the extra work easily. He made the most of short breaks during the day by taking power naps. Nishtha carried on because of her unbridled ambition. For Ridhi, it was Hobson's choice. True to their prediction, all of them were able to do more cutting.

Mayur was observing the developments very closely. Although he was a year junior to Nipun and Nishtha, he felt envious of them thanks to his anomalous mind which focused more on the lives of others. Meanwhile, he came to know that both of them had got the chance to do surgeries by leaving aside their egos and entreating the chief in a manner that closely resembled begging.

I also deserve to operate, at least an appendicectomy or hernia repair, he thought.

A few days later, a case of appendicectomy was on the list. Mayur went to the surgeon's room, where he found the chief alone.

'Sir ji, Good morning. It is my humble request that I may be allowed to do an appendicectomy,' Mayur said with folded hands.

Dr Ujjwal, who found Mayur's manner too melodramatic for his comfort, raised his brows. 'If the appendix is retrocaecal in position and you are not able to deliver it, what will you do?' he asked.

Mayur looked puzzled, as if he had been asked to explain the Keynesian Theory of Money.

'Sorry, Sir. I will go and read about it.'

'Never ask to perform a surgery until you are thorough about its theoretical aspects. There is no room for error while dealing with the human body. Get lost!'

Mayur rushed out of the surgeon's room.

'Nipun must have talked behind my back to turn the chief against me,' he grumbled.

The chief remembered the first appendicectomy he had done during his MS course. Two beautiful women, a staff nurse and a junior doctor, had assisted him. He had been dying to impress them with his precocious surgical talent.

Dr Ujjwal had made a small incision to reach the abdominal cavity. Then, he had used his index finger and tried to deliver the appendix out into the operative field.

But even after struggling for ten minutes, he couldn't find it.

There was no choice but to call Dr Jagdish, his boss. 'Yes, what is it?' he had said.

'Sir, the appendix seems to be absent in this case,' Dr Ujjwal had replied.

'*Abe gadhe* (You, donkey)! If you can't find an organ during a surgical dissection, it doesn't mean the patient was born without it!'

Dr Jagdish had scrubbed up and delivered the appendix in a minute.

That day, Dr Ujjwal had realized the true worth of his boss, and he had stopped making fun of him behind his back.

22

Arranged Marriage Jumble

The process of arranging marriage basically entails finding faults in the prospective spouse and then determining whether these faults can be ignored.

A lot of time had elapsed since Nipun and Ridhi's ill-fated birdwatching trip-cum-date. But Nipun's admiration for her was so resilient that it had survived, like a microorganism in a spore.

Over the last month or so, Ridhi and Nipun had once again reached a basic level of friendship, which entailed pulling each other's legs at least once a day. Nipun attributed this to time, the master healer.

He felt like taking another chance. In the next few days, Nipun prepared the ground to propose another date to Ridhi. He took extra pains to teach her the surgical steps and was also liberal with his compliments. However, his attempts to use similes to praise her often ended in disaster.

The opportunity to have a go at it came when both of them were alone in the seminar room.

He asked, 'Ridhi, how about dining together this Saturday?'

'Why don't we see a movie, sitting in corner seats, in

the last row?' Ridhi replied with a wink.

Nipun couldn't believe this.

But when Ridhi began to laugh, Nipun felt that she basically thought of him as a laughable character and nothing more.

'Okay, don't stress yourself. If I go crazy for you, I will give it to you in writing!' Ridhi said.

Nipun remained muddle-headed. Although Ridhi had given him the cold shoulder, she was still leaving options open. Was he a stepney, to be kept in reserve?

At Nipun's home, his parents were fervently plotting to terminate his bachelorhood. His sisters were also eager to dance their heart out at Nipun's wedding.

His dad spoke to him, 'We have received a marriage proposal for you through a common friend, from the parents of a girl by the name of Saundarya. She is doing her MD in radiology in Jodhpur. Saundarya is one in a million. Even your fussy mom approved of her. Being the only child, she is also the sole heir to her parents' property. I told her father that you are so valuable to your boss that he can't afford to send you away from his department! So they have agreed to meet you in Delhi.'

'Dad, give me a day to decide. I'll call you tomorrow.'

He thought about the proposal. Nishtha and Ridhi had stuck their tongues out at him multiple times, and in the future they were likely to supplement this with kicks on his butt. He had to move on.

He called up his dad. 'Fix up a meeting on any Sunday and let me know. I don't care about the property and I will agree to the match only if I like the girl,' Nipun said, feigning idealism.

Of course, I won't insult her by refusing the property! he thought.

After two weeks, Nipun and Saundarya met face to face at a restaurant in the Royal Jewel Hotel. Both their families were accompanied by their relatives. Some relatives had been chosen for their skill in detecting microscopic flaws with the prospective bride and the groom, while others were mind readers with lie-detection capabilities. There were a few interrogators too.

True to her name, Saundarya was a classic Indian beauty. After looking at her, Nipun felt like breaking into the song, '*Kitna haseen chehra, kitni pyari aankhen* (What a beauty! Such a pretty face and so striking eyes).'

Imagine the look on the faces of Ridhi and Nishtha after they catch a glimpse of Saundarya! Nipun thought.

Nripendra, Saundarya's father, often intervened when Nipun's parents asked Saundarya a question. He seemed to be a psycho.

But he is not going to stay with us. So why should I bother? Nipun thought.

Nipun and Saundarya were told to shift, by themselves, to a separate table in the restaurant.

Initially, they made small talk.

Then Nipun broke the ice. 'What do you expect from a husband?'

'He should be very loving and affectionate,' Saundarya said.

'An adorable girl like you deserves to be showered with a lot of love and affection.'

'I also want him to encourage me to progress in my career.'

'Okay.'

'What are your hobbies?' she asked

'Listening to music,' Nipun replied.

He concealed his other hobby, birdwatching, as he wanted to tell her about only those hobbies which were not supposed to take a man away from his lady.

Nipun also avoided joking. He knew girls were more finicky about choosing their life partner than patients deciding on their surgeon.

Just before they were about to return to their families, Saundarya gave Nipun a seductive smile. Then she gazed directly into his eyes, making words irrelevant. Nipun felt that she liked him. But he had to contend with her father, the snake hovering around the jewel.

Nipun told his father, 'I am ready to marry her right now! Please talk to her parents.'

'The dam of your emotions has burst!' Nipun's dad said. 'How can you go crazy about a girl after meeting her for just a few minutes? Are you marrying the girl or her looks?'

'Dad, please. By dilly-dallying, we will lose her,' Nipun asserted.

Nipun's parents walked towards Saundarya's family.

'We agree to the match,' his dad said. He expected a laddoo would be shoved into his mouth, followed by chants of 'Congratulations!'

But nothing of that sort happened.

Saundarya's dad folded his hands. 'Please give us some

time to decide.'

He, along with his relatives, spent a good fifteen minutes having a discussion which often turned animated. During this period, Nipun remained in suspended animation.

Then, Nripendra announced, 'Everything is okay. However, we need to get their horoscopes checked by our family astrologer before taking the final decision.'

'If you had informed us beforehand, we would have brought the horoscope. Anyway, we will send it to you,' Nipun's dad said.

Nipun was disappointed. But he was hopeful that the horoscopes would indicate that they were a match made in heaven.

Saundarya had told her parents that Nipun had breezed through her assessment. However, her dad didn't want to take any chances. The man, who avoided lifts because he was afraid of getting trapped in them and who forced his wife to share all her passwords with him, wouldn't let his darling daughter be handed over to a guy without thoroughly researching his character. His suspicious nature had rubbed off to some extent on Saundarya too. So the family decided to buy time by using the plausible excuse of matching horoscopes.

On the suggestion of a relative, they decided to take the help of Eagle Eye Agency, run by Rameshwar Singh, a retired intelligence officer.

They had expected to run into a moustached old man wearing a hat. But the clean-shaven guy looked like a scheming villain from old Hindi movies. Plus, he didn't have a babbling female assistant, wearing a siren red lipstick, by his side.

'We want you to confirm if the boy we are considering as a match for our daughter is spotless,' Saundarya's father said.

'Contrary to the general perception, solving murder mysteries is not our main job. In fact, we do lot of matrimonial enquiries. But the fastest-growing segment is assignments to catch cheating spouses! Regarding your case, I assure you prompt and accurate detective work. I've got a brilliant team of boys and girls who can even find out what goes on behind closed doors!' Rameshwar asserted.

The deal was signed. Saundarya hoped that Nipun would be categorized as virginal.

Rameshwar gave the task to Samarth, his key man. He was a master of disguises, having posed as a transgender in the last assignment. Samarth felt the assignment would be a cakewalk because doctors, being public figures, were sitting ducks for a detective.

Armed with Nipun's photograph and a lot of acumen, Samarth entered Nirog Hospital posing as a patient's attendant. Just when he was about to enter the OPD, he heard, 'Hey, Samarth!'

He looked around and was pleasantly surprised to find Mayur. Mayur and Samarth were distant relatives but were often seen together near the drinks trolley during the family celebrations. Samarth was overjoyed to see Mayur because an insider was the most effective mole.

'I am investigating Dr Nipun on behalf of his prospective in-laws,' he told Mayur.

Mayur couldn't believe this. Finally, he had the chance to avenge at once all the humiliations meted out to him by Nipun, which he had duly noted, date-wise, in a diary. His eyeballs started oscillating rapidly.

'Let us go to the cafeteria. We might be able to get a clue,' he told Samarth.

They entered the doctors' section. Mayur was relieved to find Nipun and Ridhi chatting with each other. Samarth and Mayur sat at a nearby table.

'That is Nipun with Ridhi, the girl wearing the yellow top. Both of them are going steady. Take a photo,' Mayur pointed out.

Samarth took out his pen-cum-spy-camera and took a photo of what he thought was foolproof evidence.

'I think you need not investigate further,' Mayur whispered.

'The assignment has been completed in a flash. The time saved can be put into the account of my girlfriend—I'll watch a movie with her. In the evening, I will present the evidence to my boss. Thanks a lot,' Samarth said.

The detective agency reported back, with photographic evidence, to Saundarya's father.

Nripendra immediately rang up Nipun's dad. 'What the hell is going on? Why are you trying to destroy my daughter's life?'

'How? I don't understand a thing.'

'Your son is going around with a girl. Make a surprise visit to the hospital and see for yourself.'

'I am really sorry, but I have actually not been aware of this.'

Sarwan called his son. 'Your alliance with Saundarya

is off. Idiot, if you were already in love with a girl, why didn't you tell us?'

'Dad, there is some misunderstanding. I think they are just making an excuse to back off.'

'Are you sure?'

'I swear, Dad. Let us forget about them.'

Nipun felt thunderstruck. For the last few days, he had been fantasizing about Saundarya waking him up every morning with a kiss and being pulled back into bed by a pair of strong arms. Nipun opened a notebook and wrote 'Why me?' hundreds of times till his hand cramped.

For the next few days, Nipun looked funereal. Mayur judged that his sinister plan had worked. He danced joyfully on the ruins of Nipun's broken alliance.

23
War with No Rules

Surgeons believe in action in the operation theatre as well as outside it.

Dr Ujjwal took Ayana along to the National Conference on Biliary Surgery in Goa. The conference organizers often chose Goa as the venue, as if the heavy academic sessions could only be dealt with by letting one's hair down at a beachside bar later in the evening. Initially, many delegates inferred that Dr Ujjwal had made a young lady elope with him as this was thought to be child's play for him. It was only after a while that everyone came to know about Ayana being his wife.

While the couple were on the return flight, Dr Ujjwal said to Ayana, 'Coming back from such a breathtaking conference venue hurts. Goa remains with the Goans. One is left wishing for a siesta but that too remains elusive.'

Back in the department, Dr Ujjwal was surprised to find that there were vacant slots in his operation list. Previously, during the first few days after returning from a conference, he would end up working past sunset to clear the backlog of surgeries.

After reaching home, he told Ayana, 'I don't understand

why patients have started avoiding me.'

'You are paying more attention to your wife than the patients, that's why!' she said.

'I don't know. Let's see.'

However, his work continued to suffer. Then, Candy gave him a vital piece of information—Dr Vishesh's unit had operated on more cases than them.

'How could that butcher become more popular than me?' Dr Ujjwal said.

He called an emergency meeting of all the doctors of his unit.

'Sir, I suspect that our patients are being misguided by the other unit,' Candy suggested.

'Divide into teams and work on different angles. Wear a disguise if required! Otherwise, I will have to take the help of a professional jasoos,' the chief said.

Two days later, Candy, along with Nipun and Ridhi, entered Dr Ujjwal's office.

'Sir, we have solved the mystery of the missing patients,' Candy said.

'What did you find?'

'We suspected that someone from the front desk might have been misdirecting the patients. To ascertain this, Ridhi told her cousin to come to the hospital on Monday, which is your outdoor day. Ridhi's cousin posed as a new patient. The predictable happened. She was advised to consult Dr Vishesh. The rationale given—your hands tremble during surgery!' Candy revealed.

'That bloody bastard!' Dr Ujjwal shouted. He clenched his fists and rushed towards Dr Vishesh's office like a mad elephant. Others followed. They wanted to stop him but did not have the guts to do so.

While they were on their way, many bystanders were filled with admiration for the chief, presuming that he was rushing to treat a critically ill patient.

After reaching Dr Vishesh's office, Dr Ujjwal kicked the door open. Dr Vishesh, sitting on the sofa, was looking through some files. Before he could figure out what was going on, Dr Ujjwal gave him a stinging slap. Dr Ujjwal's hand moved again, but Dr Vishesh recovered just in time to dodge it by moving his head backwards. Dr Ujjwal lost his balance and fell into Dr Vishesh's lap. For a moment, they were both in a compromising position. They quickly disengaged from each other. Then, Dr Vishesh returned the slap with dividend by kicking Dr Ujjwal's shin. By now, a number of onlookers from both camps had gathered. Luckily, there were some level-headed individuals among them. The warring bulls were restrained by a few sturdy men, while others formed a buffer zone by standing between them.

'I'll get you dismissed from this hospital,' Dr Vishesh shouted as Dr Ujjwal was leaving.

'You can even file molestation charges against me as no one thinks you to be a man!' Dr Ujjwal yelled.

The director, who had often arbitrated in their cock fights, decided to meet them separately. Like many other physicians, he felt that most surgeons barely used their brains. The surgeons retaliated by asserting that they were men of action while the physicians were just stethoscope-wielding theorists.

Dr Vishesh was the first one to reach the director's office.

He pleaded, 'Sir, Dr Ujjwal barged into my office and assaulted me for no rhyme or reason. During the last conference, after my talk had finished, he asked a number of uncomfortable questions just to embarrass me.'

Fifteen minutes later, Dr Ujjwal came to present his defence.

'Sir, Vishesh has stooped so low that he has started bribing the hospital staff to direct all surgical patients to him. During the conferences, he presents his talk with photos stolen from the internet. I lose my cool if I observe someone lowering the prestige of our hospital.'

The enquiry held by the director confirmed Dr Vishesh's conspiracy. He was served a show-cause notice. However, Dr Ujjwal was also warned not to exhibit dadagiri (hooliganism) in the hospital.

Soon, Dr Ujjwal's unit was able to recover its normal patient intake. However, Dr Vishesh was smarting for revenge after Dr Ujjwal's assault, topped up by humiliation from the director. His previous attempt to drive a wedge between Ayana and Dr Ujjwal by getting a fake letter sent to Ayana had come to nothing.

In desperation, he called for Balwan, a former wrestler who was now grappling with law enforcers. The history-sheeter felt more at home in prison than outside it.

'How do we teach this Dr Ujjwal a lesson?' Vishesh asked Balwan, who was his old patient.

'Just like there are specialists among doctors, in my profession too there are experts for different crimes! I am more comfortable with extortion, blackmail and honey traps!

We could get him embroiled in a case of molestation. I have a woman called Munni in my gang. She can pose as a patient with breast disease,' Balwan said, in the manner of a salesman making a pitch.

'But that wily bastard always keeps a female attendant around him while examining ladies.'

'Doesn't matter. Munni will catch him unawares in his office. Without taking any appointment, she will enter his chamber, open the buttons of her blouse and then raise the alarm. Her accomplices, waiting outside the office, will rush inside, click photos and later act as witnesses. Most of the damage will be done by the media. There will be panel discussions on television about what punishment should be given to Dr Ujjwal and how such incidents need to be prevented in the future. Even a new law might get enacted—about the conditions to be fulfilled for examining a female patient. In short, Dr Ujjwal will achieve notoriety on a grand scale!'

'But what if Munni's allegations are proved to be false?'

'She will point the finger at me, and I will feign to be a disgruntled patient. Even if both of us are jailed, it is no big deal for us. We know how to get out of it!'

'Good idea. Okay. Work on it and execute the plan within a few days.'

'Doctor Sahib, let things cool down. We will enact this in about a month. All crimes need not be hurried! Please give me some token advance so that I can start working right away.'

Vishesh was in two minds.

'Don't worry, Sir. I will keep my word. After all, I am a man of principles!' Balwan said.

'All right. Keep 10,000 rupees for now.'

As soon as Balwan had left, Shubha, Dr Vishesh's wife, entered the living room. 'I am meeting Dr Ujjwal's wife tomorrow.'

'Are you in your senses? You know very well that I get hopping mad just at the mention of his name!'

'She wants to play the peacemaker.'

'Are you sure? There must be some catch in this. Be careful,' Dr Vishesh said, but allowed Shubha to go ahead.

'*Let us see if peace is more interesting than war!*' he thought.

Ayana had taken the initiative in reaching out to Shubha because she was afraid that an escalation of the conflict could even lead to bloodshed. She also suspected that Dr Vishesh was behind the letter which had supposedly been sent by Ujjwal's girlfriend and expected him to employ more tricks to create a misunderstanding between her and Dr Ujjwal.

They got together at an Udupi restaurant.

'Only our initiative can sort out the matter,' Ayana said.

'I couldn't agree more with you,' Shubha replied.

'But how do we do it?'

'We could refuse to sleep with them until they start behaving like gentlemen!'

'Ha ha… What if they find an alternative? I think it would be better if we persuade Dr Bhaskar, their teacher, to act as the mediator,' Ayana concluded.

Dr Ujjwal and Dr Vishesh met in the presence of

Dr Bhaskar, who let them speak their minds. Accusations and counter-accusations flew freely.

Finally Dr Bhaskar intervened. 'Enough! Both of you are equally at fault. Be good friends like you were in medical college. In the future, all your issues will be sorted out through me and not through mixed martial arts!'

Both of them promised never to raise their voices at each other, leave alone fists. Ayana and Shubha also decided to have regular family get-togethers. They knew that over drinks, men turned into ladies—emotionally speaking.

Dr Vishesh shelved his sinister revenge plan. Balwan, the gangster, felt dejected at the loss of an assignment.

The first get-together was at Dr Ujjwal's home.

Dr Vishesh said to Dr Ujjwal, 'Our wives have shown us the way. On our own, by now we would have played our roles in more "Ninja Doctors" episodes!'

'Yes. It seems we were enemies in our previous incarnation and had a one-to-one combat!' Dr Ujjwal replied.

'But who won?' Dr Vishesh asked.

Before they picked up a fight on this issue, Ayana intervened. 'None of you won. Your wives separated you!'

24

A Close Shave

Nothing is easy in our complex world—not even an activity as simple as birdwatching.

Nipun ached for a break from the routine, even if it was a short one. As if God had answered his prayers, Shanky, his birding buddy, called him.

'Hey, dude. What's up?'

'Same old story. Cutting up people and working amidst blood, pus and urine.'

'Good. Someone has got to do this dirty work! Why don't you spend a day differently? Mega Birding Day is on Sunday.'

'I will be able to make it only if I get permission from my khadoos (ill-tempered) boss.'

'Okay, wish you luck. Hope to see you there.'

Nipun decided to meet the chief. The worst possibility was that Dr Ujjwal would give him a lecture on 'Devotion to Duty' and deny leave. The chief didn't have any special power, like the ancient Indian sages, to convert him into a bird by cursing him.

'Sir, I want a day off, on the coming Sunday, to participate in the biggest birding event in Delhi, known as the Mega Birding Day. Many teams will spread out in different directions and identify as many species of birds as possible,' Nipun asked.

'Normally, I grant leave to resident doctors only if they are getting married or are *genuinely* sick. But since you have been quite regular in your duties, I am giving you a day off even though I am not sure what type of birdwatching you will indulge in!' Dr Ujjwal replied.

'I will only concentrate on birds with feathers!' Nipun smiled.

On Sunday, most of the participants rose earlier than the sun. After a power breakfast, the teams went off in different directions. Nipun and his group were in Shanky's SUV. They took a kutcha road traversing the Aravallis from the Gurgaon-Faridabad Road. Apart from Nipun and Shanky, there were two girls, Fiona and Rameeta, for whom birds were even dearer than their boyfriends.

Feeling secure in their numbers, the group members got down from the vehicle and started trekking into the heavily wooded part of the valley. They expected to find some rare bird, which could make them the stars of the competition.

'Shh... I just heard leaves rustle,' Fiona whispered.

'Careful. There might be a deer,' Nipun added.

Suddenly, two bearded toughs emerged, with sticks in hand.

'What are you people doing here?' one of them said sternly.

'Just watching birds,' Nipun replied. He was trembling with fear.

'We will show you the stars and that too in the day!' the other said menacingly.

Then both of them lifted the sticks with the intention of hitting the intruders. Nipun formed a shield by folding his arms around his face and head.

But the sticks suddenly dropped out of their hands. Nipun wondered if some superhero had come to their rescue. The toughs started coughing violently. Then he noticed the two girls triumphantly holding their chilli pepper spray cans. All of them looked at each other.

'Run!' Rameeta shouted.

Everyone sprinted as if an angry Gabbar Singh was chasing them on a horse with a loaded gun in his hand. Even after getting into their vehicle, they kept on looking back just to make sure they were not being followed.

'Hats off to Rameeta and Fiona! But for their special weapons, those thugs would have beaten us to a pulp,' Shanky said.

'Most likely, those guys were a part of the forest mafia. Must have mistaken us for press photographers because of our cameras,' Fiona added.

'Do you carry a can of chilli pepper spray everywhere?' Shanky asked.

'Yes. Except for the washroom. Safety is an issue for ladies everywhere. Of course, when you are in a forest in the company of Lecherous Nipun, you'd better be prepared!' Fiona grinned.

Nipun was surprised. 'Who told you my nickname?' he asked.

'One of your old classmates knows me. I won't reveal his name. In fact, for over an hour, he kept on entertaining us by describing your antics while you were doing MBBS. When he was leaving, he said that there was a lot more left to be told!'

'Good. I am making people healthier by getting endorphins released into their system.'

'What are endorphins?'

'Endorphins are chemicals which are good for your body. They are secreted into your bloodstream whenever you hug your boyfriend.'

'Well explained!'

The hardcore birdwatchers carried on, preferring to do the rest of their birding in the more secure environment of parks. They sighted a good number of winged creatures but also ended up disturbing many love birds of the two-legged variety.

25

Undoing Others' Mistakes

Our country is full of fake doctors, some of whom are even more dangerous than the diseases.

Even the vastly experienced professor looked puzzled. A patient, who was previously operated on for intestinal obstruction by Dr Abhik, a former student of the chief, had unexplained recurrence of abdominal pain. The CT scan showed a vague mass in the abdominal cavity.

Dr Ujjwal decided that the patient needed to be operated on. After the abdominal cavity was opened, everyone was awed to find a surgical mop that had been forgotten inside the abdomen during the previous surgery.

'Sir, how could the surgeon make such a glaring mistake?' Nipun asked.

'It usually happens in panic situations, especially if there is the deadly combination of a forgetful surgeon and a careless operation theatre staff,' Dr Ujjwal replied.

The mop was removed and the abdomen was closed. After the last stitch was applied, the chief instructed Nipun, 'Tell the attendants that their patient will be fine because the pus collection inside the abdomen has been drained. Don't mention the forgotten mop.'

Nipun did as advised, but wondered why the chief was

trying to do a cover-up.

Noticing Nipun's uneasiness, Dr Ujjwal explained, 'There is a solid reason for hiding the true facts from the relatives. They seem to be inclined to take the law in their hands. So, it is quite likely that they would try to assault Dr Abhik and ransack his premises. But I'll make sure that Abhik learns his lesson so that, in the future, he would be unlikely to forget stuff inside the abdomen.'

Then Dr Ujjwal took Nipun to his office. He called up Abhik, who practised in Sohna, a small town in Haryana. 'Hi, Abhik, this is Dr Ujjwal. You have become very matlabi (opportunistic). You haven't bothered to call on me for so long.'

'Sir, how can I forget my guru? I have kept a framed photo of yours in my office.'

'I hope you have not put a garland around it!'

'Sir, please don't use such words. May you live longer than me!'

'Although you are much younger to me, you have actually become more forgetful than me!'

'I didn't get you.'

'Today, we found a mop in the abdomen of a patient on whom you operated two months back for intestinal obstruction.'

Abhik replied in a shaky voice, 'Yes, Sir. I do remember that case. He had an intra-operative cardiac arrest. Luckily, he was revived by the anaesthesia team. Then, they advised us to close the abdomen quickly. We might have committed the error in this commotion.'

'If a fireman panics in a fire, how is he going to rescue others?'

'Sorry, Sir. I admit that there has been a major lapse.'

'I didn't tell the relatives about the mop, but an operation theatre technician, who is known to them, revealed everything,' Dr Ujjwal said, while winking at Nipun.

Nipun gave the chief an approving look for his prowess at acting.

'What was their reaction?' Abhik asked.

'The relatives, most of whom are toughs, are seething with rage, which is obviously directed at you. In fact, I noticed that one of them carries a revolver. I have called you up to warn you that they might be on the way to your hospital.'

'I think I should get out of here immediately,' Abhik said and hung up.

'Serves him right!' Dr Ujjwal smiled.

Abhik went underground and resurfaced only after a week.

He called up Dr Ujjwal. 'Sir, what is the situation now?'

Initially, the chief thought of giving another shocker to Abhik. But he reckoned that Abhik had undergone enough mental stress. So, he told him, 'The patient had a good recovery and was discharged yesterday. After a great deal of persuasion, the relatives have agreed not to rake up the matter any further.'

'I have no words to express my thanks.'

'You are welcome. But I might have done a disservice to you. You could have attained national fame if I had informed the media and the news about the forgotten mop had been highlighted on all the major news channels!'

Two weeks later, another complicated case arrived. Dr Ujjwal was called to the emergency ward by Mayur. 'Sir, this case has been operated on by Dr Jinendra in a village. I will call him inside so that you can have first-hand information.'

The so-called Dr Jinendra turned out to be a former ward attendant in Nirog Hospital in Dr Ujjwal's unit. He had left the job a year back.

Dr Ujjwal took him inside one of the cabins. 'You sisterfucker! Since when have you become a doctor?'

'Sir, please tone down your voice. After leaving my job, I gathered a few fake certificates and started practising in my village. But at least I have some practical knowledge of medical science. Bakul, a former security guard of this hospital, is also working as a doctor in my village!'

'How did you mess up this case?'

'The patient had a swelling on the back of the left knee. Presuming that there was a pus collection, I made an incision. But instead of pus, there was a gush of blood. I applied a tight bandage to stop the bleeding and shifted the patient here.'

Dr Ujjwal examined the patient.

He took Jinendra aside. 'What you diagnosed as a pus collection is actually a venous aneurysm, a swelling of a major vein. I will try my best to save the limb but can't assure you that it will be saved.'

The moment he heard that there was danger to the patient's limb, Jinendra started losing power in his lower limbs. He sat down on a chair and buried his head in his hands.

'If the patient's leg doesn't survive, the villagers will lynch me.'

He felt like running away from the emergency ward. But there was no escape as the patient's relatives were stationed outside the entrance. For the two hours that the patient was in OT, he prayed non-stop.

After coming out of the OT, Dr Ujjwal told Jinendra, 'Congrats. Operation successful. Limb will survive.'

Actually, even before starting the surgery, Dr Ujjwal had known that there was no risk to the limb. But he wanted to strike terror in Jinendra's heart.

Jinendra touched Dr Ujjwal's feet. 'Sir, please take me back in your ward.'

'Submit an application. I will try my best to get you the job. That way, I will save the people of your village from a man-eater!'

26
Parties Full of Surprises

While attending parties and celebrations, a surgeon should watch out for dissatisfied patients and disgruntled exes.

An hour before he was expected to reach home, Dr Ujjwal rang up Ayana. 'Hey, cook up some hot snacks.'

'Even hotter than me?'

'You are going to be the dessert!'

'The workaholic seems to be in the mood to be an alcoholic today.'

'Today, I have earned my drinks. I am drained out after undoing someone else's mistake.'

By the time he reached home, Ayana had readied everything for 'an evening to remember'.

'It feels as if my birthday is being celebrated in advance,' he said.

'You can't get away like that! There will be a big party on the special day. You make the juniors slog as if they were your serfs! They deserve a treat from you at least once a year,' Ayana insisted.

'Good idea. How was I managing my life all the while

without you?' he replied. Expectedly, he received a lingering kiss from Ayana.

A banquet hall was booked and all doctors of the unit, along with their families, were invited for the chief's birthday bash. Dhairya, the most docile doctor, was made the sacrificial lamb once again—he had to skip the party and manage the ward. Almost everyone arrived in time. After noticing that many doctors were acting timid, the chief announced, 'Enjoy. Indiscipline is exempt from punishment for the next six hours!'

This was a signal for Nipun to get into his naughty avatar. He mimicked everyone, including the girls. The chief didn't hesitate to laugh out loud.

There was only one latecomer. But when Ridhi entered, she made all heads turn. She was wearing an elegant evening gown, and her strut was no less than the divas sashaying down the red carpet at the Cannes Film Festival. By her side was a handsome hunk. His smile was so unwavering it seemed he had gotten a plastic surgery done to paste it permanently on his face.

Ridhi greeted the chief. 'Good evening, Sir. This is Nilay, my fiancé.'

'Why have you kept him concealed all this while? I don't think any of us would have looked at him with an evil eye!' the chief said.

'Actually, we are yet to get formally engaged.'

Nipun, who was nearby, overheard the conversation.

The first thought that came to his mind was, '*What is lacking in me?*' On the verge of tears, he retreated to a corner of the banquet hall.

Dr Ujjwal shook hands with Nilay.

'What do you do?'

'I am an industrialist.'

'Today, you can enjoy the company of doctors.'

'I am feeling a bit awkward.'

'Why so?'

'I am the only person in the gathering with an IQ under hundred!'

'You have a good sense of humour. I'm sure you will keep Ridhi very happy,' Dr Ujjwal said.

For a while, conversation reigned. Then, Candy and his wife enlivened the party with some inventive party games.

Back in his room after the party, Nipun put on the song 'Learn to Say Goodbye' and pressed the replay button. He also utilized the services of alcohol, another companion of broken hearts. After repeatedly listening to the song, he had a revelation which made him feel light again—Ridhi was a loser who had missed the opportunity of bagging a brilliant surgeon who was also a super entertainer.

It was the season of celebrations. A few days later, Dr Ujjwal was visited by Avdhesh, his old patient. The chief remembered him as the burly young man who had been admitted a few months back in a critical condition after a burst appendix. At that time, his relatives had been told that there was a 50-50 chance of survival. But Avdhesh survived, mainly because of Dr Ujjwal's intelligence, diligence and competence.

'Doctor Sahib, I am getting married on the coming Saturday in Mandna. You have to be there to bless me,' Avdhesh entreated.

Mandna, an urbanized village near the Qutub Minar, was a familiar name for Dr Ujjwal because many of his patients hailed from there.

'I'll try my best to make it,' he replied.

Avdhesh realized that this was a polite way of saying no.

'Sir, my wedding ceremony will be incomplete without you. I owe my life to you,' Avdhesh said firmly. The chief noted that Avdhesh's eyes had become moist.

This emotional fool will make a good husband and a doting father too! he thought.

'Okay. I'll be there come what may, and I will also bring along my wife. Happy?' he said to Avdhesh's delight.

Dr Ujjwal and Ayana reached Mandna on Saturday night. It was a village only in name as most of it had been gobbled up by the city. The last resistance was put up by a few traditional houses with courtyards, where groups of old men were smoking hukkahs and critiquing everything except God. Tents had been put up in a so-called park, which was actually an open plot claimed by stray dogs. They were waiting, with protruding tongues from which streams of saliva were falling like small waterfalls, to make a feast out of the leftovers. These mongrels acknowledged the vast superiority of humans, but wondered why they always left the tastiest dish, the bone with the juicy marrow, for them.

As the couple entered the venue, Avdhesh's parents

greeted them warmly. Then they were handed over to Satyam, who had been specially deputed to make them feel like royalty.

Satyam seemed to be in awe of Dr Ujjwal.

'Doctor Sahib. Avdhesh has told me that you can even make a fat person slim by making their stomach smaller.'

'True.'

'Can you make my stomach bigger? I want to become a wrestler.'

Dr Ujjwal smiled. 'Until now, no such surgery has been devised. But eating heavy meals more frequently, will serve the same purpose.'

In his enthusiasm to play the perfect host, Satyam asked a few waiters to bring different varieties of snacks. Whenever the couple told him that they had eaten enough, he would say, 'Let me serve you a small amount, please' and forcefully put some grub onto their plates. The portions were big and the cooks seemed to be madly in love with oil and cream.

In desperation, Dr Ujjwal folded his hands. 'Please, no more food.'

Satyam replied, 'Doctor Sahib, you hardly ate anything!' He thought Dr Ujjwal and Ayana were trying to show off their sophistication by eating frugally.

'Before arriving here, we attended another wedding. So, we have already eaten a lot,' Dr Ujjwal told Satyam, lying to end the mayhem.

But Satyam stood by their side, just in case they changed their minds.

'We are okay. Why don't you enjoy with your friends?' Ayana gestured.

After Satyam had gone away, Dr Ujjwal grumbled, 'An

excessive hospitality is also bad!'

As expected, the chief found a few familiar faces amongst the guests. Some of his former patients greeted him. He didn't recognize everyone, but he pretended otherwise, so they wouldn't feel offended.

An old man came to him. 'Namaste, Doctor Sahib. Avdhesh has sent me. I want to show you my hand.'

Uff! Avdhesh is exploiting me! Dr Ujjwal thought.

The old man had a tumour on the palm of his left hand. It didn't seem cancerous, but it had recurred after two surgeries that had been done by surgeons who suffered from delusions about their skills.

'Meet me at the hospital. I will refer you to our hand surgeon. Hopefully, your problem shall be solved,' Dr Ujjwal offered.

'Doctor, I am fed up of repeated surgeries. Why don't you cut off my hand and solve the problem once and for all?' he said.

Dr Ujjwal smiled. 'So, according to your logic, if someone has a disease and he is not responding to treatment, we should slit his throat to rid him of the disease?'

The grim-looking old man suddenly broke into a grin. 'Doctor Sahib. You have explained it quite lucidly! I will see you in the hospital in a few days.'

'I've had enough patients now!' Dr Ujjwal mumbled.

But within a few minutes, he bumped into Mahipal, one of his old patients. Dr Ujjwal would never forget Mahipal. Nine months ago, he had been admitted for the removal of his gall bladder, employing the laparoscopic technique. He was supposed to be discharged in a day. However, multiple complications developed because of accidental damage to the common bile duct during the surgery. The patient ended up needing two additional surgeries and had to spend four months in the hospital. On the day of his discharge he had taunted Dr Ujjwal, 'One should sell a plot of land before coming to you for getting operated!'

Mahipal's bitterness may have passed with time. Although I caused the complication, I also worked day in and day out to set it right, he thought.

Mahipal greeted Dr Ujjwal warmly. This encouraged the chief to say, 'How are you doing?'

'I am still alive, despite your best efforts to pack me off to heaven!' he said, with a wry smile.

Ayana suppressed her laughter lest Dr Ujjwal felt offended. The chief was at a loss for words. Luckily, he noticed an acquaintance waving at him.

'I will catch up with you later,' he said to Mahipal. Dr Ujjwal made a note of his dress so that he could be dodged for the rest of the evening.

He wished he had heeded the advice of his boss; 'If you meet an old patient in public, greet and recognize him. But, never ask him how he is feeling!'

But the chief was thrown completely off his balance when, in the gathering, he noticed Pratima, a former technician at his hospital, with whom he had embarked on a torrid affair five years ago. She had wanted to tie the knot with him, but Dr Ujjwal had made the sham excuse—that his mother would have never accepted her. A distraught Pratima had left her job and had disappeared forever, out of his life.

Luckily, she was looking in a different direction. But there was a distinct possibility that she would bump into him. With Ayana by his side, he was sitting on a major disaster because Pratima was that most virulent strain of exes, the wronged one.

'My abdomen feels so heavy because we've eaten too much. Let's leave.'

'Okay. But not before we've taken a close look at the bride!' Ayana insisted.

'Women are all the same!' Dr Ujjwal laughed.

Both of them went towards the stage. To call the decoration garish was an understatement. The couple were seated on an ornate sofa.

Dr Ujjwal marvelled at Avdhesh's 'catch', the bride.

He addressed Avdhesh. 'Did you search each and every house in India to find her?'

The bride smiled. This was a better compliment than the routine—'You look so pretty.' (Did anyone ever say to a bride that she was looking ugly?), or 'May you be saved from the evil eye.' (Then why call so many guests? Is there a machine to screen the visitors for an evil eye?), and even, 'May you always maintain the status of a married woman.' (This only implied that she should die before the husband.)

'If I am alive today, it is only because of the great Dr Ujjwal,' Avdhesh told his bride.

'This chap was with us for quite some time and the hospital staff sang his praises. So he is tried, tested and certified as a good human being!' Dr Ujjwal said.

Then he and Ayana stood behind the couple for a photograph.

'Sir, please move your face to the right,' the photographer motioned to Dr Ujjwal.

'My face will remain in this position. You can change

the angle of your camera,' Dr Ujjwal said with a flourish.

'Hey! He is the most renowned doctor in Delhi. Don't inconvenience him,' shouted Avdhesh. The lens man complied, but he had the last laugh. 'Sir, according to you, the eye of the needle should be moved around the thread, instead of the thread being pushed through it!'

Dr Ujjwal took his leave from Avdhesh by making an excuse that he had to attend an emergency call at the hospital. Avdhesh wanted Dr Ujjwal to participate in the post-ceremony dancing, which was about to start. The headstrong DJ was eagerly waiting to torture everyone's eardrums. If anyone requested him to turn down the volume, he raised it further. Avdhesh was disappointed because he had planned to post the videos of Dr Ujjwal dancing by his side, to make his friends and relatives aware of his 'high' connections.

The couple came down from the stage. As Dr Ujjwal looked up, he came face to face with Pratima, his ex.

'Hello, Pratima,' he said, with a forced smile and braced himself for a verbal or a physical assault. Ayana's presence was an additional complicating factor.

There were no chances of an escape except if he fell to the ground by feigning a stroke, or if God sent an alien in a spaceship to whisk him away.

'Hi, doctor, it's good to see you. After I saw you on the stage, I waited for you here. I presume this is Ayana,' she said calmly.

Then she looked towards Ayana and said, 'I have spent a lot of time with Sir!'

'Were you were working at Nirog Hospital?' Ayana asked, trying to make sense of Pratima's statement.

'Yes. In Sir's unit.'

Dr Ujjwal was relieved by Pratima's harmless talk. But he was still not out of danger because Pratima could drop the bombshell at any moment.

Then Pratima pointed to a man standing adjacent to them. 'Sir, meet my husband.'

Dr Ujjwal's sigh of relief was audible to everyone. He followed it up with a burp to make it appear to be a sign of indigestion.

After exchanging pleasantries with Pratima's husband, Dr Ujjwal left quickly, not even bothering to look around. Once his car was out of the parking lot, he started breathing easy.

Ayana commented, 'The evening was enjoyable because of the interesting conversations between you, and your old patients and acquaintances. We should have stayed longer!'

'It was *too* interesting for my comfort!' Dr Ujjwal replied.

Suddenly, it occurred to Ayana that an important matter needed to be discussed with her husband. 'Yesterday, Nishtha's mother came to meet me. Although she seems to be a hoarder of worries, her concern about her daughter's marriage is genuine. One of her cousins is a spinster, and she dreads that the way that Nishtha is rejecting marriage proposals, she might also end up one. I suggested to her that Nishtha and Nipun would make a good match.'

'What was her reaction?'

'She requested me to fix them up. I think we should help her.'

'Why doesn't she talk to Nipun's parents directly?'

'That is the crux of the problem. Nishtha insists that she is not interested in marriage at the moment.'

'And she doesn't listen to her parents. Is that right?

I know Nishtha very well. She has a mind of her own. Previously, Nipun and Nishtha have worked together for long hours on my research paper. But it seems they were also researching how to keep their natural urges in check! There is no harm in trying. Nipun might have hit puberty by now!'

'I'll talk about it with Nishtha. I am among the few people she listens to!' Ayana said.

'Why not Nipun?' the chief asked.

'If Nipun says no to a girl like Nishtha, you need to determine whether he is actually a man! So I don't need to waste my time and energy on him.'

The same evening, Ayana went to the hospital to meet Nishtha. They had so much to catch up on.

'Hey, please find a companion before all the eligible bachelors of your age are taken!' Ayana said.

'I appreciate your concern. But you sound like my mom! Since my MS exams are just three months away, I am focusing only on my studies. I may seem like a strong girl. But close to the exams, I turn into a psycho.'

'I have noticed that you and Nipun get along quite well.'

'He is a lively guy, and we're good friends. But that's it.'

However, Ayana had gotten Nishtha thinking. Nipun was now a much more desirable chap than when both of them had just joined the course. The joker could be cornered after the exam was over. She was confident that he would be as easy to catch as a fish, from a home aquarium.

27

Life in a Fast-forward Mode

When circumstances combine to create a wave in their favour, even the agnostics start believing in destiny.

For the past three months before the MS exam, Nishtha and Nipun were given lighter duties in the wards, so that they could find time to cover the huge syllabus.

Nishtha, who suffered from exam phobia, proposed to Nipun, 'Let us study together. That way, we can also clear each other's doubts.'

'If I study along with you, I will surely fail!' Nipun said.

'That won't happen if you resolve to stare at the books instead of me! Hey, I *need* your help.'

'Sure. But where do we study?' Nipun asked. He fervently hoped that she would say—'Let's do it in my hostel room.'

Then one day, exhausted from the long hours of reading, she will rest her head in my lap. That will set off an irreversible chain of events, culminating in her sweet surrender to me, he imagined.

'The library would be the best place to study. If we want to discuss a topic, we can sit in the park outside the library.'

'Can we do it in the hostel room? Yours? Or even mine?'

'Very smart!' Nishtha said with a wry smile. She saw through his game plan.

Just when their conversation was heating up, Ridhi interrupted them, in the manner of a *kebab mein haddi* (party pooper). Ridhi's face looked wooden, as if excess of Botulinum toxin had been injected all over it.

Nishtha said to her, 'You are looking so sad honey. Did the chief call you a duffer again?'

'I am actually a duffer! I can't judge people. Nilay and I are not seeing each other any more.'

'Unbelievable! It had looked like a match made in heaven,' Nishtha said, surprised.

'He was two-timing me.'

'Gosh! At the chief's birthday party, the charlatan had been portraying himself as your devotee.'

Ridhi broke down. Nipun was entirely ready to catch her precious tears in his hands and drink them, but he didn't get this privilege as Nishtha had already wiped her face with a handkerchief.

'Don't lose heart. The doors of my heart are still open for you,' he felt like telling Ridhi.

Nishtha and Nipun started studying in the library in the evenings. Although Nishtha was his competitor, Nipun never tried to conceal study material from her. The whacky guy was not wicked.

'I'm sure both of us will get through,' Nishtha said, as

Life in a Fast-forward Mode • 251

they started with their preparation for the mother of all exams.

'Amen,' Nipun replied.

Apart from acting as her agony aunt, Nipun also kept her entertained during the breaks with his self-depreciating humour. She didn't require antacids and she never had to complain to her mom about being tormented by a horned devil—her exam.

Mayur also started showing up in the library looking up the journals for references. Nishtha was surprised at the unusual surge in his academic interest. She couldn't help asking him, 'What are you looking for?'

'Dr Anuroop and I are writing a paper. Within a few days, we will send it to an international journal for publication,' he replied, with an air of pride.

Mayur and Candy! What a combination! Nishtha smiled to herself.

'What is the paper about?' She asked him.

'Dr Anuroop has devised his own technique for the laparoscopic repair of umbilical hernia.'

'He has also developed many techniques to fall over someone! Anyway, all the best!' Nishtha replied with a wry smile.

They had another unexpected visitor a few days later. Ridhi took a seat beside Nishtha and Nipun.

'Can I study in your company? I won't be able to come daily, but I shall show up now and then.'

'Don't give us more respect than we deserve! Just say you are going to join us,' Nipun replied.

'Thanks. I want to brush up my theory well in advance so that I don't have to toil at the last moment, just like you guys.'

'You are too organized, almost Spartan!' Nipun chuckled.

During the next few days, Nipun noticed that Ridhi was warming up to him. But she didn't show any signs of having lost her head over him.

Does she have feelings for me or is she just trying to get over her break-up? A woman is a tough puzzle. But the stakes are also very high! he thought.

A month passed. Nipun and Nishtha bumped into Mayur in the ward.

'So, has the paper been accepted?' Nishtha asked.

'Dr Anuroop had sent the paper with lot of expectations and he even named his technique after himself. But it was returned within a week by the editors of the *European Surgical Journal*. They had reasoned that it had nothing to add to the existing knowledge!'

'If Dr Anuroop wants to be famous, he could sing a song dressed just in his boxer shorts and post the video on YouTube!' Nishtha laughed.

During this period, Nipun and Nishtha continued with their surgical work. They were pleased at being given a free rein. The chief was trying to make them confident about operating without supervision before they were stamped with their MS degree.

In turn, Nipun and Nishtha were mentoring Ridhi and Mayur. Nipun taught Mayur the steps involved in many surgeries. Finally, Mayur was convinced that he had misjudged Nipun. He no longer felt any malice towards him. In fact, he felt so guilty about playing a dirty trick to break Nipun's engagement that he decided to unburden himself. Mayur rang up Samarth, the private detective who had previously shadowed Nipun. 'Do you remember doing a matrimonial enquiry of Dr Nipun?'

'Yes, the playboy trying to trap a decent girl!'

'Actually, Nipun is the opposite of a playboy! The poor guy hasn't dated a girl in ages. I was mistaken. Ridhi, the girl whom I presumed to be his girlfriend, was subsequently engaged to some other guy.'

Samarth reinvestigated and confirmed Mayur's information. He contacted Saundarya's father, gave him a good character certificate for Nipun and apologized for the previous mistake. During this period, Saundarya's family hadn't been successful in their search for a boy with the combined traits of Einstein, Gandhi and Hercules. Her dad was becoming desperate. But even after Nipun had been given a clean chit, he didn't run to Nipun's parents because that would make him seem like a 'despo'.

Ridhi was treating Nipun in the cafeteria after he had made her perform a surgery—independently.

'Nipun, please take me on a birdwatching trip again!'

'What!' Nipun exclaimed, almost spilling his hot coffee because his hands were trembling. After a few seconds' silence, he said, 'Nice joke!'

'It is not a joke! I want our relationship to soar high, like an eagle! Actually a week ago, a cousin of mine, who is an avid birder, visited us from the UK. My mom and I accompanied him. Just like you had done on our date, he made a dash to photograph a rare bird, leaving us unattended. So I guess all birders become semi-lunatic on a birding trip!'

'Yes, but they behave normally in other environments, including home! Long live your cousin!' Nipun smiled.

Then she looked at him so lovingly that he forgot her past excesses.

While walking through the corridors of his hostel, Nipun sang so loudly that the onlookers thought he had come back heavily drunk.

After entering his hostel room, he clenched his right fist, raised it and shouted, *'Yessssss... She is mine!'*

Nipun dropped his socks in the dustbin and deposited the room key in the refrigerator.

The next day, Nipun and Ridhi went birdwatching. This time, Nipun chose the Sultanpur Bird Sanctuary which had fencing all around it to keep animal predators as well as human loiterers at bay. Unlike the last birding trip, when he had left her alone, he made sure not to exceed a gap of six inches between him and Ridhi. However, for most of the time, they remained even closer, as Ridhi leaned against him while they walked hand in hand. Within half an hour, he had showed her more than twenty species of birds, including some vividly coloured ones.

Nipun focused his binoculars on a starling. However, the hyperactive bird flew away.

'The starling has flown into that bush,' Nipun pointed out. He took Ridhi into a grassy patch surrounded by dense shrubbery. Ridhi was aware that there was no starling there.

Nipun couldn't help embracing her and Ridhi was only too willing. Soon, the lovebirds were smooching wildly. However, they separated after hearing a group of birders chatting nearby. Their lip-lock would have shown up as a coincidental finding through the binoculars of the birders.

To recharge, they went to the restaurant in the adjacent tourist complex.

'You know, you have tormented me so much for the last one year,' Nipun said.

'Sorry.'

'Mere words will not do. To compensate for the mental agony, you are sentenced to give one hundred kisses to the victim!' Nipun whispered.

'If you want to give out this type of punishment, even a harsher one will do!'

They moved back to the sanctuary and found a secluded spot where Ridhi served her 'sentence'.

The next day, Nishtha was sitting in the garden in front of the library, waiting for Nipun to arrive. Like any other Indian, she was on a high because of the dark clouds and a cool wind. From a distance, she saw Nipun walking towards her along with Ridhi. This was a bit unusual. Then, she noticed that they were hand in hand.

Was she hallucinating?

She focused again. The image of Ridhi clutching Nipun's hand became clearer as they drew closer. The only time Nishtha had felt so badly shaken was when she had broken up with her boyfriend three-and-a-half years ago.

I have no one but myself to blame for losing Nipun to Ridhi. He had literally begged me for a relationship so many times, she reflected.

She said to Nipun, 'You have to keep holding her hand, come what may.'

'Ridhi also needs to do the same for me!' he replied.

After a while Nishtha left, citing the excuse of a headache to mask her heartache.

Later in his room, when Nipun opened his Facebook account, he was startled to find Nishtha's message, which she had sent earlier in the day—'You are the best medicine for me', it read.

Nipun mumbled, 'Oh God! First you brought about a long drought of women in my life, and now you are ending that! With a flood!'

The next day, he didn't talk to Nishtha about the Facebook message. Nishtha too refrained from asking Nipun to narrate the unabridged version of his entanglement with Ridhi.

Meanwhile, Saundarya's dad, after having dilly-dallied for a few days, decided to call Nipun's dad. 'With folded hands, I request you to reconsider Nipun for Saundarya. In the past, a misunderstanding was created between the two families by some vested interests. Let us begin anew.'

'Let me talk to my son. Frankly, I am only the ceremonial head of my family. Not only is my advice not binding, lately I have been barred by my wife from giving any unsolicited advice!'

After having taken his wife into his confidence, Sarwan called Nipun, who didn't pick up his phone since he was in the operation theatre.

He then sent Nipun a WhatsApp message—'Rejoice, my son! Saundarya's parents are eager to have you as their son-in-law. Call me whenever you are free'.

After reading his dad's message, Nipun became as crazy as a pauper who had won the lottery. He took out a notebook, opened a blank page and wrote his name. He drew three lines that began from his name and ended in—'Ridhi', 'Nishtha' and 'Saundarya' respectively.

'Ha ha ha ha!' he laughed, like Raavan. 'I am the luckiest guy on earth. Three fairies are vying to be my consorts. Alas, I have to choose just one.'

He thought of an objective method. *I can devise a scoring system, based on various physical and mental attributes and go for the one with the highest total!*

Then, he had an even zanier thought. *Why not marry all three of them? Create a small harem! Nipun the King, can then gradually expand the harem to 365 women. One queen for each day of the year!*

But after dinner, he came to his senses because he had to reply to his dad. He reasoned, *Ridhi loves me from the bottom of her heart. She has never let me down, except for that one incident, when it was my fault. When I had the plaster on my ankle, she stood by me. Nishtha, on the other hand, has always treated me as if I was her lackey. Saundarya, I barely know.*

He called up his father, 'Dad, I'm sorry. It is too late. Just two days ago, Ridhi and I have decided to spend our life together because we are in love with each other. Tell Saundarya's dad that your son is not a yoyo!'

'If I hadn't called you, you might have informed me

only after *marrying* Ridhi!' Nipun's dad said sarcastically. His head was spinning. But he was relieved that his son had finally found a match.

He rang Saundarya's father, 'Sorry. Nipun just got fixed up two days back with Ridhi, one of his juniors.'

It was Nripendra's turn to feel dizzy. The private detective had told him a few days ago that Nipun and Ridhi were not in a relationship. He cut the call, sat down on the sofa and asked for a glass of water. The bizarre chain of events related to Nipun seemed to be never-ending. He deleted all the phone numbers of Nipun's family.

Fed up of this hullaballoo, Saundarya told her parents that she would find a boy on her own.

The news about Nipun and Ridhi reached the chief through one of his departmental secret agents. He passed it on to Ayana.

'The fact that Ridhi and Nipun have become close despite our best efforts to set up Nipun and Nishtha proves the saying that love can neither be forced nor extinguished,' Ayana commented.

'The same was true for you and me!' Dr Ujjwal smiled.

A month later, Nipun and Nishtha were taking the practical exam for their MS. With two internal and two external examiners, the examiner-to-candidate ratio was 2:1. So both of them were in for some solid grilling. The external examiners included Dr Tapas from Delhi and Dr Suvir from Chennai.

On the first day of the exam, short cases were given to both the candidates to prepare. Nishtha was called first. As a convention, the external examiners were supposed to ask most of the questions in the viva. The internal examiners voluntarily chose to keep a low profile because they were quite likely to bestow undue favours upon their students, having been buttered up by them for over three years.

Dr Tapas hardly participated in the viva, leaving Dr Suvir to ask most of the questions. Dr Ujjwal noticed that he was leering at Nishtha.

The oldie seems to be infatuated with her. But this phenomenon is well known! Dr Ujjwal thought.

Then, it was Nipun's turn to appear for the viva. His performance was as good as Nishtha's since both of them had covered most of the topics together.

During the evening tea, Dr Tapas whispered to Dr Ujjwal, 'I want to talk to you in private.'

'Sure. I will come to your hotel room in about two hours,' Dr Ujjwal replied. He wondered what Dr Tapas was up to.

Dr Ujjwal reached the hotel room right on the dot.

Dr Tapas wasted no time getting to the point. 'I just wanted to know if Nishtha is single.'

'Yes, she is. But something is grossly wrong with you! I thought you were happily married!'

'Your dirty mind can never think straight! I am looking for a match for Mannat, my son, who is doing his MCh in plastic surgery. Nishtha has such a rare combination of stunning looks and superior-intelligence. Please do me a favour. Act as the matchmaker and pursue the matter with her parents.'

'Sure. My wife knows her mother. We will initiate the

process. The rest is up to the families and the prospective partners.'

The next day, the candidates were given long cases. Except for a few minor mistakes, both of them did well. In the evening, before leaving, the examiners announced the unofficial result. Nishtha and Nipun were overjoyed at having been assessed as competent enough to be let loose on the public as surgeons.

The chief gave them the option to continue in the department as senior residents. Neither of them had to think twice before saying yes. The Gang of Three remained intact. When Nipun was asked what his present position was, he replied, 'Same as before! It's an inverted triangle and I'm still at the bottom!'

Ayana got in touch with Nishtha's mom.

'There is a matrimonial proposal for Nishtha from Dr Tapas, for his son, who is a budding plastic surgeon. It would be great for Nishtha to be a part of this illustrious family.'

Nishtha's mom had already heard a lot about Dr Tapas. She and her husband got in touch with him. They met his son, whom they assessed to be quite high on the groom scale. But that was the easy part. They were worried about Nishtha playing truant again. Ayana was requested to act as the lubricant.

Nishtha and Ayana met at the Cup of Joy coffee house.

'Hey, Dr Tapas wants to take you home,' Ayana smiled.

'What?' Nishtha frowned.

'I mean as his daughter-in-law.'

'But how did he presume that I'd like his son. Am I marrying the boy or the family?'

'In our country, one marries both, even if it is a love marriage. The proposal is from one of the most reputed families in Delhi. The ball is in your court.'

'But still, I feel I should know the boy pretty well before deciding to be incarcerated with him for life! Right now, I am in a mental logjam. We'll talk about this tomorrow,' Nishtha said.

As soon as Nishtha had given the nod, Ayana, Nipun and Ridhi met Mannat. They apprised him about Nishtha, emphasizing on her pet cravings and pet peeves. Before leaving, they warned him not to make any conversation suggestive of women being appendages of men.

Nishtha and Mannat met shortly afterwards. At the outset, she looked for the usual indicators with which she initially assessed a man. His nails were trimmed, his shirt was neatly pressed and he didn't make slurping sounds while sipping tea. Mannat, on the other hand, was totally smitten by her and had already made up his mind to spend his life with her.

After a few meetings, Nishtha felt that she didn't need to look any further. Most of his views were similar to hers, although she felt a bit eerie upon knowing that even his favourite colour was the same as hers. She had absolutely no idea that Ayana and company had leaked the question paper to ensure Mannat's stupendous performance.

Meanwhile, Nipun and Ridhi had also decided to be man and wife. But she put forth a condition—no more than four birdwatching trips in a year.

'Okay. But what if I convert you into a bird watcher?'

'That will be a win-win situation for us both.'

Nipun and Ridhi married first. Mannat and Nishtha followed two weeks later. After Nishtha had come back from her honeymoon, the Gang of Three had their long-overdue meeting.

Nipun teased Nishtha, 'Ha ha… I am smarter than you. I had a love marriage, and you had to settle for an arranged marriage.'

'But I had no other choice. Out of Ridhi and me, only one could have grabbed you!' Nishtha replied.

Nipun chuckled, 'I don't agree. There were many ways to divide me between the both of you—odd and even days, alternate months or even alternate years!'

'It's impossible to change this guy. He will always remain lecherous!' Ridhi said.

And they faced life light-heartedly ever after.